D0192922

WHEN THE CRICKETS STOPPED SINGING

WHEN THE
CRICKETS
STOPPED
SINGING

Marilyn Cram Donahue

CALKINS CREEK
An Imprint of Highlights
Honesdale, Pennsylvania

For information about permission to reproduce selections from this book,
please contact permissions@highlights.com.

Calkins Creek
An Imprint of Highlights
815 Church Street
Honesdale, Pennsylvania 18431
calkinscreek.com
Printed in the United States of America

ISBN: 978-1-62979-723-6 (hc)
ISBN: 978-1-68437-137-2 (eBook)
Library of Congress Control Number: 2017949839

First edition
10 9 8 7 6 5 4 3 2 1

Design by Tim Gillner
The text is set in Bembo.
The titles are set in LeOsler.

This book is for the storytellers of my family—grandparents, parents, aunts, uncles, and cousins—who so often sat around the kitchen table, telling tales that inspired me to write about the past and help me understand who I was to become.

WHEN THE CRICKETS STOPPED SINGING

CHAPTER ONE

MESSINA, CALIFORNIA
JUNE 13, 1939

It was so hot outside the dogs quit panting. They just rolled over, lay quiet, and let their tongues hang out. My brother, Eddie, cracked an egg and fried it on the sidewalk. Mr. Abbott, the mailman, collapsed on Palm Avenue right in front of Dodie Crumper's house, where I never slowed down if I could help it. The weather report said "more of the same," which was no different from what we all expected, it being the middle of June.

I was lying on my stomach on the front room floor. It was the coolest place in the house. The big apricot tree spread its leafy branches above the roof, and the wide front porch was protection from the midday sun. I felt the roughness of the carpet against my elbows, felt the sweat behind my ears, heard the static when Mama turned on the radio.

"In these troubled times . . . ," a voice began.

I didn't feel troubled. Just hot, and that was OK. Hot was supposed to be uncomfortable, but for me, it wasn't. Not so long as the fan kept working. Hot meant summertime, and summertime meant vacation. Long days and longer twilights. It was the time of year when the frogs over by Willow Pond croaked all night. The time of year to steal slivers of ice from the ice truck, drink Kool-Aid all day, and play kick the can in the street until the moon came out.

I rummaged around in the cigar box that held my favorite things and found my four-leaf clover, dried and put away in a smaller box. Half a walnut shell sat on a wad of cotton. It looked like a little brown boat floating on a white cloud. I found the scattered nasturtium seeds that I kept meaning to plant. My fingers closed over an irregular stone. A moonstone. I had found it at La Mirada Beach when we went there after a storm. It had washed up with the seaweed and sand-crab shells and just seemed to be waiting to be found.

I rolled over on my back and held the stone up to the light coming through the living room window. The soft, warm glow shone through milky patches like a full moon shining through the spaces between drifting clouds.

That's the way summer was supposed to be. A warm glow in the middle of the year. I didn't want it to ever change.

". . . escalation of the war in Europe . . . ," said the voice. Then the words, *". . . only a question of how long America can stay out of the conflict."*

But not now, I thought. *Not here.* I was glad Europe was far away. I closed my eyes and thought of the silkworm moths, safe in their cocoons in the shoebox on the back porch. I felt like that. Wrapped in the cocoon of my hometown, Messina, with the warm glow of the whole summer ahead of me.

I was waiting for the electric rotating fan to blow on me again when I heard the commotion outside. Somebody was whooping at the top of his lungs. Other somebodies were screaming and yelling.

I ran to the window. It looked like the new preacher, Reverend Adams, had a family. I counted two little girls the same size, a girl about my age, and a boy who looked to be a year or so older.

I opened the front door and slipped out. I took a copy of *Calling All Girls* magazine with me so I could sit on the porch swing and pretend I was reading. I kept the swing as still as I could because it had a squeak, and I didn't want to miss a thing the newcomers said.

That house had always been a quiet place. Whenever I visited there with Mama, she warned me to talk soft and not clump my heels on the polished hardwood floors. We always sat on the rose velvet love seat and sipped mint tea out of flowered china cups and nibbled butter cookies with walnut halves pressed into the top. Mrs. Linfield, the preacher's wife, would ask, "So how are you these days, Angelina?"

I always answered, "Very well, thank you, ma'am."

I said those words even though I might have had a bleeding blister on my right heel and a sty in my left eye. I knew if I was very well, thank you, Mrs. Linfield would proceed to talk to Mama while I helped myself to another cookie.

Reverend Linfield was what people called an academic. I guessed that meant he had a lot of education. From our front porch, we could see him at his desk in an upstairs room at night.

"Working on his sermon," Daddy would say. "Let's hope it will be an improvement over the last one."

I couldn't remember what Reverend Linfield had said in any of his sermons. They were full of long words, and he had the habit of letting his eyes wander when he spoke. He seemed to be inspecting the organ, the stained glass windows, a cobweb in the corner of the ceiling. He was more interesting to watch than to listen to.

When Reverend Linfield finally retired, the church members sighed with relief. The search committee that looked for a replacement said they wanted a lively family to fill the old parsonage. It looked to me like they were getting what they'd ordered.

Mrs. Adams, the new preacher's wife, came out of the house and began shaking her finger at the boy. He paid no attention. "Charles," she insisted, "we must cooperate!"

From what I could see of Charles Adams, he didn't look like he was big on cooperating. *Testing the waters,* I thought. *Just testing the waters.* I had heard my dad say that about Eddie when he caught him smoking Mr. Flannery's dried grape vines along with a bunch of boys he wasn't supposed to hang around with.

"You can't get away with *anything* in this family," Eddie had told me. I thought he and Charles Adams might have a lot in common.

Now Charles hung his head, but only until his mother went into the parsonage and shut the door behind her. Then he put his hand in his pocket and pulled out something. It was wiggling.

The girl my age started drawing a hopscotch pattern on the dirt driveway. Charles came up behind her, holding that wiggling thing in both hands, trying hard not to drop it. Quick as a cat's wink, he reached out and slipped it down the back of her neck. I could see it kicking before it disappeared.

The girl yelped and started jumping around like she was standing on an anthill. She started patting herself all over to make sure nothing was hiding in her clothes, then gave another yelp and pulled at her blouse.

"You creep!" she yelled. "Your stupid toad peed all over me!" She turned and aimed a kick at a place that would have made Charles double up and fall in the dirt if it had made contact.

"You," she shouted, "will go to the BAD PLACE if I have anything to say about it!"

"You won't," he answered.

"How do you know?"

"Because you, Reba Lu, don't have any *authority*."

She turned red and slammed into the house. Charles was busy gathering some leaves from the front lawn when she came out a few minutes later, wearing a clean blouse. She went right up to him and shouted, "You'd better keep away from me. Don't talk to me. Especially don't touch me!"

"It's your own fault," Charles said. "You shouldn't have carried on like you did. You know that toads only pee when they get excited. You scared the poor thing."

It was at that moment, when she whirled around and went back to her hopscotching, that I decided to wander across the street. I was halfway there when Mrs. Adams came to the front door and put both hands on her hips. She spoke in the same kind of voice Mama uses when she says she's at the end of her rope.

"Really, Reba Lu . . . ," she began.

"He started it." Reba Lu stood on one foot and bent over to pick up her marker stone.

"Turn the other cheek," Mrs. Adams advised.

"Ha!"

Then Reba Lu saw me. For a few seconds we stood there, measuring each other up. Reba Lu had red hair and freckles and what Mama called "oomph." She looked at me like she doubted if I had any. I guess she decided to take a chance because she said, "What's your name?"

"Angie."

She raised one eyebrow. "Must be a nickname."

I nodded. "It's really Angelina."

"I'm Reba Lu."

"I heard."

"It's really Rebecca Louise, but that's too big a mouthful. The monster is Charles. Those others over there are the twins."

I saw them up close for the first time. Two identical little girls, about five years old, pretty as pansies. They were making mud pies and trying to feed them to a mangy cat with big eyes and a crooked tail. They had their hair braided in short pigtails tied at the ends with colored ribbons.

"Keep your distance from those sisters of mine," Reba Lu said. "The one holding the cat's head, that's Violet.

The one with the mud pie is Rose. My mother makes them wear purple and pink ribbons so people can tell them apart. Don't let their names fool you. If you get too close, they'll bite."

From the look of the cat's tail, they could do more damage than that. I decided to take her advice. I changed the subject. "What happened to that toad Charles put down your back?" I asked.

She shrugged. "It hopped into those bushes by the front door. It'll probably give me warts." She glanced over at Charles, who was putting a large leaf on the sidewalk. "Don't pay him any mind. He has a missionary complex."

"What?"

"He doesn't want to be one and he's trying to prove he isn't the type. It's a good thing, as far as I'm concerned. By the way, we're the new preacher."

"You mean your father is."

"Nope. He says we're all in this together."

I wondered what the Reverend Adams would say if he could see Charles spitting on the sidewalk, which was what he was doing now. He put a leaf a few feet in front of him. *Splat.* "Perfect shot," he said. Then he backed up two steps. *Splat.* "Almost perfect."

He walked over to the edge of the grass and picked up something fat and black. It looked like a stinkbug. He put it carefully in the middle of a sidewalk crack, where it began to move slowly away. Charles wiggled his mouth around to work up some spit and shot it straight at the bug. He raised both fists above his head. "Bull's-eye!" he shouted. Then he gave me a sideways glance.

"That was pretty good," I said. I measured Charles with my eyes and saw that he was a little taller than me.

He shrugged. "Stinkbugs are pretty easy because they're so slow. But a grasshopper—now that takes some practice. They're liable to hop away before I have enough spit."

I thought Charles had a real talent, but Reba Lu didn't. "Ignore him," she advised. She squinted at me. "How old are you?"

"Twelve."

She nodded. "I'm almost twelve and a half. I guess we'll be in the seventh grade together come September." She gave me a questioning look. "You like to hopscotch?"

I picked up a smooth stone, tossed it onto the first square, and did two singles and a double over it. That's how our friendship started. With names, and being the same age, and liking to play hopscotch in the preacher's dirt driveway.

CHAPTER TWO

The next day, Mama and I made her famous meat loaf, scalloped potatoes, and Waldorf salad to take across the street to the parsonage. It was my favorite meal, and I was glad when Mama said, "Let's double the recipe, and have enough for our own dinner tonight."

It took most of the morning because there was so much mixing and chopping to do. We boiled potatoes, then skinned them and cut them into thick slices and put them into a big bowl. Mama made the white sauce while I grated cheese. We took turns chopping onions, first putting a slice from the hairy end on top of our heads to keep from crying.

"It's a mystery to me why this works," Mama said. She had learned about it from a cooking demonstration at a meeting of the Messina Woman's Club. We had to stand up straight while we chopped so the slice wouldn't fall off. I didn't care why it worked. I was just glad it did, because I was always the one who had to chop the onions, and I was sick of red eyes and a snotty nose.

I loved cooking with Mama. She never scolded me for doing something wrong, just showed me the right way instead. And I loved the way she plunged her bare hands right into the bowl of ground meat and raw eggs and onions and bread crumbs to mix up the ingredients because that meant I didn't have to do it. Getting raw meat and eggs under my fingernails was not my idea of a good time.

Mama put her arm around me. "This is a welcoming dinner, Angie," she said. "Folks have been doing this for new neighbors for longer than I can remember." She gave me a hug. "It's a kind of sign that this is a good place to live. That our town is full of good people." Messina did have a lot of good people in it, but I thought there were some exceptions. Miss Hallie Harper, my sixth grade teacher, for example. There were times when she was downright mean.

That afternoon, when I went over to the parsonage with Mama to deliver the food, nobody came to the door when we rang the bell.

Ding-dang-ding-dong. The four brass chimes hung just inside the front door on the entrance wall. Mrs. Linfield used to polish them with a soft cloth and Vaseline. "This is the kind of music angels make," she had told me. But angels weren't making the kind of noise I heard now.

"Look what you've done!" Reba Lu shouted from somewhere inside. A door banged, or maybe it was somebody's head hitting the wall. "Get out of my room! Get out, get out, *get out!*"

"Give me back my rat!" Charles yelled.

"I already gave it to the cat."

"Argh! I'll get you. You'll be sorry!"

Reba Lu shrieked, and the door slammed again.

"Now, Charles. Reba Lu. I have heard enough." It was Mrs. Adams, speaking in a low, controlled voice.

Mama rang the bell again. A horrible yowling filled the air, and the Adams's cat streaked around the corner of the house with the twins close behind it. Its crooked tail stuck up like a zigzag bolt of furry lightning.

Mama turned to go home, but the door opened wide and there was Mrs. Adams with a red kerchief wrapped around her hair and a dust mop in one hand. She looked at the twins and shook her head. She didn't try to stop them. I didn't think anybody could. She just pulled the kerchief off, smoothed her hair, and held out her hand to Mama.

"I'm Deborah Adams," she said.

"And I'm Sally Wallace," Mama answered.

They both looked at Mrs. Adams's outstretched hand and started to laugh because Mama had the meat loaf in one hand and the Waldorf salad in the other. Mrs. Adams leaned the dust mop against the wall and took the meat loaf. Then they joined hands and smiled at each other as if they were old friends.

When we handed over the rest of the food, you would have thought we were delivering Christmas presents. "Oh, Sally, you've saved my life," Mrs. Adams exclaimed. "The children aren't usually so wild. Reba Lu, especially, knows when to turn on her good manners. But all four of them are acting like savages today. I hope it's the confusion of moving that's done it. I'd hate to think they'll be like this permanently." She invited us right into the kitchen, put the food on the counter, and filled the teakettle.

"You'll stay for a cup of tea? Of course you will. I'm dying to visit. Everything about this town is still new to me."

We sat at the kitchen table, and Mama began to tell her things about Messina, like how you could get your groceries delivered free if you paid your monthly bill on time, and how the children's shoes at Hanson's dry goods store were every bit as good as the ones you could buy in the city and not nearly so expensive.

But I kept thinking about how she had called her children *savages*. I liked that. I couldn't wait to tell my friend Geraldine, who was always the one to be telling *me* new things. I wondered if Mrs. Adams got her information about savages firsthand—if they had been missionaries living among savages before they moved to Messina.

Mrs. Adams seemed so friendly I got up my nerve to ask.

Mama acted shocked and said, "Angie, what a question!"

Mrs. Adams put her hand on Mama's arm. "It's all right, Sally. We have some friends who are doing mission work in New Guinea. But whenever my husband gets to thinking we might do the same, I remind him there's plenty of missionary work to do right here at home. Anyway, I have quite enough to deal with trying to keep peace among our own four."

The teakettle began to sing, and she put the tea things and a plate of cookies on a tray. "We'll have tea in the parlor, like proper folks do," she said. She laughed like she'd made a joke, and I saw Mama smile. This was sure a lot different from having tea with Mrs. Linfield.

It wasn't but a few minutes before Reba Lu came in and shook Mama's hand. When Charles came in, I could hardly believe he was the same person who had just put a toad down his sister's blouse. He wore a clean shirt that was tucked into his pants, and it looked like he had put water on his hair and combed it flat on top. He sat down and ate about a dozen cookies and talked to Mama about his hobbies, which included reptiles, stamps, and camping out.

Charles didn't mention spitting. I decided he could be polite when he wanted to. Mrs. Adams said he and Reba Lu were just one year apart, so I figured he would be starting eighth grade come September.

I couldn't stop thinking about Charles after we went home—how he could put a toad down Reba Lu's blouse, then turn right around and have good manners while he ate cookies and talked to Mama. But mostly, I thought about his spitting. Men spat on the sidewalks and in the street. It was a dirty thing to do. Everybody knew that. Still, men got away with it and so did boys. They spat in the wastebasket at school, at the bushes on the playground, and on the railroad tracks on a hot day, so they could make them sizzle. They even spat at us girls and at each other.

But Charles took the cake. I'd seen him hit a leaf, dead on, and he had marked that stinkbug even when it was crawling away. Reba Lu had told me that he once had to memorize five Old Testament Bible verses for spitting in the Sunday school drinking fountain from three feet away.

I made up my mind to find out what real spitting felt like. The kitchen sink wouldn't do. It had to be outside in broad daylight. I was walking alongside our house on the narrow sidewalk that went by the kitchen window when it came to me that this was as good a place as any.

I looked along the walkway and saw a large stinkbug moving slowly across the concrete about two feet away. *A moving target,* I thought. If Charles Adams could mark a moving bug, so could I. And this one was even bigger than his, which ought to make my job easier. I sucked the insides of my cheeks to work up a good wad of spit, leaned over, and aimed.

My saliva landed in front of the stinkbug. The bug backed off a bit and began to detour around the wet blob. I leaned over to try again, but I suddenly felt something was wrong. Probably it was that conscience thing that I kept hearing about in Sunday school. I turned around and saw Mama, staring at me from behind the kitchen window screen.

The back porch door slammed, and she was standing on the sidewalk. She looked at the stinkbug and then at me. I swallowed what was in my mouth.

"Angelina, were you trying to spit on that poor bug?" she demanded.

I nodded.

"It was not a good idea," she said quietly. Which told me quite clearly that ladies do not spit at all. Not anywhere. Not even on stinkbugs. Then she made me move the bug, which was beginning to stink something awful, to a safe place. Then I had to get the hose and wash down the sidewalk.

I told myself this was all Charles's fault, but I knew that wasn't true. He hadn't told me to spit on the stinkbug. I had just wanted to see if I could do it myself. When I finished hosing, I went out to sit on the front steps and play jacks. I had just done foursies when I looked across the street and saw a stranger coming down the sidewalk. He looked to be a bit older than my daddy. He was wearing a dark suit. Even on a hot day like this! It looked a little shabby, but he had put a red carnation in his buttonhole. He walked kind of funny, favoring one leg. He stopped a minute and leaned over to rub it. Then he took a few more steps and stopped by the low-clipped privet hedge that bordered the lawn of the Clement house right next door to the parsonage.

I'd never seen him before. We didn't have many strangers in our small town. When we did, people wanted to know why they were there. Were they somebody's kin? An old friend from out of town? A new shopkeeper? Congregational or Baptist? This man cleared his throat with a gurgling sound, leaned over, and spat a yellow wad that looked like pus into the gutter. I turned my head and looked the other way. It was clear that he was not a gentleman.

His spitting made me feel sick. Not like when I watched Charles trying to hit a leaf. That had made me go right home and try it myself. But this was disgusting. The spit seemed to come from somewhere deep inside him, somewhere dirty.

I was picking up my jacks to go inside when Mama came out on the front porch. She looked across the street, and raised one hand to shade her eyes from the sun. Then she went right down the front steps and walked over to the curb.

"Jefferson?" she called out. "Is that you?"

I stared. I couldn't believe Mama knew that man.

"It is you," she said. "It's been a long spell since you were in Messina. Are you back to stay?" I didn't think she sounded too friendly.

He tipped his hat to her, the way men do when they talk to ladies. "Hello, Sally," he said. But he didn't answer her question. He just turned and walked up the steps of the Clement house and rang the bell. It was a three-bedroom bungalow where the choir director, Lucy Clement, lived with her mother and a boarder named Gisele Martin who taught first grade at the grammar school.

When nobody came, he knocked hard on the door. Mrs. Clement opened it. As soon as she saw him, she commenced wailing. She sounded as distressed as my dog, Buster, did when he got bit by a snake last summer. But that Jefferson person just stepped inside and shut the door behind him.

Mama came back up the porch steps. She was shaking her head the way she sometimes did when Eddie and I didn't act the way she thought we should. "That man," she told me, "never did have good sense. Always taking chances. One time, he raced his old Ford out on the City Creek Road and ended up in the river." She looked thoughtful. "I suspect he's come on hard times."

Then she put her hand on my shoulder. "Mr. Jefferson Clement did his bit in the army, and he got decorated for it. He must have done something to deserve that medal, and we oughtn't to forget it."

So that's who he was. But Mrs. Clement sure hadn't sounded happy to see him. I started to ask Mama about that, but she marched right past me and into the house. The screen door banged shut behind her.

CHAPTER THREE

We were eating watermelon on the front porch that evening when Geraldine Murlock came by. "Hey, Geraldine," I yelled. She came up to the porch, flipped up the skirt of her sundress from behind, and sat on the concrete steps next to me.

"Ahhhh," she sighed.

I knew right away what she meant. Those steps stayed cool even on the hottest days, and they sure felt good on your backside.

Geraldine and I had known each other since the first day of kindergarten. I had been standing in the playground deciding whether to swing or slide when she came up and stood next to me.

"Scared?" she asked.

"Of what?"

"The bars. Sissies sit in those swings and go down that baby slide. I'd rather hang from the bars."

She bent over and scooped up a handful of soft dirt from under the swings, then rubbed it into the palms of her hands. She went over to the bars, grabbed hold of one, and swung back and forth a bit. Before I could figure out what was happening, she was hanging by her knees with her underpants showing. "Come on," she said. "Try it."

I tried, and tried again. I got a blister on the palm of my hand and a skinned knee from falling in the dirt. But when I finally hung from the bars by my knees, just like Geraldine, I didn't care if my underpants *did* show.

From that day on, we were friends. Geraldine was the one who always wanted to try something new. I was the one who could calm her down when she got carried away. Like the time she dialed "one" and asked Dr. Thomas if his refrigerator was running. When he said yes, she laughed real loud. "HA! HA! HA! You'd better go catch it."

"That wasn't very nice," I'd told her. "Dr. Thomas might have been with a sick person, giving a shot or something."

"I never thought of that."

"That's the trouble, Geraldine. It's a good thing you have me to do your thinking for you."

She put an arm around my shoulders. "We make a good team," she said. High praise, from Geraldine.

"Have some watermelon," I offered now.

"Can't have any this late in the evening," she said. "It makes me wet the bed."

That's the way Geraldine was, always blurting out the truth, no matter what it was. My father cleared his throat and started to cough. I saw his mouth twitch the way it always does when he's about to laugh out loud, but Mama gave him a poke. My brother, Eddie, who was fifteen, made a choking sound and went into the house.

"Really, it does, Mr. Wallace. My mama says she never saw anything like it. I just go to sleep and wake up in a puddle, and she says if she catches me eating any watermelon after four o'clock in the afternoon, she'll tan my—"

"Look there!" Mama exclaimed. "I thought I saw a shooting star!" Everybody looked, but nobody saw anything.

"That's too bad," Mama said. "You must have just missed it." She reached out and took my plate of watermelon that I hadn't even finished. "Why don't you and Geraldine go take a walk? It's real nice this time of evening."

Geraldine's eyes lit up. "Come on, Angie," she said.

I thought about asking Reba Lu to come along because she hadn't met Geraldine yet, but taking a walk around the block was my favorite thing to do with Geraldine. Just the two of us. It meant freedom, though Mama didn't know that. It meant sharing secrets and promising never to tell, cross your heart and hope to die.

Sometimes it also meant stopping at the drugstore and letting Johnny Henderson fix you a double-chocolate-cherry coke. Geraldine had a huge crush on Johnny, who was going into the ninth grade and was way too old for her. But I had sworn to keep her secret.

So we set out by ourselves. As we walked up the street

that evening, Geraldine decided she wanted to drop in on the revival at the Baptist church and watch the souls being saved. We could hear the bell ringers tuning up as soon as we turned the corner by the drugstore. They weren't real bells, just goblets of water, each one filled to a different level. The players tapped them with the backs of silver spoons and produced a waterfall of sound that made the back of my neck tingle. Half the town went to those revivals, just to hear the music.

Geraldine and I sat in the back row of pews. It was the best place to be when people started getting the spirit. That was my favorite part of the show, even better than the water goblets.

I looked around while we waited. The Congregational church, where my family went, had white walls and a pretty, stained glass memorial window behind the altar. The center aisle was covered with blue carpet.

The Baptist church, on the other hand, needed an inside paint job, and the windows along the walls were filled with mustard-colored glass that gave everybody a jaundiced look, the way people get when they eat too many carrots. The wood floor was worn and scuffed, probably from so many sinners walking down the center aisle to be saved.

The little pump organ, operated by a perspiring Miss Barnable, began bellowing out music, and the congregation swayed and sang, *We shall come rejoicing, bringing in the sheaves.* Geraldine and I stood and swayed along with them so we wouldn't attract attention and look too obviously like Lutherans.

After the singing was done, we sat down and listened to some water glass music. Then the visiting preacher, a man called Brother Otis, with slicked-back hair, got up and began to give the message. He started off soft and slow, but pretty soon he began carrying on like he had a hot brick in his pants.

He said, in a voice that trembled as it roared, "I'M HERE . . . TO CURE YOU . . . OF YOUR SPIRITUAL . . . ILLS!"

Miss Barnable eased in the stops and started playing "The Old Rugged Cross" real soft so we could hear what the preacher said above the music. But really, we could have heard him if she'd played a lot louder.

"ALL YE WHO ARE WEARY AND HEAVY-LADEN, COME FORTH AND CONFESS YOUR SINS!" Brother Otis thundered.

One by one, people started down the aisle toward the altar. Not everybody, of course. Only the worst sinners. That's why Geraldine and I were there. We wanted to see which ones had been so bad they had to confess in public.

Old Man Snyder was first. Geraldine poked me, and I poked her back. We had heard the way Mr. and Mrs. Snyder used to yell at each other right out in the front yard where everybody could hear them. Some folks said she got on the bus one day and never came back. But we figured he had killed her and buried her in the cellar.

Miss Hallie Harper was next. She had given me a D on my geography test. It was about time she repented!

My mouth dropped open when I saw Mrs. Clement marching down the aisle shoving Mr. Clement in front of her.

"Get along there!" I heard her say. "You've got plenty of confessing to do." He was red in the face, but he did what he was told. Right that minute, he didn't look much like a war hero to me. He looked more like he wanted to hightail it for the door. Even so, I noticed that he pulled his shoulders back and nodded to people he passed on the way to the altar.

I whispered to Geraldine, "I saw that man spitting in the gutter this morning."

Geraldine didn't blink an eye. She stood up and followed him down the aisle.

"Geraldine! What are you doing?" I stood up and tried to grab her, but missed. What was she thinking of? What terrible sin could *she* be guilty of?

I started down the aisle after her, but somebody reached out and grabbed the waistband of my skirt and wouldn't let go. I twisted my neck and saw Mrs. Clement's daughter, Lucy, our Congregational choir director, sitting at the end of a pew. She had the same kind of look I had seen on her face when the sopranos in the choir couldn't hit their high notes. Kind of determined, like life was trying to get her down, but she was putting up a good fight.

"Sit down, Angelina," she whispered. "Congregationalists don't confess their sins in public. If you take one more step down that aisle, I'll tell your mother on you."

I leaned over and whispered back. "But your mother went to get saved."

"Mama doesn't need saving," she told me. "It's my father who needs to have a talk with the Lord."

I had a lot to think about while I waited for Geraldine.

Brother Otis raised his hands in the air and began singing, *Mine eyes have seen the glory of the coming of the Lord.* Everybody joined in, and the sinners started back up the aisle to their seats. We had just reached the *glory, glory, hallelujah* part when Geraldine plopped down beside me.

"What did you confess?" I asked.

"I didn't confess anything. I just stood there and looked sorry and listened to the sinners." She gave me a look. "How else am I going to find out about things?"

On the way home she told me, "That man with Mrs. Clement confessed that he deserted his family. He left them to get along the best way they could. *And* he philanders."

I knew what deserted meant, but *philander* was a new word. "What does *that* mean?"

Geraldine gave a little shrug. "I'm not exactly sure, but I know it's something you're not supposed to do. I think it's why Brother Otis and Miss Barnable went behind the church this afternoon."

"They were probably talking about the revival hymns."

"Back behind the church? In the bushes? Honestly, Angie, you've got to start noticing what goes on in our town. They weren't talking about music. They were . . . you know."

I knew, but I didn't want to talk about it right then. We were quiet a minute. Then I said, "Well, guess who that man with Mrs. Clement turned out to be?"

"Who?"

I hugged myself inside. Geraldine didn't know *everything*. "He's her husband," I said calmly, just like I was asking somebody to pass the salt. "That makes him Miss

Clement's father. His name is Jefferson. He got a medal in the Great War, but he needs to have a talk with the Lord."

Geraldine stopped in the middle of the sidewalk and stared at me. "How do you know all that?" she demanded.

"Why, I just listen, Geraldine. How else am I going to find out about things?"

CHAPTER FOUR

We were saying good night at the corner of Pacific Avenue and Mulberry when Geraldine suddenly said, "Are you OK? You look kind of puny."

I did feel downright puny. Kind of like I'd walked too far too fast and my knees needed to rest. By morning, I had a cough that rattled like Dr. Thomas's Model T Ford when he backed it out of the driveway. Mama picked up the telephone and said, "One, please."

It was the doctor's number. Geraldine's was one-one, and we were four-four. Messina wasn't a very big town, and the telephone office had only so many plugs in the switchboard. Most people listened in on their party lines long enough to find out the news.

My bedroom door was open, and I could hear Daddy

and Mama talking in the kitchen. "She's not so sick that she doesn't look forward to seeing the doctor," I heard Mama say.

Everybody loved Dr. Thomas. He had a black leather bag, worn thin around the edges, but shiny all over. Geraldine said she thought he wiped it with shoe polish. In it he kept his instruments. When I was younger, he always put the stethoscope earplugs in my ears so I could listen to his heart. Then he let me rap his knee with the knee hammer and watch his leg kick up in the air. I was too old for that now, but not too old to feast my eyes on his little bottles of different-colored sugar-coated pills, small and round, with flat sides.

They worked wonders, he told me. He said they even cured people who only thought they were sick. "Do you want pink or blue?" he asked now.

I didn't hesitate a second. "Pink!"

"I'll leave a bottle of cough syrup with your mama," he said. "You swallow a teaspoonful, then suck on a pink pill to kill the taste."

I often wondered why he didn't give some pink pills to his daughter, Miss Emma. Probably it was because he knew she wasn't sick the regular way. She was *strange* sick.

It must have made him sad to go home at night and see her strangeness because Miss Emma was all he had left after Mrs. Thomas "passed away."

I knew that meant she had died, but I thought it was a silly expression. It was like passing the potatoes, or passing gas, or passing the corner where you meant to turn. Wherever she had passed to, I thought it was too bad that Dr. Thomas had to cope with Miss Emma alone.

Sometimes Miss Emma seemed all right. She loved to answer the phone when Mrs. Dawson, Dr. Thomas's housekeeper, didn't get there first. She could sweep the walks and go to the store if someone went with her. On Sundays, she went to church and wore her boa, a fur scarf with real little fox heads hanging from it. She liked to pat them, but Dr. Thomas had to give her a nudge when she started talking to them.

I was lying in bed thinking about Miss Emma when Mama came into my bedroom. I was hoping she was bringing me some of her homemade lemon drops or a piece of the pineapple upside-down cake that she baked in a heavy black frying pan. But it was a mustard plaster, evil-smelling and sinister-looking. She had spread the mustard mixture on one-half of a piece of red flannel, then folded it together to make a kind of envelope.

She held it out in front of her, and I could feel the heat coming at me as she lowered her arms to plop that flannel on my chest. Mama pulled my blanket up under my chin, and I got hotter. She made me sip some steaming chicken broth, and I started to sweat. By morning I was feeling better. "Dr. Thomas's cough syrup usually does the trick," I heard her say to Daddy. "But a mustard plaster is a sure thing."

I was well again when Geraldine came to visit on Saturday afternoon. We were playing jacks on the front porch, cooling our legs on the cold cement steps, when Mama came back from calling on Mrs. Hewitt, who was just out of the hospital. She was all sweaty and out of breath, and she began talking to my father before she got the front screen door shut behind her. We kept on playing and listened.

"It was terrible," she gasped. "There was poor Mildred Hewitt, lying on her sickbed, frozen with fright, and Emma Thomas sitting there talking a mile a minute with that awful thing around her neck!"

"You mean her boa?"

"Not the fur one!" Mama exclaimed. "The *real* one. The one she keeps in a cage. It crawled around her neck and up in her hair and down her arms and onto the bed."

Geraldine and I quit playing jacks and inched a little closer to the screen door. We loved hearing stories about Miss Emma.

Mama hugged herself and shuddered.

"So what did you do?" Daddy asked. I could hear the laughter bubbling up in his voice.

"*Do?* I was as scared as poor Mrs. Hewitt, who looked like she was having a stroke. All I could *do* was call Dr. Thomas. He came and got her, poor man. I know Emma loves to go visiting, and it's good for her to get out, but he's going to have to make her leave that snake at home."

After that, they lowered their voices, so we slipped around to the back and went into the kitchen, where we poured some grape Kool-Aid and listened through the crack in the swinging door.

I didn't see anything wrong with what we were doing. Geraldine said listening was important. It was a good way to find out things grown-ups wouldn't tell us. We had learned a lot about the people in our town by paying attention to what they said, and the way they sounded. Geraldine wasn't as good a listener as I was. She got sidetracked by little things—like hangnails, or a wart on her knee. But now she was as interested as I was to hear the latest about Miss Emma. So she kept quiet and put her head close to mine against the crack in the door.

"It's those animals," Mama insisted. "That nasty little pug-faced dog and all those cats. She feeds them at the table, in chairs. And they sleep with her at night, in her bed. The boa, too, I'll bet. Lord knows what else she's got living with her. The worst of it is, she thinks they're people. Mrs. Dawson told me so, and she ought to know. She's the one who has to clean it all up."

"Poor Miss Emma," said my father.

"Poor Mrs. Dawson!" I whispered to Geraldine. We slipped out the back door, and I whistled for Buster. Then we walked up the street, hoping we could get a glimpse of Miss Emma with the snake around her neck.

When we did, we almost dropped dead in our tracks. There she was in the upstairs window. Her head reminded me of a plump yellow apple, smooth all over but with frizzled brown hair that resembled dried leaves. She wore a clean white blouse with a crocheted lace collar, but she had a soiled look about her. Dark smudged spots hollowed out her eyes.

I stood there, staring back, until Buster began to whine and push between my bare legs. But when Miss Emma smiled and waved, I didn't think she looked so strange after all. I was waving back when the snake around her neck began to move. Its head swayed as she fondled it, and in the window beside her was the ugly face of her nasty little pug dog, Lily-Poo. She scooped it up and kissed it smack on the mouth.

Geraldine and I turned and ran, with Buster at our heels. I didn't stop until I reached my front steps, and Geraldine kept right on going. I threw my arms around Buster's neck. I would let my dog sleep at the foot of my bed if he wanted to. But Buster would think it was undignified if I tried to put him in a chair at the table. Besides, Mama would take a switch to both of us.

That was the whole difference, I decided. Poor Miss Emma didn't have a mother to lay down the law. She didn't know when to stop playing games.

The fortunate thing was that the strangeness didn't keep me from loving Dr. Thomas. He bore his cross well. I wasn't sure what that meant, but it had to be true because I had overheard Reverend Adams say so when Reba Lu and I were hopscotching in the parsonage driveway.

CHAPTER FIVE

All the Congregationalists went to church the next day to hear Reverend Adams give his first sermon. Even my dad went, and he hadn't been inside the church since the Sunday that Reverend Linfield decided to preach for over an hour on hellfire and damnation.

Reverend Adams and Mrs. Adams had been doing a lot of visiting around the neighborhood. When they came to our house, Reverend Adams and my dad rolled up their sleeves and tinkered with our Plymouth sedan until Mama and Mrs. Adams made them come sit on the front porch and have some iced tea and oatmeal cookies.

"Nice folks," my dad said after they had gone home. I figured Mama wouldn't have too much trouble getting him into his good suit come Sunday morning, and it turned out I was right about that.

There was a big crowd for the new preacher's first Sunday. It seemed like half the town was filling the pews. I was in my seat when I heard a kind of commotion in the back of the church. I turned around and saw that Mr. and Mrs. Clement had come in. You never saw so much hand shaking and carrying on. People smiling and nodding and patting him on the back like he'd won first place in a popularity contest.

The sermon started with a funny story. Reverend Linfield had never done that. He always just plowed into sin like he knew folks had a pile of it in their own backyards. But Reverend Adams, after he had got people laughing and feeling comfortable, commenced talking about ordinary problems and how we should do the best we could every day. He ended up telling everybody: *Love your enemies, turn the other cheek, hate the sin, and love the sinner.*

Out of the corner of my eye, I saw my dad nodding his head.

"Mighty fine ideas," he said later, after we got home. "Too bad the preacher didn't go a little farther."

"How do you mean?" I asked.

"Well, he told us what we should do, but he didn't give us any directions. Folks need some hints as to how they can go about doing those things."

I was still thinking about what he said when Geraldine came over on Monday afternoon with a pile of *Calling All Girls* magazines. The two of us liked to sit together on the porch swing, thumbing the pages and arguing about which outfits would look good on us.

"Look here!" She held up an advertisement. "The girl in that skirt and sweater looks just like you." She pointed to a page with a girl carrying an armload of books. Her dark brown hair was shoulder length and straight, like mine. She was wearing a big fake smile that made her look like studying must be fun.

Well, I *was* a little like that, except I didn't think my smile was so fake. I *did* like school, and I liked to get good grades. I might groan along with everybody else when we had homework, but that was just for show.

Geraldine hated homework. She came over almost every afternoon so we could do it together. Sometimes I got real impatient with her when she picked at a fingernail or made whistling sounds between her teeth while I was explaining an arithmetic problem.

"You've got to pay attention," I would say. "You're just copying my answers, but you don't know how I got them."

"Well, they're the right answers, aren't they?"

"That's not the point. What are you going to do when we have a test?"

She sat back in her chair and gave me her exasperated look. This meant bulging her cheeks out and staring at me real hard. "I'll manage," she said. "I always do."

I knew she "managed" by sitting behind me and peering over my shoulder, but I didn't say anything. Whenever Geraldine got on my nerves, I thought about that day when she'd taught me how to hang by my knees from the bars in the playground. And I remembered that we were best friends.

The front door slammed across the street. Reba Lu

picked up a stick and started drawing a new hopscotch pattern in the driveway. She never looked our way.

Geraldine peered over the top of *Calling All Girls*. "Who's that redheaded girl across the street?"

"Reba Lu Adams. She's one of the new preacher's kids. She's pretty good at hopscotch."

"She sure has a funny name." Geraldine raised one eyebrow, and I remembered how Reba Lu had done the same thing when I told her my name. I could only raise both eyebrows at the same time, but I reminded myself to pick up on my eyebrow exercises in front of the medicine cabinet mirror, starting again that night.

"Let's see if she wants to come over here and look at magazines." Geraldine turned a page. I sighed. That's the way it was with Geraldine and me ever since I'd bawled her out for that phone call about Dr. Thomas's refrigerator running. Now, whenever she got an idea, she sat back and waited for me to act on it.

I went down the front steps and stood on the sidewalk. "Hey, Reba Lu!" I called. "Come on over."

She dropped her stick and hightailed it across the street. She stood a second on my front porch until I said, "Reba Lu, this is Geraldine." Then Geraldine scooted over to one side of the porch swing and I sat on the other so Reba Lu could fit between us. We three sat and thumbed the pages until we came to an article called "Does Your Voice Charm?" We practiced using *low, vibrant tones* for a while, then we looked for new ways to fix our hair.

Geraldine found a picture of a girl with long blonde

hair. "That's what I want to look like," she said. "But my mother won't let me. She cuts it so short I look like a boy."

"It is short," Reba Lu said, and we explained that a couple of years ago, some new kids had brought head lice to school. The kids moved away soon after, but the lice stayed. Our mothers took us to the barbershop to get our hair cut real short so Dr. Thomas could treat our scalps. My hair grew out, but Mrs. Murlock, Geraldine's mother, never really believed the doctor when he said we were cured.

"I'm not taking a chance on lice," she had said. "They could come back any time." And she made Geraldine wear her hair real short so she could spot the dirty things if any more of them dared to raise their heads.

I'd overheard Mama say, "Mrs. Murlock is a fearful kind of person, but she means well."

I took that to mean that being fearful was why she was always saying *no!* whenever Geraldine wanted to do something. That didn't stop Geraldine. She just went ahead and did what she wanted without asking her mother first. I thought things might have been different if Geraldine's daddy had lived. He died when she was just a baby, and Mrs. Murlock was bringing her up all by herself. I thought if I had that job, I might turn into a fearful kind of person, too.

Personally, I thought short hair suited Geraldine, but it would never be as blonde as the girl's in the picture. Geraldine's was pale brown. She squeezed lemon juice on it after she washed it and sat in the sun to let it dry, but it didn't help. "No matter what I do to it," she said, "it's as dull as mud."

"Nothing wrong with that," Reba Lu told her. "Rich people put mud packs on their faces to purify their skin."

Geraldine looked impressed that Reba Lu would know a thing like that, but I didn't believe a word of it. Nobody with any sense would put mud on their face. I began turning pages by myself because the two of them were talking a mile a minute and ignoring me. It felt like they were sitting on the porch swing together, and I was sitting somewhere else. I bet if I went in the house, they wouldn't even know I was gone. I started flipping through the pages faster and faster until, all of a sudden, I came to an article called "What It Takes to Be Popular."

"Look here," I said. "This is what we need to read."

Reba Lu took the magazine and spread it open in her lap. She pointed to a boxed-off area titled "HELPFUL HINTS." The first hint was *Be Nice to Everyone.*

Geraldine read the words out loud. "That sounds like something your daddy said in his sermon last Sunday."

Reba Lu sighed. "He says that all the time. Especially to Charles and me."

"Let me get this straight," Geraldine said. "If you act nice to people—even the ones you don't care about—then they'll like you and you'll be popular?"

Reba Lu nodded. "That's the general idea." She folded her hands and looked from one of us to the other. "Besides that, it's a surefire way to get on God's good side."

Geraldine scrunched up her face. "Why would I want to do that?"

Reba Lu stared at her. "Everybody wants to get on God's good side."

Geraldine narrowed her eyes, the way she always did when she was about to start an argument. But I spoke up before she could say a word.

"What exactly did you have in mind?" I asked Reba Lu.

Reba Lu pursed her lips like she was kissing air and squinted her eyes. We waited for her to speak, figuring that she had an inside track, her daddy being the preacher and all. Finally, she said, "I thought we might do what my daddy said. You know, make God happy by loving our enemies and all that. Loving your enemies is almost the same as turning the other cheek, so we'd be killing two birds with one stone."

I felt uncomfortable about turning the other cheek. It was like inviting somebody to slap you two times in a row. "What about hating the sin and loving the sinner instead?" I asked.

Geraldine really liked that idea. "They won't be hard to find," she said. "There must be plenty of sinners in Messina."

This was starting to sound complicated to me, but I decided to go along with it because the two of them wanted me to.

"Let's make a list," Reba Lu said.

"Yeah!" Geraldine exclaimed. "Let's get their names down on paper."

They looked at me until I went in the house and came back with a notepad and a pencil with some eraser still attached. Reba Lu reached for it before I had hardly gotten settled on the swing. When Geraldine and I started telling her about some of the folks in our town who did bad things, Reba Lu licked the tip of the pencil and wrote down their names. I noticed she had neat penmanship and dotted her *i*'s with perfect little circles. I admired that.

"Even though we like him a lot, and he always takes time to talk to us kids, we probably ought to start with Willie Jack Kelly," Geraldine said. "Everybody knows that's not grape soda that he carries around in his paper sack."

I pinched myself to keep from grinning because I was in on Willie Jack's secret. I had overheard Dr. Thomas tell Daddy that the bottle Willie Jack kept in his brown paper sack was filled with tap water instead of whiskey like people thought. "He's been prone to kidney infections ever since the war," Dr. Thomas had said. "Now that we have that new sulfa drug, he's some better, but I told him he still needs to drink lots of water."

The doctor had laughed. "He just keeps his water bottle in that sack because it irritates the tarnation out of those old hens like Mrs. Hewitt and her crony, Hallie Harper, to see him drink from it. Willie Jack doesn't care much what people think about him. He says he did his bit to help his country because it was the right thing to do. He knows that, and it's enough for him."

It was enough for me, too, and I decided right then and there I wasn't going to tell what was in his sack.

"What about Miss Hallie Harper?" I said real quick, just to change the subject. "There's no way you can please that teacher!" I told Reba Lu to write her name in capital letters.

Geraldine nodded. "And then there's Mr. Flannery. He chased me out of his yard when I was only trying to taste a couple of grapes off his arbor.

"And Old Man Snyder," Geraldine went on. "He told

Johnny Henderson to stop snooping around his property, and Johnny wasn't doing anything but walking up the street to go to work at the drugstore. Probably he was afraid Johnny would discover Mrs. Snyder."

"Where is Mrs. Snyder?" Reba Lu wanted to know.

"In the cellar, where he buried her after he killed her. Everybody knows that."

Geraldine reached across Reba Lu and gave me a nudge. "Remember how Mr. Jefferson Clement had to go to the revival and confess he's a philanderer?"

"That's not all," I said. And I told them about his disgusting spitting and how Mrs. Clement had wailed when she opened the door and saw him standing there.

"But Mama says he did his bit in the war, and we oughtn't to forget that. She says he was decorated. That means he got some sort of medal."

"For doing what?" Geraldine asked.

I shrugged. "Something brave, I guess. Don't you have to do something brave to get decorated?"

"It depends," Reba Lu said. "You could get a Purple Heart if you were wounded. That might mean you were brave, and it might not. What if you got shot while you were running away? Or you might have accidently shot yourself in the foot."

I looked at Geraldine. She lifted one shoulder. "He's still a sinner because of the philandering."

Reba Lu wrote down his name. We were quiet a minute. Then Geraldine gave a big sigh and said, "We forgot somebody." She gave me a gagging kind of look, and I knew right away who she meant.

"Dodie Crumper," I said. I sat back and waited for the explosion.

"Dodie Crumper!" Geraldine agreed. "I can't stand her. She's a disgusting human being. I hate everything Dodie Crumper does."

I said I did too, so we talked a while, educating Reba Lu about how Dodie picked her nose when she thought no one was looking and popped the pimples on her chin.

Reba Lu turned red. "I do that sometimes."

"So do we," Geraldine said, "but Dodie does it in public."

That made all the difference, so we hooked little fingers and swore to love Dodie and just hate the nasty things she did in public. I didn't even want to think about what she might do in private.

"Aren't we going to love anybody else?" Reba Lu asked. "There must be lots more sinners all around us."

Geraldine frowned. "Would we have to love them *all*?" She sounded like that might be more than she could handle.

Reba Lu turned to a fresh page and drew three columns. "How about if we start with a few of the worst ones and practice on those?"

It hadn't been so hard to come up with the names and the bad things people did. What stumped us was how to show love. I thought this was what my dad had meant when he said the preacher should have given us some hints. We finally came up with something to do for everyone except one person.

SINNER	SIN TO HATE	HOW TO SHOW LOVE
Willie Jack Kelly	Drinks whiskey from a paper bag.	Bring him apples and bananas.
Miss Emma	Loves that evil snake.	Visit her and teach her to crochet.
Miss Hallie Harper	Gives terrible grades.	Tell her she is a good teacher.
Jefferson Clement	Philanders.	Help him find a hobby, like collecting stamps.
Dodie Crumper	Picks her nose in public. Pops her pimples, ditto.	? ? ? ?

I put one finger on that empty space in the last column. How could we find a way to love Dodie? How could we find a way to *like* her? "This isn't going to be easy," I said.

Geraldine reached across Reba Lu and poked me. I poked her back. We both looked at Reba Lu. She looked exasperated. "We could start by being nice," she said.

"How?" Geraldine and I said the word at the same time without much enthusiasm.

"Honestly!" Reba Lu exclaimed. "We say 'Hi!' or 'How are you?' or 'What's new?' That's what my father would tell us to do."

"No offense," Geraldine said, "but your father hasn't met Dodie Crumper. Last time I spoke to her, she threw a rock at me."

"Why did she do that?" Reba Lu asked.

Geraldine looked down and shuffled one foot like she was squashing a spider.

"Could be because I called her fat-headed and stupid."

Reba Lu nodded wisely. She seemed to like to play it up that she was a few months older than Geraldine and me. "This has gone too far to be solved by saying 'Hi!'" she said. "Not only do you hate Dodie, but she hates you right back. There's only one thing to do. We have to go all the way."

I had a bad feeling about that. I knew Geraldine did too because she said, "Just how far would that be?"

Reba Lu folded her arms across her chest and looked serious. "We have to include her."

"Include her in *what*?" I asked.

"In something kids really like to do. Something so special it only happens once a week."

Geraldine looked horrified. "You don't mean . . . !"

"Yes." Reba Lu nodded. "The Saturday matinee."

"You only go to the matinee with your best friends!" I protested.

"Exactly," she answered. "With the people you love."

Geraldine made a gagging sound. I know how she felt. The matinee was sacred. It meant popcorn and Royal Crown Cola, the exciting fifteen-minute Buck Rogers serial before the main feature, the intermission, when we climbed the stairs of the Ritz Theater and visited the restroom with its red brocade drapes and velvet padded stools where ladies could sit and powder their noses.

It meant the twenty-minute bus ride from Messina to San Andreas, the bus ride back, the independence and grown-up freedom, the tingling fear of what might happen if you missed the bus or got off at the wrong stop. The possibilities for excitement were endless. San Andreas was a big town, with two picture-show theaters, a Woolworth store, and Rexall Drugs, where you could get a cheeseburger, fries, and a cola for twenty cents. All this would have been fun to share with Reba Lu, her being a newcomer and all. But now we would have to share our fun with Dodie Crumper.

Later, when the three of us went up the street to her house to invite her, I was hoping she would refuse. I crossed my fingers behind my back and said to myself, *Say no! Say no! Say no!*

We found her on her front steps, bouncing an old tennis ball with most of the fuzz worn off. She had on an old pair of shorts with the hem coming out of one leg and a man's sleeveless undershirt several sizes too big. Her hair wasn't combed. It looked dry and scruffy, as though it belonged to a stray dog.

She looked at Geraldine and me, then at Reba Lu. "Who are *you*?" she asked her.

Reba Lu didn't even blink. "Reba Lu Adams. The new preacher's my daddy."

"I don't go to church," Dodie said.

She began to pick at a brown, crusty scab on her knee. A big piece came off, and she examined it carefully before putting it on the step next to her. Then she gave a long, wet sniff.

It was quiet, except for the sound of Dodie sniffing. "So . . ." Dodie looked at us one at a time. She had an expression like she was cleaning out a junk box and figuring out what to throw away. "What do you want?"

Geraldine turned her head and looked at me. I turned mine and looked at Reba Lu. After all, this had been her idea. Reba Lu cleared her throat.

"We're going to take the bus to San Andreas and see the matinee at the Ritz Theater on Saturday. Do you want to come?"

Dodie squinted the way people do when they're taking aim before shooting at a row of bottles on a fence. "Why should I?" she asked.

Reba Lu squinted right back at her. "Because it will be fun," she said.

"Oh," Dodie said. She started picking at what was left of that scab. She picked at it for what seemed like a long time. Finally, she looked up at us, her pale blue eyes squinted half shut against the sunlight.

Say no! Say no! Say no!

I thought the words so hard I was sure Dodie would get the message.

"Well, I guess that would be OK," she said.

We three turned and made it down the street in record time. We sat on my front porch swing and looked at each other. I, for one, wasn't sure we had done the right thing. But at least Reba Lu hadn't lied and said *because we like you and want to be friends.*

CHAPTER SIX

That Saturday, we put our nickels in the slot on the bus, rode to San Andreas, and got off at the corner nearest the Ritz Theater. We each bought hot, buttered popcorn in a paper sack and Royal Crown Cola in a paper cup. Except for Dodie, who said she wasn't hungry.

We found our seats and waited for the lights to dim. Maybe this wasn't such a bad idea after all, I thought. I was beginning to get a warm feeling inside about making the effort to like someone when I glanced over at Dodie sitting beside me. She put her hand in my popcorn bag and stuffed some in her mouth without even asking.

She kept on eating, and I let her have the whole thing. I didn't want to put anything in my mouth that Dodie Crumper had touched.

She began to crack her knuckles while Buck Rogers and his Rocket Rangers were rescuing Wilma Deering from Killer Kane and his mob of space gangsters. The cracking got louder and faster as Buck snatched Wilma from a moving conveyor belt just as the jag-toothed chopping wheel was about to slice her down the middle. *Crack, crack* went Dodie's knuckles.

I stood it as long as I could, but when the Fox Movietone News came on, I leaned over and whispered, "Cut it out." She gave me a dirty look and crossed her arms so she could put her hands in her armpits. I tried not to stare, but I couldn't help it. Even in the dim light, I had seen that Dodie's hands were red and sore-looking, and some of the skin was peeling off.

Dodie had gone to school with Geraldine and me since kindergarten. But I didn't have any idea how she spent the rest of her time. I never talked to her if I could help it. Sometimes I even crossed the street when I saw her coming.

Now that I couldn't hate her anymore, I wondered how I was supposed to act. Did I have to feel sorry for her? Should I ask her what she did to make her hands look like that?

I decided not to think about Dodie and focused on the news report, which was mostly about the war in Europe. The film showed Hitler giving speeches in Germany. At first, I thought he was funny, the way he yelled and threw one arm in the air, but when I saw trucks full of sad-looking people being driven to the trains, where they would travel to places called concentration camps, I didn't see anything funny about that.

I thought back to that morning when I was lying on the floor waiting for the fan to blow cool air on me. The voice on the radio had talked about the war in Europe, and said, ". . . only a question of how long America can stay out of the conflict."

Did that mean Hitler could come here and try to put Americans in trucks like he did in Germany? Did it mean people in my town would have to fight him? I kept telling myself that Europe was far away, and he wouldn't bother to come all the way to Messina. At the same time, I wondered how he was getting away with the things he was doing. And if he was so bad, why was America staying out of the conflict? Why didn't our president stand up and say, "That's enough!" It was what my dad said when he thought Eddie and I were getting out of line.

I took a long drink of Royal Crown Cola. I was glad when the Porky Pig cartoon came on. We laughed right up to the end when Porky said, "Th-th-th-that's all, folks!"

The main feature was *Days of Jesse James* with Roy Rogers and his sidekick, Gabby Hayes, who needed a haircut and shave real bad. When Roy Rogers finished singing "I'm a Son of a Cowboy," Dodie started to clap. I gave her a poke and said, "He can't hear you."

She put her hands in her lap. "I know that," she said. "I'm no dummy."

When I sneaked a look at her a couple of minutes later, her sore-looking hands were balled up into fists. I didn't know if it was to keep from cracking her knuckles or if she was mad and felt like punching something. I leaned a couple of inches away to give her some space.

After the show Geraldine said, "Let's ride the streetcar." It seemed like a good idea, especially since it was free on

Saturdays. We rode it all the way north to the end of the line at Hill View Pioneer Cemetery. Just because we had never done it before, we got off and walked around among the gravestones.

We were in the middle of a heat wave, but black clouds formed over the mountains to the north and nosed across the valley, casting dark, creeping shadows over the withering grass. It was covered with mounds that were sure signs of gophers. I had stopped to count them when thunder sounded off in the distance. Hot as it was, I felt a shiver in the middle of my back, and I made up my mind not to miss the next streetcar out of there. I hurried to catch up with the others.

The graveyard was really old. Most of the gravestones were in bad condition, with big chunks broken out of the marble and the words hardly readable. Miniature pink and white cemetery daisies grew close to the ground, almost hidden. They were the only fresh flowers I could see in the whole cemetery.

"This is a disgrace," Reba Lu said. "Look here at poor *Jessie Ann Watkins 1865–1910*, with weeds growing all over her."

"It says *Eternal Peace*," Geraldine said. "I guess she isn't bothered by a few weeds."

"That's not the point," Reba Lu snapped.

"Look, there are lots of words on this one," I said, to keep Reba Lu from getting carried away.

She shrugged. "They're too faded to read."

But Dodie got right down on her hands and knees with her nose almost touching the old marble. "I can make out most of it," she said.

Carolina Mary Clarke 1871–1883

Beloved daughter
Here lies our angel, taken away

From her earthly home to sing
In the heavenly chorus.

"Twelve years old," Geraldine said.

My age, I thought. I wondered what the stone would say if *I* were buried there.

Here lies Angelina Wallace
Who got a D in geography.

I felt a raindrop on my arm and shivered. Maybe it would rain hard and wash the dust from all these old stones. But the clouds moved eastward, taking their shadows with them.

We were quiet until Dodie said, "I sure wouldn't want to be buried in this place."

"It probably looked a lot nicer all those years ago," Reba Lu told her.

"Nobody gets buried here anymore," I told them. "This place is all full up. My daddy said so. Anyway, our church has its own burying place in that land out back under the elm trees."

"Do you have to be a member to get put there?" Dodie wanted to know.

I looked at Reba Lu, then at Geraldine. They both

shrugged. "What's the difference?" I asked. "None of us is going to be dying anytime soon."

"*She* did," Dodie told me, pointing to Carolina's gravestone.

Suddenly, visiting the cemetery didn't seem like such a fun thing to do.

"Let's go," I said, and nobody argued. We caught the next streetcar on the corner and opened the windows so the breeze would blow through our hair.

"I hope we get back to town in time to stop at Walden's drugstore for some ice cream before we have to catch the bus," I said. "I still have a dime to spend."

"I'd rather have a root beer float, and it only costs a nickel," Reba Lu said.

Geraldine began to count her money. "I think I'll have enough to buy a couple of comic books. They last longer than ice cream. I can read them over and over."

We all looked at Dodie, who was taking off one shoe. She turned it upside down and shook out two nickels and a dime. She put the dime back in her shoe and the nickels in her pocket. Then she stared out the window and didn't say a word.

I sneaked a poke at Geraldine. She made a sound in her throat that sounded like "*hmm-hmm.*" Then she said, "Dodie, how'd you get so much money?"

Dodie gave her a quick look. "I earned it," she said. She went back to looking out the window.

The rest of us stared at each other. I'd heard Mama say that Mrs. Crumper did a load of clothes for ten cents, and she ironed for fifteen cents an hour. Mama said she could buy a pound of ground round steak, a bunch of carrots, and four baking potatoes for that much money.

But nobody was going to get rich taking in washing and ironing. Especially since rumor had it that Mrs. Crumper drank up most of the profits. So it was a pretty sure thing that Dodie didn't get her money from her mother. Yet here she was with an extra dime in her shoe. It just didn't add up.

By the time we got back to Walden's drugstore, I had a headache from all that thinking. "I'll have a peppermint cone," I told the soda jerk. "Two scoops." I figured I'd earned them.

I sat next to Reba Lu at the counter. She was already sipping root beer through a straw. Dodie sat next to me and ordered a lemon phosphate. Now and then she blew into it through her straw so that the bottom of the glass filled with big bubbles.

"That sounds like someone passing gas," said Geraldine, who had chosen her comic books and sat on a stool next to Reba Lu.

I knew if we were back in Messina, Geraldine wouldn't be talking about gas or thumbing through comic books. She would be leaning with one elbow on the counter, smiling at Johnny Henderson, and getting an extra squirt of chocolate in her cherry coke.

"What a rude thing to say," Reba Lu said.

Geraldine leaned forward and gave me a grin. For a minute, it was just the two of us, the way it had always been. Then Dodie started blowing more bubbles, and Reba Lu offered Geraldine a sip of her root beer.

When we climbed on the bus that would take us back to Messina, I made sure that Reba Lu sat next to Dodie.

Geraldine and I took the seat across the aisle from them. Reba Lu began asking Dodie what Mr. Crumper did for a living.

"He's a geological engineer," Dodie said.

Geraldine and I nudged each other. "I wonder where Dodie got big words like that," I whispered.

Everybody in town knew that Mr. Crumper had come upon hard times and had to travel around the county digging outhouse holes for people who couldn't afford septic tanks. And the reason Mrs. Crumper took in washing was because the outhouse holes didn't put enough food on the table to feed the backyard crows.

I waited until the bus blew out a belch of gray exhaust fumes and started to move. Then I leaned over and whispered into Geraldine's ear.

"Have you seen Dodie's hands?"

She gave me a surprised look. "I'm not blind."

I took that to mean that everybody in the world had noticed but me. And that I should have noticed. And that I was actually a little slow for not noticing. Geraldine really made me mad when she said things like that.

"Well then, what's the matter with them?" I asked.

"My gosh, Angie. Everybody knows what Dodie does at home."

"What? What does she do?"

"She does all the washing and ironing that Mrs. Crumper would do if she was sober."

CHAPTER SEVEN

We were coming home from Sunday school the next morning when Reba Lu suddenly said, "Who's next on our list?" She was really into loving sinners. I could see we had a busy summer ahead of us.

"How about Miss Emma?" I suggested. "Every time I walk past Dr. Thomas's house, I see her sitting by that upstairs window peeking out. I bet she'd like company. We could go and get acquainted first and teach her to crochet later."

I didn't really want to go, but I was dying to see Reba Lu's face when she saw what Miss Emma kept for pets.

"Not me," Geraldine protested. "I hate snakes."

Reba Lu gave her a stern look. "We all agreed to work together on our list of sinners," she reminded her. "We can take Dodie with us. We'll call first and ask Mrs. Dawson to make sure the snake is in its cage."

"Ugh!" Geraldine said, but Reba Lu had already lifted the receiver down from the wall and was waiting for the operator.

When we started up the street, the front door of the Clements' house banged open. Mr. Jefferson Clement came out on the porch, saw us watching, and waved a greeting from across the street like we were all old friends.

"Ho, there, ladies," he called. "Out for a little Sunday walk?"

It was the first time I'd come face to face with Mr. Clement since he arrived back in town. I wondered if he remembered that I had stood there watching and listening while Mama talked to him. I didn't know what to say to him, but, as usual, Reba Lu did.

"Good morning, Mr. Clement, sir. It's a fine day, isn't it?" Then she gave Geraldine and me a push to hurry us up.

Mr. Clement glanced back at his house, then crossed over and followed us up the street. "Oh, ick!" I whispered. "Having him back there where I can't see him makes me feel like a spider is crawling in my hair."

"Ignore him." Reba Lu made a quick turn up the front walk to Dodie's door. She turned to look at me. "If you can't say anything nice, don't say anything at all. That's what my daddy would say." Then, before we could stop her, she gave the bell key a twist. "Dodie?" she called. "Come on out here."

"Can't," came from inside. "I'm scrubbing clothes."

The three of us looked at each other. I remembered

what Geraldine had told me, and I figured this must be one of the days when Mrs. Crumper was on the bottle. I wondered which neighbor's clothes Dodie was scrubbing. I was considering what to do next when Geraldine opened the patched screen door and walked right in.

I never would have done that. It was the worst kind of manners. Apparently, neither would Reba Lu because she stood firmly beside me. Out of the corner of my eye, I saw Mr. Clement passing us on the sidewalk in front of Dodie's house. He slowed down a little, seemed to hesitate, then went on. Reba Lu and I stood there and listened, and pretty soon we heard Geraldine say, "You're washing *whose* dirty drawers?"

We couldn't hear Dodie's answer, even with our ears against the screen. Reba Lu shifted from one foot to the other. "I'm thinking Geraldine might need our help," I said.

"I was thinking the same thing." Reba Lu reached for the door handle.

Neither one of us was prepared to see Mrs. Crumper asleep on the couch with her mouth hanging open and an empty glass in her hand. The cotton stuffing that was coming out of the holes in the cushions was about the same color as her dyed yellow hair. We tiptoed on through the kitchen and found Dodie and Geraldine out on the back screened porch.

The Crumpers didn't have a washing machine, just two big standing tubs. One was for washing. The other, with a wooden wringer clamped on its side, was for rinsing. The washtub held a big scrub board, and Dodie leaned over it with soap up to her elbows. Up and down went her skinny arms, rubbing somebody's old union suit against the bumpy tin panel.

"I wonder who in Messina still wears old-fashioned underwear like that," I said.

Geraldine stared at me. "What do you know about men's underwear?" She sounded surprised and a little angry. She never could stand it if I got a step ahead of her.

"I hang my father's and Eddie's on the line, don't I?" I almost told her that Eddie wore modern boxer shorts with stripes, but thought better of it.

Geraldine didn't have a father or any brothers, so I knew a lot more than she did about *some* things. It felt real good to get the advantage now and then.

Dodie pulled the cloth out of the water and twisted it so that most of the soap oozed out, then dropped it into the rinse tub. She dunked it up and down a bit, then stuck the end of the dripping cloth in between the rollers, tightened the lever, and started turning the handle with both hands. I could see it was hard work.

"How long is this going to take?" Geraldine asked.

"Until I get done." Dodie jerked her head at a dirty pile on the floor. "Then I have to hang them on the line. What do you want?"

"We're on our way to visit Miss Emma," Reba Lu said. "We thought you might like to come, too."

Dodie shook her head. "I won't go in any house that has a snake in it. No way!"

"We took care of that," Reba Lu told her. "It's caged up."

"Miss Emma's crazy," Dodie protested. "Mr. Jefferson Clement told me she hasn't got the sense to tie her own shoelaces." She gave the handle another couple of turns. "He's a nice man, Mr. Clement is. He helped me hang out the wash the other day. He says he likes to be friendly to people. He says . . ."

"Are you coming or not?" Geraldine interrupted. I wished she had held her tongue. I was dying to find out what else Mr. Clement had said. After all, he was on our list of people to love, and we needed to find out as much about him as we could.

Dodie pulled a man's shirt out of the soapy water and began to rub it up and down against the scrub board. Finally, she dropped it in the rinse water and turned to look at us.

"Why are you all of a sudden asking me to do things with you?" she demanded. She was using her testy voice. The one that said *don't fool with me.*

Geraldine shuffled, and Reba Lu cleared her throat.

"Why not?" I said. Just those two words. But I was amazed that they had come out of my mouth.

Reba Lu started to say something else, but Dodie held up one hand and cut her off just like she was slicing bread with a sharp knife. She looked at me with a kind of half smile.

"Yeah," she said. "Why not?" Geraldine and Reba Lu could have been in China for all the notice she gave them.

Dodie wiped her hands on her shorts and went to peek at her mother. When she came back, she said, "She'll be out a while longer. I can't be gone too long, though."

We walked up the street in twos. Geraldine and Reba Lu first, then Dodie and me coming along behind.

We were about to ring Dr. Thomas's doorbell when Geraldine said, "Wait a minute. Who's going in first?"

We hadn't thought of that.

"If we all push in together, we could get caught in the doorway and never get out," Geraldine said. She was trying to act like she was in charge, but she was scared. We all were, a little, but Geraldine was the only one who would never admit it. That's why she was stalling by asking questions like that.

Geraldine picked a few long blades of grass, broke them into different lengths, and held them up so we could see only the tips. "We'll draw straws," she said. She gave Dodie first choice. Poor Reba Lu got the short piece. She would have gone home right then, except we pushed her up next to the front door and made her ring the bell. Mrs. Dawson must have been waiting on the other side because the door flew open like a gust of wind had hit it. She ushered us upstairs before we could change our minds.

"This is a real occasion," she said. "Miss Emma doesn't get many callers. Now, you just settle in and make yourselves at home. Stay as long as you like."

Reba Lu went up the stairs so slow we had to give her a couple of shoves to get her to the top. Miss Emma's door was closed, probably to keep the animals from running loose. We stood in front of it and looked at each other. "Do you smell something funny?" Reba Lu asked.

We did. It was a warm, musty smell, kind of sweet in a sickening sort of way. Dodie tapped at the door. When it opened, the smell came out to meet us.

"Welcome," Miss Emma said. "How thoughtful of you

to call. She motioned to two chairs and a love seat. "Do sit down."

I didn't see how we could. Two cats sat in one chair and hissed. That ugly little dog, Lily-Poo, was on the love seat, licking herself. Miss Emma sat in the remaining chair and stroked the brown monkey that sat on her shoulder and wrapped his tail around her neck. White mice skittered from under the dresser and across the carpet. I spotted the snake in a tall cage in the corner. It was looping itself in and out of shapes that never stopped moving.

"That's Cleopatra," Miss Emma said. "Isn't she lovely?"

Geraldine gave me a shaky look and sat on the edge of the bed as far from Miss Emma's green parrot as she could. The rest of us perched beside her. I noticed that the pink satin coverlet was spotted with white splotches of parrot poop. I tried not to sit in any.

The parrot began to squawk, "Help! Help! Somebody save me!"

"Henry is afraid of strangers," Miss Emma said. She smiled at him fondly. "Wise old bird, aren't you, Henry?"

Reba Lu and Geraldine looked at me. Dodie opened her mouth, but no words came out. I cleared my throat, but I couldn't think of anything to say. I gave Reba Lu a nudge.

"Well," she said, "how are you today, Miss Emma?"

Without blinking, Miss Emma said, "I'm not quite right. Didn't they tell you?"

I wanted to ask who "they" was, but I didn't dare.

"They've been saying that since I was only as big as Joseph here." She lifted the little monkey off her shoulder and bounced him on her knee like a baby. To my amazement he put his thumb in his mouth, just like he was human.

"Miss Emma's not right," she told Joseph, patting his furry little head. "That's what they said about me. I heard them through a crack in the door."

Joseph chittered back at her. *Chika-chiky-chika.*

I glanced at Reba Lu. Her eyes were open wide, and she looked like she would never shut them again. She edged a little closer to me to get away from the fresh parrot poop that Henry was depositing on the coverlet.

I stared at Miss Emma with her face like a plump apple and her frizzled brown hair. She looked anything but lovable to me. We really had our job cut out for us if we wanted to keep her on our list. I could just imagine trying to teach her to crochet while Joseph chattered and tangled the thread and mice ran across the floor.

"Want to see my new teeth?" she asked suddenly. Before we could decide, she opened her mouth into a big doughnut shape and leaned toward us. Her false teeth were large and wet and shiny.

I said a prayer for God to keep them in her mouth.

When the door creaked open, I half hoped it would be Him, coming to take charge. But it wasn't God. It was Dr. Thomas, which seemed to me almost as good. His eyes were on Miss Emma while he talked, but I had a feeling he was speaking to us girls.

"Nice for you to have company," he said. "The girls can catch you up on what's going on in our town."

I didn't think we could tell Miss Emma anything she didn't already know. From that upstairs window, she could see everything that happened on Palm Avenue. I bet at night she could even look in a lot of lighted windows.

As if she were going to demonstrate how much she could see, Miss Emma went over and peered out the window. She stiffened and held her breath. Then she began to rock back and forth, hugging herself with both arms. She turned and took a step toward Dr. Thomas. "Papa," she whimpered. "He's back." Her eyes had grown big, and her lips trembled. Her voice rose higher until she sounded like a little girl.

The little monkey squealed excitedly, and the parrot began to squawk. "Help! Help!" it screeched.

"Help! Help!" mimicked Miss Emma. Over and over.

Before we could see what Miss Emma would do next, Dr. Thomas took me firmly by the shoulders and pointed me toward the door. "You all better run along now," he said. "It's time for Miss Emma to have her rest."

We ran, and I led the way. I wanted to get outside to see what had scared her so. I could still hear her whimpering. And the sound of Henry squawking "Help! Help!"

As soon as I opened the front door, I saw who she was carrying on about. Jefferson Clement was leaning against the wall of the bank building on the corner, right where Willie Jack Kelly usually stood. He wasn't doing anything wrong, as far as I could tell.

But he sure seemed to have gotten Miss Emma riled up.

CHAPTER EIGHT

Crack! Sizzle! Boom!

The Fourth of July announced itself early in Messina and kept right on sparkling and banging until the moon was high.

Eddie and my father had bought Roman candles, whirligigs, and firecrackers over a week ago. They were saving the showiest ones for later, to set off at the town picnic. But I could hear the firecrackers early that morning while I helped Mama make the potato salad.

Everything sizzled and popped on the Fourth of July. The chicken crackled in the frying pan. Onions crunched as Mama chopped them into tiny, shiny pieces. Even the Rice Krispies I had for breakfast seemed to get into the spirit as they snapped and crackled.

American flags waved in front yards, and downtown Messina had a huge red, white, and blue banner that stretched all the way across Main Street from Flannery's Grocery Store to Verna's Beauty Parlor.

By eight o'clock in the morning, it was eighty-nine degrees outside, and inside it wasn't much cooler. The radio said it would be a scorching Fourth of July, and the announcer wasn't talking about fireworks.

Across the street, the Adams twins, Violet and Rose, were busy tying strings of firecrackers together. When they had a good collection, they eyed my dog, Buster. He eyed them right back and crawled under the house.

I saw Violet grin and point a finger in Buster's direction. She said something to Rose, who started hugging herself with excitement. That was when I remembered how Violet was the one who had held the cat's head while Rose tried to feed it a mud pie. I got the picture! Violet was the one who got the ideas, and Rose carried them out.

As soon as I had that figured out, I marched right over and told the twins I knew what they were planning. I made them look at me, one at a time. Then I had my say. "I skinned the hide off the last mean kids who tried such a trick." It was a fib, but I figured it was for a good cause. They looked disappointed, but scared, too, and that suited me.

Then I went back home and tried to lure Buster out from under the house with a lamb shank bone from last night's supper. But he knew all about firecrackers tied to his tail, and he wasn't taking a chance.

The next thing I knew, the twins were digging up a patch of dirt at the side of the driveway. Charles was helping, so I went over to watch. He showed Violet how to drag the hoe in a straight line to make a furrow. Then he pulled a long string of firecrackers out of his pocket and showed Rose how to plant it.

She began jumping up and down. "I get to plant the firecrackers!" she yelled. She looked at her sister and stuck out her tongue. "You have to dig the hole."

"Lay the line down real careful," Charles said, "and cover the crackers with that nice loose dirt. If you water them good and keep the weeds pulled, they'll sprout next spring and be ready to pick by summer. You can sell the ones you don't want and make some money to buy Abba–Zabas."

Reba Lu had come out to watch with me. "The twins are crazy about Abba–Zabas," she explained. "They chew at the taffy until they make a hole, then suck the peanut butter out."

"I'm surprised your father let Charles get away with that," I told her. "What are they going to do when the firecrackers don't sprout?"

Reba Lu shrugged. "They'll be into some other mischief by then." She grinned. "My dad was the one who put him up to it. He said there won't be any Sunday sermon if those two don't give him some peace."

Geraldine came by, and we three stood around looking at each other until I said, "I can't stop thinking about Miss Emma. While I was slicing the salad potatoes this morning, I kept remembering how she sounded when she saw Mr. Clement outside her window."

"You don't know for sure if Mr. Clement is the reason she was scared. Anyway, everyone knows Miss Emma is tetched." Geraldine held one hand up to her head, made a circling motion with her index finger, and laughed. But it wasn't a ha-ha laugh. I could tell by the tone of her voice that she was in one of her arguing moods.

"Nobody else was out there!" Reba Lu said.

"That's right." I stared at Geraldine until she lowered her eyes. "We all heard her," I went on. "She said, 'He's back!' and she sounded like a little girl having a bad dream. I can't get it out of my mind."

I didn't think they could, either. We stood there looking at each other a few minutes more. Finally, we meandered up the street to say hello to Willie Jack and take him a shiny apple that had been picked fresh last fall from one of the mountain orchards and stored in our cellar where it kept nice and cool.

Willie Jack was the town handyman when he actually worked, and folks said he was a real craftsman. He painted, repaired, and could build things from scratch. I remember when Daddy hired him to make my dollhouse when I was little. He even carved some furniture for me—a tiny bed and a kitchen table with four chairs. Then he made a sofa and an easy chair for the front room. He put tiny soft pads on those because he said my doll people would be more comfortable with cushions to sit on.

Willie Jack didn't have any family of his own, which my dad said was a pity because he would have been a good father. He dressed himself in overalls, a plaid shirt with long sleeves, and heavy boots all year round. When Mama took me up to Artie Longmire's barbershop to have my hair cut real short back when we had that head lice scare, I heard Artie say that all those clothes helped cover Willie Jack's battle scars.

"It's too bad what his injuries have done to him," Artie said, and all the men waiting to get shaves and haircuts nodded their heads up and down.

Eddie told me Willie Jack had been shell-shocked in the Great War. He was fighting in the trenches in France when a German bomb dropped so close it blew him out of the hole he was in, and it was a miracle he didn't go to kingdom come. They sent him home to Messina instead. After all this time, he still jumped at loud noises and sometimes got the shakes. The worst times were what folks called his black spells. They didn't happen so much anymore, but when they did, he talked out loud to himself and thought he was still in the war. When he got like that, Dr. Thomas would go and sit with him, and after a while he'd be himself again.

I liked Willie Jack. He talked to me like I had a lot of sense, which was more than my brother, Eddie, did.

"Do you think I need my hair trimmed, Angie?" he once asked.

I told him he did. "When you let it grow long and it hangs over your ears," I said, "you remind me of that actor, Gabby Hayes, in the Roy Rogers movies. Why don't you go see Artie Longmire at the barbershop? He can give you a haircut and a shave, too."

He thanked me for the advice. What's more, he took it, and he looked pretty good until it all grew back.

When we got to the corner, Willie Jack wasn't alone. He had his ugly old chow dog, Duke, with him. Duke mostly stood in front of Willie Jack's old frame house and drooled when we walked past. But when Duke saw a bicycle, he opened his mouth and showed his pointed teeth and long, purple tongue. He always looked like he'd been chewing indelible pencils.

Reba Lu said he looked harmless to her. My mouth dropped open when she walked right up and started petting him. "Nice Duke. Good dog," she said, and he rolled over on his back like he wanted his stomach scratched.

That's the way Reba Lu was, always trying to see the best in people. And dogs, too. I guessed that was the way you got to be if you were a preacher's daughter.

Geraldine and I edged over to say hello to Willie Jack, but he had more important things on his mind. He leaned back against the whitewashed stucco wall of the Bank of America building, waved one arm in the air, and motioned for God to come on down. He patted the dusty window ledge next to him and scooted over a bit to make more room.

"It's a fine day, ain't it, Lord?" he said to the empty space beside him. He always started his conversations with God that way, even if it was pouring rain. Then he would get right on with whatever it was that troubled him.

"I smell something fishy," he said now. Reba Lu stopped petting Duke and wiped her hands on her shorts. Geraldine and I sniffed the air, but Duke didn't seem to smell any worse than usual. Not fishy, anyway.

Willie Jack raised his paper sack to his lips, then changed his mind and put it down. "What I'm saying," he explained, "is that *somebody* is up to no good." He said *somebody* like he was sure God knew who he was talking about.

He gave his dog a nudge. "Ain't that right, Duke?" Duke didn't make a sound, just lay on the sidewalk, hoping for more petting. Reba Lu sighed and began rubbing his stomach with the toe of her shoe.

"What I'm asking, Lord," Willie Jack continued, "is for you to protect your little lambs. I'll do my part, but I can't be everywhere at once like you can."

He raised the paper sack again, and this time he took a long drink out of the open bottle that was inside. I still hadn't told Geraldine and Reba Lu that Willie Jack's hooch bottle was full of water. I gave myself a little hug for being in on his secret.

"Willie Jack Kelly got a medal for heroism in the Great War," I'd heard Daddy say. "He saved a lot of American lives, including mine. Any time he wants to stand on the corner and talk to God, it's all right with me."

Reba Lu gave Geraldine and me a poke. "This is not a good time to talk to Willie Jack about sin," she whispered. I had to agree. I didn't want to compete with God for Willie Jack's attention anyway.

We backed away slowly. As soon as we got out of earshot, Geraldine asked, "Who were the little lambs he was talking about?"

"Don't you ever read the Bible?" Reba Lu asked her. "God's little lambs are young people, like us."

"Well, *I* don't need protecting from *anybody*," Geraldine said.

I thought that wasn't entirely true. It was just Geraldine, acting like she knew all the answers. But we didn't have time to discuss it. The sound of drums was coming from the parking lot of the Congregational church across the street, and folks were hurrying over there to take their places in line.

The parade always began and ended at the church, and if you missed anything, you could see it right there: Dr. Thomas in his black and yellow clown suit, wearing a big red nose; the Messina marching band, which gave Geraldine goose bumps because Johnny Henderson was in it; Old Man Snyder riding the dappled mare that lived in the shed over the cellar where we suspected he had buried his wife; Eddie and my father on the Harley Davidson that Mama hated.

Jefferson Clement drove Mrs. Clement's old Ford convertible with the top down. He had polished it until it was as shiny as black ink. He wore a shirt so white it must have been bleached twice. And his tie matched the red stripes in the American flag tied to the radio antenna. Mrs. Clement sat in the front seat with him, but she didn't smile and wave her hand like he did. When they passed us, he took off his straw hat and lifted it high in the air. Some people behind us began to cheer, yelling, "Welcome home, Jeff!"

Geraldine started to wave, but Reba Lu got hold of her hand and pulled it down.

"What's the matter with you, Geraldine? Have you already forgotten how Miss Emma cried and carried on when she saw him?"

Geraldine shrugged. "She might have been mixing him up with somebody else. Anyway, you've got to remember that Miss Emma isn't quite right. She said so herself."

"Just the same," I said, "she's on our list of people to love."

"So is he," Geraldine reminded me. She was wearing one of her know-it-all looks, so I ignored her and went back to watching the parade. But I was beginning to wish we had left Jefferson Clement off our list.

The highlight of this year's parade was Reverend Adams dressed as Uncle Sam in red, white, and blue and wearing a fake goatee that kept slipping sideways on his chin. It didn't slip all the way off, and I figured that God must be looking out for him, and if that didn't give him a Sunday sermon, I didn't know what would.

When the parade was over, we all went to the American Legion Park east of town. Mulberry trees grew along the little stream that was fed by a spring. The berries were deep red, almost black. If we didn't pick them soon, the birds would eat them. The stream emptied into Willow Pond, where the trees trailed long branches in the water and frogs hid and croaked their night songs.

Tall eucalyptus trees stood along the north side. They were so old that their roots had risen far above the ground, making a kind of jungle that smelled like Mentholatum. Geraldine and I used to explore there, hunting for the little eucalyptus pods that looked like round heads wearing hats.

Dodie was over there now, wandering around among the trees. I saw her pull off some leaves and sniff them, then stick them in her hair. It gave me a funny feeling to remember doing the same thing myself. Then she climbed over some roots to a place where two eucalyptus trunks grew close together and made a kind of slanting V shape. She leaned back against one of those trunks and put both feet against the other. I could tell by the look on her face that she was just soaking it in. That this was a place she loved. I watched her a minute, then went to help Mama with the picnic food.

We were starting to set our potato salad and fried chicken on one of the long tables in the shade when Mr. Jefferson Clement came walking up with an angel food cake. He was wearing the same straw hat that he'd waved in the parade. It had a red band around it. And that white shirt of his just about made me blink when he stood in the sun. He came over to our table, smiled at Mama, and set the cake down. "The rest of my family will be along," he told her.

She gave Mr. Clement a smile before she said, smooth as silk, "Oh, Jefferson, Dr. Thomas and Miss Emma are eating with us today, along with Angie's friends Geraldine and Reba Lu." She began setting the table, then managed a little laugh. "You can leave the cake if you like."

Mr. Clement's mouth looked like he'd bit into a lemon. But only for a second. "Maybe next time, Sally," he said. Then he picked up his cake and walked away.

I could see he wasn't going to have any trouble finding someplace else for his family to eat. He started going from table to table, tipping his hat to the ladies and grinning from ear to ear, just like he was running for mayor. Mr. Flannery, the grocer, pumped his hand up and down and patted him on the back. And I saw Mr. Temple, our druggist, heading his way with a big smile on his face. Mrs. Hewitt started waving her hand at him and moving the plates at her table to make more room.

But Mama wasn't impressed. She leaned over and whispered to me, "Quick now! You go and tell your friends and the Thomases that we saved a place for them. Hurry up."

I hurried. But not so fast as to miss the look on Mama's face. She wasn't sorry she'd told a lie. Not a bit. There was something strange going on with Mr. Jefferson Clement, and I didn't know why she didn't just come right out and say so.

CHAPTER NINE

The day after the picnic, Reba Lu had to stay in her room until it was clean. Geraldine had a toothache, and Mrs. Murlock took her to the dentist. I sat on the front porch swing by myself, but it wasn't much fun. After a while, I told Mama I was going up to the American Legion Park to collect some eucalyptus pods. "You know, the ones that look like tiny hats," I said. "If I poke holes in them with a darning needle and string them on some yarn, I can wear them around my neck."

Mama smiled. "That's a good idea. We could dip them in some beet juice to add a little color." Mama was good at coming up with ideas like that. "While you're there," she said, "you could pick some mulberries. I noticed yesterday that they're ripe enough."

Mama made real good mulberry muffins, and I was tired of oatmeal mush for breakfast. I took a pail with a long handle and started up the street. When I got to the park, it was so quiet I could hardly believe all the commotion that had gone on there yesterday. I started collecting eucalyptus pods in a paper sack I'd brought and nearly jumped out of my skin when I saw two feet hanging from a tree limb above me. I could tell they were Dodie Crumper's feet without seeing the rest of her.

"You'd better come down," I told her.

"Why?"

"You could fall and break a leg."

"I could do that walking down the street."

"Maybe so, but it's more likely when you're in a tree."

Dodie jumped down and landed on both feet at the same time. "You're a fearful kind of person, aren't you?"

"I am not, and that's a rude thing to say."

Dodie shrugged her skinny shoulders. "I was only saying what I think." We stood there a minute. Then she said, "That day we went to San Andreas . . . it was OK."

I nodded. "I love going to the movies. Too bad Messina doesn't have a movie house."

Dodie scratched her head with both hands, then examined her fingernails for dandruff or something worse. "But then we wouldn't get to take the bus. That's the part I liked most. Going somewhere different. A place where nobody knows your name, and you can pretend to be anybody you want to be."

I had to think about that. I wouldn't want to be anybody else, but maybe I would if I was Dodie. "Who would you be?" I asked her. "You know, if you could choose."

She picked up a handful of pods and dumped them in my sack. "That's easy. I read about a girl in a book. She went to live at a farm where they expected a boy who could help around the place. But they kept her anyway. And she got to do all sorts of things and be outdoors a lot."

I didn't say anything. I was surprised that Dodie had read a book all on her own. But I wasn't surprised that she liked a book where the character lived with strangers instead of her mother.

She squatted down and began to draw squiggles with a stick in the soft dirt at the edge of the stream. Then she looked up at me sideways. "I've got that Geraldine figured out."

"What do you mean?"

"She acts like she knows everything, but she's really the kind who likes to sit behind people in school and look over their shoulders to get the answers."

I felt my face turn hot.

"Huh," Dodie said. "I thought so. I bet you let her do it, too."

It was hard to keep from smiling. I was thinking about the time we had a spelling test and Geraldine copied my words. But she wasn't careful, and she got some of them wrong. When Miss Harper passed back the papers with the grades on them, Geraldine's face turned red, and she said, "This isn't fair."

"Is that so?" Miss Harper said, and she sent Geraldine to the blackboard to write the words she missed ten times each. Some of the kids made chortling sounds, but Geraldine didn't care. She never minded having to get up in front of the classroom, even when she didn't know the answer. I wasn't like that. I never liked going to the front of the room. Sometimes I thought Geraldine and I were more different than we were alike.

She'd been mad at me for not writing clearer so she could cheat easier. She said she wouldn't come to my house for a whole week, but she didn't mean it. She was behind in writing her spelling sentences, and she needed my help.

All this thinking about wrongdoing reminded me of something I wished I could forget. Whenever I thought about it, I wanted to go back and change things. To speak up when I had the chance. But it was too late.

"What's the matter?" Dodie asked. She moved a few feet away. "You look like you're about to lose your breakfast."

I swallowed. I did feel a little queasy. I didn't like remembering the time I had acted like a coward, but every now and then it came sneaking back into my mind like a slug in a pot of geraniums.

I took off my sandals and went and stood in the cool water that ran through the park year round. I hoped my feet would get so cold I would have to sit down and rub them to get the feeling back. But they didn't.

"Did you ever do something you're ashamed of?" I asked.

Dodie scratched her head. "Maybe. Depends on what you mean by ashamed."

"You know. Something you feel really bad about."

Dodie scratched her head again. "You mean like stealing grapes from Mr. Flannery's vines? I've done that lots of times, but I'm not really ashamed. It's more like I'm sorry I got caught."

"This was different from stealing grapes." I began to wish I hadn't started this conversation.

Dodie looked at me as if I had suddenly become a more interesting person. "So what did you do?" she asked.

"Do you promise never to tell?"

Dodie crisscrossed her fingers over her chest in the general direction of her heart. "Promise. Hope to die."

I shook my head. This was Dodie Crumper I was dealing with, and I needed more than her promise. "You have to tell me something back," I said. "Like a secret thing you've never told anybody."

She narrowed her eyes. "OK."

So I told her how I had seen some mean kids teasing a new girl at school because she had a cheese and bell pepper sandwich. "Her parents were from another country, and I guess that was a normal lunch for them instead of peanut butter and jelly or baloney and mayonnaise like the rest of us had. But these kids dumped her lunch box in the schoolyard dirt. And they teased her about her name, just because it was hard to pronounce. I knew I ought to tell them to cut it out, but I was afraid to. She looked so scared. I'll never forget it."

Dodie didn't react the way I'd hoped she would. I had wanted her to say that I was being silly about the whole thing. But she didn't. She said, "I don't like to see somebody get picked on." Which told me right there that she would have done something, and I was a coward for standing by.

I didn't want to talk about it anymore. "It's your turn," I said.

She made me cross my heart and say "hope to die," then

as soon as she found a low rock next to the stream where she could sit and dangle her feet in the water, she began.

"In the middle of the night, I had to go to the—you know—and I tripped over a chair and fell flat on my face. I stayed on the floor a little while. Stayed real quiet, just to make sure nothing but a chair had tripped me up. Then I got up and felt around on the wall for the light switch. But when I flipped it, nothing happened. I was in the dark. Totally. There wasn't even a moon that night. That's when I figured that Mama hadn't paid the electric bill, and they'd shut our lights off again. I—I never went back to bed. Just pulled a cushion from the front room couch and sat in a corner. I held that cushion in front of me just in case something was waiting to pounce on me. I kept hearing noises in the walls."

I thought that wasn't surprising, considering what the Crumper house was like. Those noises were probably mice—or worse. "So what finally happened?" I asked.

"I sat there until the sun started to come up. I never knew how pretty the sky could be early in the morning, with all that light chasing the night away."

I stared at Dodie. Who would have thought she could say something almost like a poem. But I didn't tell her that. Instead, I said, "Where was your mother?"

"Out cold with her bottle."

Dodie said it like it was the most natural thing in the world to have a mother who was out cold with a bottle. I wondered if it was her bottle that made her feel poorly so much of the time, but I wasn't going to ask.

"I've never told anybody, Angie. That Geraldine would

probably laugh her head off at the idea of someone my age being afraid of the dark. Remember you promised not to tell."

"So did you," I reminded her. We both stood there with the cold spring water up to our ankles and stuck out our little fingers. I hooked mine around hers, and we pulled hard to make our promises stick. Then we got busy picking those mulberries that Mama wanted. When we'd finished, we began to walk down the street together.

"I'll save you a mulberry muffin," I told her.

At Dodie's house, she turned and looked at me just before she opened the door. "Save me two?" she asked. Then she grinned.

I grinned back. When I'd gone to collect mulberries that morning, I'd never expected to get to be sort of a friend with Dodie Crumper. But that's what had happened. Now she knew something about me that nobody else knew. And I knew something about her. Somehow I was sure Dodie would never tell my secret. And that was more than I could say for Geraldine.

CHAPTER TEN

A couple of weeks later, Reba Lu and Geraldine and I were looking for something to do and decided we wanted to camp out. We wanted it even more after our mothers said no. We sat on my porch swing and tried to figure out what to do.

"Mama wouldn't even let me explain," I complained. "She just shook her head before I had even finished asking."

"Same here," Geraldine said. "Only mine said, 'Of course not!'"

Reba Lu gave the swing a big push with both feet, and we all put our legs straight out and coasted. "Want to hear what mine said?"

Geraldine and I didn't bother to answer. We knew Reba Lu well enough by now to know she would tell us, no matter what.

Reba Lu jumped out of the swing. "Mama looked at me like this . . ." She put one hand on each hip and gave us the kind of look Mrs. Adams usually reserved for Charles. "And then she said, 'Really, Reba Lu!'"

We burst out laughing. We had all heard Mrs. Adams sound exactly like that. Suddenly Reba Lu started doing a little dance, putting her arms in the air and turning around in circles. "I've got it!" she shouted. "They said no separately. That's our answer."

Reba Lu might have got it, but I didn't. And from the look on Geraldine's face, she didn't, either.

"Don't you see?" Reba Lu demanded. "We have to get all three of our mamas together. That way, we'll have a better chance to find a chink in their armor."

"What chink? What armor?" I glanced at Geraldine. She raised both eyebrows and shrugged her shoulders.

"It's an expression. If a knight's armor has a chink—a little piece broken out of it—he's more vulnerable."

I knew that word! Miss Hallie Harper said small nations by the sea could be vulnerable to attack by ships. That meant they would probably lose the battle. So maybe we could win the battle if we made our mothers more vulnerable by getting them together while we joined forces. I never thought I would thank Miss Harper for anything. But this might make it easier for me to love her.

"OK," Reba Lu said. "Here's what we're going to do. We'll bake oatmeal cookies and make sweet iced tea. Then we'll get our mothers to come sit on Angie's front porch. It'll be easy to convince them to let us camp out when they see how capable we are."

She did her little dance again. "What are we waiting for?" she asked.

So we baked the cookies that afternoon at the preacher's house because he was out making visits to the sick, and Mrs. Adams was teaching a Bible study class up at the church.

Reba Lu found her mother's recipe, and we worked on the cookies all afternoon, sifting and mixing and blending. But when Reba Lu pulled the first cookie sheet out of the oven, we just stared at them. Not one of us even wanted to taste one. "We followed my mama's recipe," she said, "but her cookies never looked like this."

Geraldine reached out and poked one with her finger. It was mushy in the middle and singed at the edges. The raisins looked like black flies. "Your oven must be broken," she said.

Just then the twins came in the kitchen, all sweaty and dirty from digging up some of their firecrackers to see if they had sprouted yet. They took two cookies apiece, one for each hand, and ate them right down, burnt edges and all.

We cut away the rest of the black edges, but it didn't help much. We would have made another batch, except we had already used up all Mrs. Adams's oatmeal.

"Mama is always telling me not to eat cookies fresh from the oven because they need to rest a while for the flavor to develop," I said.

Privately, I thought these would take a considerable amount of resting to improve. But we hoped for the best and put them in a shoebox lined with waxed paper and hid them in Reba Lu's closet so Charles and the twins couldn't find them.

The next day, Geraldine told her mother, "Mrs. Wallace has invited you to her house this afternoon." Reba Lu did the same. I just waited until Mrs. Murlock and Mrs. Adams were coming up the front walk, then told Mama we had unexpected company.

After they had nibbled some on the cookies (which tasted like they needed a lot more resting), and washed down the crumbs with iced tea, we brought up the campout. It went like this:

Mama: "You'll catch your death of cold." We reminded her it was the middle of July.

Mrs. Murlock: "You don't have a tent, and I'm not buying one." We explained how we could hang long sheets from the low limbs of a tree.

Mrs. Murlock: "Not one of my sheets, you won't."

Mrs. Adams: "The coyotes will get you." That was something we hadn't considered, but we assured them we could throw rocks and make enough noise to scare them off.

Then they all started asking questions.

Mama: "Whose backyard did you plan to camp in?" Reba Lu's. She had some trees with low branches that would be perfect to hang sheets from.

Mrs. Adams: "What are you going to eat?" Peanut butter sandwiches and grape Kool-Aid, donated by Mrs. Adams, though Reba Lu was just getting around to telling her that.

Mrs. Murlock: "Where will you go to the bathroom?" "Wherever."

That was from Geraldine, and our mothers had a fit until Mrs. Adams said she could leave the back porch door unlatched.

Mama and Mrs. Murlock held their ground. They were still shaking their heads when Daddy came home.

"Camping?" he exclaimed. "I did that when I was a boy. Fine idea. Good, healthy fun."

There wasn't much our mothers could do then except load us down with instructions.

"Lights out at nine." What lights?

"Take plenty of blankets." It was still July.

"If you see a coyote, don't run. Yell for help as loud as you can." I intended to climb the nearest tree as high as I could.

This was on a Thursday. We figured we could make our plans, get our equipment together, build our tent, and be ready to camp out on Friday night. We sat on the scrubby grass that grew under the big elm trees in the preacher's backyard while Reba Lu made a list and Geraldine stuck her two cents in and was bossy, as usual. I had always been the list maker when it was just Geraldine and me, but Reba Lu had taken that over because of her nice handwriting.

After a bit, Reba Lu began to read out loud. "Chewing gum, Nancy Drew books, flashlights, snacks." She chewed on her pencil a bit, then added pencils and paper.

"What for?" Geraldine and I said it together.

"You want to keep a diary, don't you?" Reba Lu sounded surprised that the two of us hadn't thought of that. "It's the most important part of having an adventure. Writing about it, so we won't forget all the things that happened."

I glanced at Geraldine. She was getting that narrow look about her eyes that meant somebody was starting to push her too far.

"In a diary," I told her, "you can write down anything you want. You can even write things about *other people*." I shifted my eyes toward Reba Lu. Geraldine brightened up considerably and gave me a thumbs up. I could have hugged myself. This was the Geraldine I knew.

"What about the campfire?" Geraldine asked.

We stared at each other. "We could roast marshmallows," Reba Lu said.

"And cook weenies on a stick," I added. "That's better than peanut butter sandwiches for camping out."

"Do you think our folks will let us light a fire?" Geraldine asked.

"They will if Eddie builds it and makes sure we don't burn up," I said. "The trouble is, he'll probably want to hang around and eat roasted weenies and marshmallows."

"That's OK with me," Reba Lu said. "I think Eddie's nice." I tried not to grin when I saw how red her face was getting.

Geraldine started walking around the backyard. "You don't have much kindling wood here," she said. "I've got a big pile at my house. It's what's left over from the old outhouse that fell down. My mama will be glad to have it hauled away."

Reba Lu gave her a pinched-mouth look that said as plain as day what she thought of cooking weenies over wood that had been used for such private purposes. But she gave in when Geraldine said it had been sitting in the sun for over a year and had all the germs baked out of it.

"Did we forget anything?" Reba Lu wanted to know.

It came to me with a jolt. It reminded me of the way I had felt the time I used a knife to pry burnt toast out of the toaster while it was still plugged in. We *had* forgotten something. I thought of our list of sinners. "Dodie," I said. Just that one word. The two of them looked at me like I needed to wash my mouth out with soap.

"Maybe her mother won't let her come," I said. I was starting to get a bad feeling of what it would be like with Dodie in the same tent with Geraldine and Reba Lu.

Geraldine let out a snorting sound. "Her mother wouldn't even know she was gone."

Once again, we trudged up the street to Dodie's house and rang the bell. When the door opened, we expected to see Dodie, but Mr. Jefferson Clement came out instead. Bits of what looked like straw stuck out of his hair. As he limped past me, I caught a whiff of something spicy—like the aftershave lotion I had smelled up at the barbershop.

He looked startled to see us and never said a word. Just kept going down the sidewalk, and across the street toward his own house.

He didn't move too fast, though, and he had his left hand on his right shoulder, rubbing it like it was hurting him. Before we could blink twice, Dodie came stomping out of her house. Her face was red, and her fists were clenched. She started up Palm Avenue, moving fast, as if someone was shoving her from behind. She never even glanced at us.

"You come back here!" we heard Mrs. Crumper yell.

"Hey, Dodie!" Geraldine called.

Dodie never slowed down. Her shoulders were hunched, and her bony elbows jabbed the air.

"I wonder what happened?" Reba Lu said, eyeing the front screen door. "Do you suppose we ought to see if Mrs. Crumper is all right?"

Geraldine and I looked at each other. Neither one of us cared a hoot about Mrs. Crumper.

"It's our Christian duty," Reba Lu insisted, and marched up the front steps.

Geraldine sighed. "Next thing we know, she'll be telling us to love the whole sinning Crumper family."

I uh-huhed in agreement, but we went ahead and followed her into the house.

Mrs. Crumper wasn't in her usual place on the couch. She was sitting on a hardback chair, holding the sweeping half of a broken broom in one hand. The other half was standing broken-side-up in a fishbowl filled with dirty water. The water moved, so I figured it must have a live fish in it. Poor, trapped thing.

Mrs. Crumper's face was a sight, all red and puffy, and she was taking great gulping breaths that made her chest rise and fall. Her pink chenille robe fell apart in front, and we got a good look at what she wasn't wearing. Geraldine and I stared, but Reba Lu went over and pulled the robe back together.

Mrs. Crumper ignored her. "Dodie's real mad at me," she told us. "She says I've ruined everything because I told Mr. Clement not to bring any more dirty clothes over here. Now she won't be getting any more of their money. Well, she'll just have to do without. I don't want that man coming around."

That was the longest speech I ever heard Mrs. Crumper make. Her mouth twisted, and I thought she was going to start crying, but then I saw she was trying to smile. She stared at the broken broom she was holding and put it on the floor next to her chair.

"How about you girls sit yourselves down a while. Dodie will be back. She always comes back." She tried to get up and fell back into the chair. "I could make some lemonade," she said. Then she gave a loud hiccup.

I wanted to get out of there fast, but my feet seemed glued to the dirty Crumper floor. Geraldine took hold of my arm and gave it a pull. We had taken a few steps toward the door when Mrs. Crumper clutched at her hands, twisting and rubbing them like she was washing a dirty shirt she couldn't get clean.

"I take care of my Dodie. She's a good girl, a hard worker. She's going to make something of herself."

Reba Lu opened her mouth, but even she couldn't think of a single thing to say to that.

Mrs. Crumper picked up the piece of broken broom and started waving it in the air. Then she narrowed her eyes at me like she was trying to figure out who I was. When she tried to get up off the chair again, I started backing toward the door. Geraldine got there before me, and Reba Lu was right behind us.

We stumbled down the front steps, getting our arms tangled around each other. I was wondering how that broom got broken. But before I could say anything about it, Reba Lu found her voice. "Maybe we should add Mrs. Crumper to our list of people to love." She sounded doubtful, which was unusual for her. She started to say something else, but Geraldine had had enough.

"You can forget it, Reba Lu," she said. "Dodie is all the Crumper I can stomach, and I'm having trouble with that one."

I thought that was a little unfair, but I nodded and said, "I don't ever want to go back in that smelly house again. I think Dodie's mother might be a little tetched in the head."

Reba Lu put her hands on her hips and jutted her chin out at us. "You're both thinking about yourselves," she accused us. "Is that any way to get on God's good side?"

We stood there on the Crumpers' front walk glaring at each other and scuffling our feet on the sidewalk. Then something came out of my mouth that surprised me.

"We came here to ask Dodie about camping out, and that's what we're going to do." I started up Palm Avenue. I looked back once and saw that they were trailing along behind me.

"We don't even know where Dodie went!" Geraldine yelled.

"I do!" I yelled back. I hoped I was right.

By the time we reached the American Legion Park, Geraldine and Reba Lu had caught up with me, and the three of us were walking together again. It was the first time in our friendship that *I* was in charge. I was beginning to like the feeling.

I led the way past the picnic benches, then stopped and pointed toward the eucalyptus forest on the north side. Dodie sat on one of the giant roots that had grown almost flat on top like a long bench. I saw that she had stuck some eucalyptus leaves in her hair the same way she had at the Fourth of July picnic. She faced away from us, her back hunched over like she was hunting for something in the dirt.

"How'd you know she'd be here?" whispered Geraldine.

"I just knew." I didn't feel like explaining.

We walked over to Dodie and stood around, waiting for her to look up. She didn't. She was scratching up piles of dirt, moistened with water from the creek, and mixing in small rocks and broken-off bits of eucalyptus bark. As we watched, she scooped up handfuls and pressed the dirt mixture into the shape of four walls around an empty space in the middle. The whole thing was about as big as a shoebox.

"Are you OK?" I asked.

"What do you care?"

"I just wondered. Mr. Clement came tearing out of your house and your mother is really mad."

"Not your business."

"What are you making?" Geraldine asked her.

"Fort."

"Why are you putting rocks and leaves in the wall?" I asked.

"Makes it stronger."

Then she took a single eucalyptus pod with the hat attached and put it in the center of the square. It looked lonely, I thought, sitting there all by itself. We watched as she began laying sticks in a crisscross pattern across the top.

"I guess that's the roof," Reba Lu said. Dodie glanced sideways at her, but kept on working.

I cleared my throat. "We came to find you because we want to ask you something."

"Ask me what?"

I raised my eyebrows at Geraldine. She gritted her teeth. "We're camping out in Reba Lu's backyard Friday night. We came to invite you."

Dodie steadied the roof of her fort, then covered it with rows of long eucalyptus leaves.

"What for?" she finally asked.

Reba Lu took over. "Because it will be fun. Don't you want to have fun?" I remembered that Reba Lu had said almost the exact same thing when we asked Dodie to go to the matinee. Dodie might not be very likeable, but she wasn't stupid.

She narrowed her eyes at Reba Lu, then stared at Geraldine. I might as well have been on the moon for all the notice she took of me. Then she said, "You two don't like me, do you?"

Reba Lu was struck dumb. So was Geraldine. Even though she put both hands on her hips and got that look on her face that meant business, she didn't seem able to say anything. Reba Lu got her voice back and plunged right in with her best missionary voice. "We're *trying* to like you," she said. "We *want* to like you, Dodie, but you always . . . you make it hard to be nice!"

Dodie's eyes seemed as pale as rain. You could almost see right through them. It made me feel sad to look at her eyes. But it was hard to feel sorry for Dodie Crumper for very long.

"I don't like you, either," she said. "We're not friends, so why don't you two leave me alone?"

She turned back to her little hidden fort. We stood in

silence, not knowing what to do. "Go away," she said. Even though she had said "you two," I was sure she meant to include me now.

Reba Lu and I started to leave, but Geraldine had found her voice and wanted to have the last word. "Hey, Dodie," she taunted, "if you don't put a door or windows in the walls, your little eucalyptus pod can't come out."

Dodie never turned around, but we could hear her clear as a bell. "That's right," she told Geraldine. "And nobody else can get in."

CHAPTER ELEVEN

On the day of the campout, I had to face a bowl of mush before Mama would let me outside. I looked at Eddie for help, but he grinned and said, "It's been bubbling on the stove for about an hour. Ought to be nice and slimy by now."

When Mama dished it up, it dripped long threads of slobber, all soft and shiny like the undersides of the snails that crawled under wet leaves in the garden. When I looked at it, I wanted to gag.

I covered it with sugar, put a hunk of butter in the center, and stirred it around until Mama told me I was too old to play with my food.

"I'm always too old for some things and not old enough for others," I said. I was going to say what I thought of that mush, but she gave me one of her *don't be sassy* looks. I left the table as soon as I could and went outside. Buster was waiting by the front door. I scratched his neck. "Come on," I said.

Geraldine and Reba Lu were already tying ropes to some low-hanging tree branches when I got to the Adams's backyard. "You're late," Geraldine told me.

"Mama made mush," I said.

"Nasty, slimy stuff." Geraldine shivered.

Reba Lu sighed. "It's good healthy food, and it doesn't cost much."

"Neither does snot," I said, "but I don't eat it."

I was thinking how nice it was to have the last word as we hung up the old sheets Mama had found at the back of a cupboard. We clipped them together with clothespins, then pinned back a flap on one side to make an opening for going in and coming out.

"You should have put your blankets on the ground before you hung the sheets," Charles said. "Now you have to crawl inside and drag the blankets through that narrow opening."

He was chewing on a piece of toast. I wondered how long he had been sitting on the back steps watching. I reached around my waist to make sure my shirt was tucked into my shorts.

Reba Lu rolled her eyes. "Don't pay him any mind. He's jealous because he doesn't get to camp out."

"Do too," Charles said. He walked over to the far side of the backyard and began hanging sheets over the rows of clotheslines where Mrs. Adams hung her clean washing to dry. He had already spread a blanket on the ground. "This is my territory, Reba Lu, and don't you forget it." Then he looked at me. "I can help you drag those blankets inside when you're ready."

I smiled, but I didn't answer. I seemed to have lost the connection between my brain and my tongue.

"Why didn't we think of that?" whispered Geraldine, pointing to Charles's side of the yard. "With no covering on top, Charles can lie there and look at the stars all night!"

"And the bats and owls can come in," Reba Lu said.

Pretty soon, we began to hear a soft clucking, and a pretty little speckled hen stepped out from behind a bush. "Chick–chick–chick," Reba Lu called, and it came right up to her. She picked it up like it was a cat and stroked its feathers.

"I never knew you had a pet chicken," Geraldine said.

I could tell she was impressed, and so was I. Lots of people had chickens, but they were for laying eggs and frying. If you made a pet out of one, and it ended up on your dinner plate, it could turn you off drumsticks forever.

But Reba Lu didn't seem worried. "Her name is Gloria," she said. "My daddy says when she brags about an egg she's laid, it sounds like she's praising the Lord. He says he's considering taking her to church to sing the Gloria Patri with the choir."

She scratched Gloria's head and got up to put her in the chicken coop for the night. "We'll never cook Gloria," she said. "She's too good a watchdog. If anything comes in this yard that doesn't belong here, she'll let us know. You should hear her when she gets worked up!"

We heard her when Reba Lu put her back in the coop.

She made such a fuss of cackling that Buster put his nose down with one paw over his head.

We all went home to get some lunch and gather the extra things we would need: a bag of chewy Walnettos, homemade sugar cookies, and a package of Twinkies with banana cream filling.

When we returned to Reba Lu's backyard, I saw that Charles had picked up a lot of small rocks and put them in a pile near the opening to our tent. "Ammunition to throw at coyotes," he said. I noticed he had already dragged the blankets inside our tent.

"Thanks," I said.

He shrugged and looked at his feet. "No problem." He went back to fixing his camping gear, and I walked over to where Reba Lu was fussing with the sheets.

"That was pretty nice of Charles," I said.

"He's in love with you. That's why he's acting like that."

"*In love?* What do you mean *in love?* Charles hardly knows me."

"Maybe so, but he sure looks at you a lot. Talks about you, too. He thinks you have 'expressive blue eyes.' He says that's his new favorite color."

"Well, I never heard of such a thing. It's just . . . just ridiculous."

"I'm only telling you what I know."

I ignored her and began fussing with a sheet that kept coming loose. But while I fussed, I thought about Charles and decided I could do worse. Charles was taller than me by at least two inches. He didn't have bad breath. And Reba Lu said he was good in arithmetic, which I hated.

I took a good look at him when he was busy catching an alligator lizard. I didn't dwell on what he might be going to do with it, but concentrated on his chin (it didn't recede), his fingernails (not too dirty), and his hair (dark brown and combed flat on top).

"When did Charles start doing that to his hair?" I asked Reba Lu.

"When he got goofy about you."

I changed the subject. "I wonder what Dodie is doing?"

"Who cares?" Geraldine asked.

"That's a bad attitude," Reba Lu said. "God is probably listening to you right now."

Geraldine looked uncomfortable. "Do you want me to lie and say I'm sorry she isn't here?"

Reba Lu looked thoughtful. "I can't really say I miss her."

I didn't say anything. I was wondering what Dodie was doing right that very minute when we were looking forward to having a good time. Was she scrubbing somebody's dirty laundry? I was starting to feel bad for her, and I kind of missed her. Dodie was different from Geraldine and Reba Lu. I could be myself around her and not worry about making mistakes.

After a while, Eddie came over to start the campfire, and we got to talking about the weenies and marshmallows we were going to roast. Reverend Adams had dug a shallow pit and put large rocks in the bottom and pieces of Geraldine's outhouse wood on top. Eddie got the flames going, and we sat around watching them reach out to lick the summer air. Pretty soon Reverend and Mrs. Adams brought the twins outside. Before you knew it, there were my folks, and Mrs. Murlock, all sitting on blankets on the ground, waiting for the flames to die down and become embers, and I didn't think about Dodie at all.

Charles came out of the house carrying hot dog buns, a couple of packages of weenies, and a jar of mustard. All of a sudden, everyone seemed to be hungry, and we put those weenies on long sticks and turned them slowly over the embers. Mama, Mrs. Adams, and Mrs. Murlock took charge of opening the buns, spreading mustard on them, and putting them on paper plates. Those embers were just right, and before I knew it, Charles had taken my stick and was turning it slowly so the weenie got cooked on all sides.

When it was done, he handed it to me. "Thanks," I said. I gave him a quick smile. Then I got busy putting the weenie in the bun. I took a big bite and tried to pretend that Reba Lu and Geraldine weren't watching and poking at each other.

Reverend Adams began to sing an old camp song.
Tell me why the stars do shine,
Tell me why the ivy twines,
Tell me why the sky's so blue,
And I will tell you why I love you.

Mrs. Adams joined in. Then we all started singing. It felt good to sit in the open air, with twilight coming on, and the sky so big above us. Pretty soon it would be full of stars, sparkling up there like somebody had salted the universe.

I put a marshmallow on a pointed stick and held it in the embers until it was toasted on the outside and gooey in the middle. Then I popped it whole into my mouth and let the sweetness fill me. Geraldine burned one and ate it anyway, charred parts and all.

"I like it this way," she said, but I knew she was showing off a little.

Pretty soon, Mrs. Adams took the twins into the house. They were carrying on, screaming and kicking, because they wanted to camp out, too. Then the others wandered off home, except for Charles, who was rustling around in his corner of the yard.

It was getting dark, and the stars were coming out fast. Geraldine and Reba Lu and I lay on our backs in the grass and found the Big Dipper, and argued about how to find the North Star.

Then we went into the tent to read about Nancy Drew in *The Hidden Staircase*. Buster came with us and stretched out by my blanket. It wasn't long before we turned off the flashlights.

"You always know it's safe outside when the crickets sing," Reba Lu whispered.

"Everybody knows that," I said. "It's when they stop that you have to watch out."

"Crickets are good luck," Reba Lu continued. "You don't want to kill a cricket."

She went on, telling us about things we already knew. Geraldine glanced at me. First chance we got, we changed the subject and began talking about what was on all our minds.

"Mama doesn't like Jefferson Clement," I said. "She told a fib at the picnic to keep him from sitting with us."

"Good for her," Reba Lu said. "I'll never forget the way Miss Emma cried when she looked out her window and saw him. What do you suppose he did to make her so scared?"

Geraldine sniffed. "Might be nothing at all. You can't trust everything Miss Emma says."

"Well, I trust Miss Emma more than I trust Mr. Clement," I said. "Maybe we ought to take him off our list."

"You mean just give up on him?" Reba Lu sounded shocked. "We can't start changing our list of sinners just to suit ourselves."

"I'm not sure he's a sinner worth saving," I told her.

We were quiet for a bit. Then Geraldine said, "Smell that honeysuckle?" We all sniffed. "It has a heavier smell at night."

We sniffed again. Cool air from the canyon drifted softly across the yard, carrying the scent. I felt as though the flowers were sighing. I was thinking I might even write a poem about sighing honeysuckles when Reba Lu broke the spell by saying, "Sometimes I'm scared of the dark."

"Me, too," Geraldine said, and she began to tell about the shadows that lived under her bed.

"I've got them in my closet," I said. "They open the door, a little at a time, slowly . . . slowly . . ." I reached out and grabbed Geraldine's arm.

She screamed, and so did Reba Lu, even though I hadn't touched her. We looked at each other a minute, then started to laugh. Reba Lu grabbed a flashlight. "I'll show you what monsters look like!"

She had me hold the flashlight while she made shadow pictures against the hanging sheet of our tent. She was good at it. Her fingers formed arms and legs, and her fist made a witch's head with a pointed hat and crooked nose. Then she did something with both hands together that looked like a big coyote with its nose pointed to the sky as if it were howling. Finally, she made a little dog that danced.

Geraldine and I were impressed, but Reba Lu shrugged. "My daddy taught me," she said. "When I'm afraid of the dark, I can form a shadow monster. Then I can send it away and make something funny instead."

We were all quiet for a long time. I was thinking about how a shadow can be scary sometimes and funny other times. Then I remembered Dodie's secret. She said she had been scared of the dark, but I couldn't help wondering if she had more to be afraid of than a few shadows.

Despite the gentle breeze outside the tent, I was sticky with sweat. I kicked off the light blanket that Mama had made me bring and lay without moving, trying to get my skin to cool down. I could hear Geraldine and Reba Lu breathing. Long, deep breaths that meant that they were either asleep or close to it. Then I heard a strange sound, like a chicken starting to cackle. It stopped almost before it got started, and I didn't pay any more attention. I wished *I* could go to sleep. I closed my eyes. It was so hot that the crickets had stopped chirping.

I opened my eyes. That wasn't right! Crickets didn't stop chirping because it was hot. They stopped when they heard something, or someone, coming. And then I heard it, too. Slow, careful steps across dry grass. I wondered why Gloria didn't sound an alarm. Buster made a soft sound, deep in his throat. I took hold of his collar with one hand.

With the other, I pulled the blanket back up, covering all of me right up to my nose. I would have covered my head, too, but if it was a coyote, I was determined to get a look at it. One good look before I yelled. I tightened my fingers around my flashlight. I saw the shape through the sheet of our tent. Large and looming. Not at all like the hand shadows we had laughed about. This one looked solid and seemed as big as a horse.

I watched the shadow move to the flap that we had fastened with clothespins. One by one the pins were quietly pulled away. He stood, outlined in the moonlight, not a horse at all, but a man. Probably it was Reverend Adams, I told myself, checking to see that we were all right.

"Reverend Adams?" I asked softly.

There was no answer. Buster began to growl, low down in his throat. I tightened my hand on his collar. The shadow moved . . . the tent flap opened . . .

"Help!" I yelled. "Help!"

Geraldine and Reba Lu sat straight up and bumped heads. Buster's throaty rumbles turned into angry barking. I let loose of his collar.

"Sic 'em, Buster. Sic 'em!" I shouted.

Buster leaped forward and fastened his teeth into the backside of the intruder, who had turned to run but got caught in the ropes that we had strung to hold the tent up.

"Get him, Buster!" I yelled. "Get him, boy!" Buster hung on as the man gave a loud yell, scrambled to his feet, and staggered away.

"Attaboy, Buster. Hang on!" It was Charles's voice. His footsteps thumped across the yard as he chased after the man.

The three of us all tried to crawl out of the tent at the same time. Geraldine stepped on my hand, and I put my elbow in Reba Lu's eye. Reba Lu began to cry.

Then we heard a yipping sound. A few seconds later, Charles was back, carrying Buster. When I reached out to pet him, saying, "Good boy, good Buster!" and touched him on his side, he yelped in pain and began shaking all over.

"Oh, he's h-h-hurt," Reba Lu stammered. Her teeth were chattering, hot as it was.

Upstairs in the parsonage, the lights went on. Reverend Adams leaned out a window. "What's going on out there?" he demanded. "Did you see a coyote?"

He didn't wait for an answer. His head disappeared, and a minute later he clattered down the back steps. "What was it? What happened?" he asked.

"Something tried to get into our tent," Reba Lu said. "Ask Angie. She was awake. She's the one who yell—"

"It wasn't *something*. It was *someone*," I interrupted. "It was a prowler!"

"I saw him, too," Charles said. "But I couldn't see his face."

"A . . . a man?" Reba Lu stammered.

Reverend Adams looked angry. He didn't ask any more questions, but made us all come into the house. "You can camp out right here on the living room floor. We'll sort this out in the morning," he said.

He wrapped Buster in a blanket and headed up the street toward Dr. Thomas's house. "The doc will fix him good as new," he told me. "Everybody says he's as good with animals as he is with people. Don't you worry."

Mrs. Adams made hot chocolate because of Reba Lu's chattering teeth. I would rather have had some cool lemonade, but I drank what I was given.

Reba Lu and Geraldine kept asking questions. "How

big was he? Did he say anything? Did you recognize him?" They had been too busy bumping heads to see what happened.

"It was too dark," was all I could say.

I closed my eyes and pretended to be asleep. For a long time, I lay on the floor, wide-awake. It was true that I hadn't seen the man's face clearly. But I did see the way he moved. And I remembered smelling something besides his sour sweat. Something spicy.

CHAPTER TWELVE

Geraldine was poking me. "Wake up, Angie. Mrs. Adams is fixing sourdough pancakes for breakfast."

Sourdough was my favorite everything. Biscuits, pancakes, bread. I loved to smell the starter Mama kept in a mason jar in the icebox, all watery on top and thick on the bottom. But this morning, I couldn't seem to work up any appetite.

I squinted at Geraldine. "What time is it?"

The mantel clock gonged nine times, answering my question. I rolled over and stared at the carved mahogany leg of Mrs. Adams's sofa and remembered why we were sleeping in the house. The sun coming up didn't help; last night was still with me.

"Where's Buster?" I asked.

"Over at your house. Eddie brought him home from Dr. Thomas's late last night, and your mama let him sleep inside." Geraldine was picking at a hangnail and giving me little sideways glances, which meant she wasn't telling me everything.

I raised up on one elbow and gave her a stare.

"He's OK, Angie. Really. At least he will be after his cracked rib heals."

"Cracked rib? That man gave Buster a cracked rib?"

"Now calm down, Angie. I told you he's going to be all right." Her eyes kept darting this way and that, and I knew there was something else she needed to tell me.

Just then, Reba Lu came in. Her eyes were all red and puffy, and I could tell she'd been crying. Before I could ask her what was wrong, she blurted out, "Gloria's dead!"

"Gloria? Your little pet chicken? What happened?"

"Somebody murdered her, that's what."

"How?"

I barely got the word out before Geraldine poked me hard in the ribs and leaned over close to whisper, "*Somebody wrung Gloria's neck.*"

With a sinking feeling I remembered that half-cackle I had heard the night before. I swallowed. It must have been Gloria, getting her neck wrung.

Reba Lu went on. "That's why she couldn't warn us that somebody was coming. She was lying there dead."

"Oh, no. Oh, Reba Lu."

Reba Lu began to cry. Geraldine joined in, and the two of them got me started. We sat on the floor and wept until

Mrs. Adams came running in from the kitchen. She got down on the floor and put her arms around us. She smelled like pancakes. I leaned against her. I wanted Mama, but Mrs. Adams felt pretty good.

"That man did it," I said between sobs. "I know he did, just like he hurt my Buster."

Geraldine wiped her nose on her sleeve. "Angie, didn't you see his face at all?"

I shook my head. "I already told you . . . it was too dark. I heard his footsteps, and I saw his shadow. I thought he might be Reverend Adams, coming to check on us. But then I saw him undo the clothespins and open the flap. That's when I yelled."

I stopped and blew my nose on a tissue that Mrs. Adams handed me. "I never saw his face," I went on, "but I'm sure it was a man."

I was glad when Mrs. Adams said, "Well now, your pancakes will be getting cold. We can talk about this later." Her voice sounded too cheerful, like somebody practicing for a part in a play.

"I should go home and see Buster," I said.

"Not yet, dear. I promised your mother I would give you a good breakfast."

Geraldine and Reba Lu had already eaten, but they sat with me at the table and had another glass of fresh-squeezed orange juice apiece. Reba Lu kept sniffing and saying, "Poor Gloria."

"Charles and Reverend Adams are over at your house," Geraldine told me. "They went to talk to your daddy about what happened."

Then she said what I already knew. "Something real bad is happening in our town."

I didn't answer, for Mrs. Adams put a plate in front of me. I was surprised to find that I could eat two stacks of pancakes and three pieces of Canadian bacon. As soon as I finished, Mrs. Adams told us to go out and clean up the mess in the backyard.

First we visited the little mound of dirt where Mr. Adams had buried Gloria under the shade of a Cecile Brunner climbing rose bush. We picked some pink buds and stuck them in the soft soil, then watered them good so they wouldn't wilt quite so fast. Reba Lu wanted to have a memorial service, so we stood around while she said a few words.

"You were a good chicken, Gloria. A true friend. I'll always remember what big eggs you laid and how soft your neck feathers were."

She gulped and swallowed. I thought talking about neck feathers wasn't such a good idea in light of what had happened to Gloria.

"You were a real hero . . . uh . . . heroine," Reba Lu went on. "You would have tried to save us, but you didn't get a chance to cackle. We'll never forget you."

We didn't talk much while we took down the tent. We were rolling up the sheets and blankets when Geraldine threw hers in a pile and sat on it. It seemed like a good idea, so Reba Lu and I did the same thing.

"So," Geraldine said.

Reba Lu looked at me, waiting.

"I'm not exactly positive who it was," I told them.

"But you have an idea," Geraldine said.

"It's more of a feeling. There was something about the way his shadow moved. It seemed like he was trying to hurry, but couldn't go too fast. It made me think of the first time I laid eyes on Jefferson Clement. He was walking funny then, kind of limping like one leg hurt. Just like the man who opened the flap of our tent. And I smelled something spicy. Like aftershave. Mr. Clement smelled that way one day in front of Dodie's house."

"That doesn't prove anything," Geraldine said. "Artie Longmire uses that stuff on just about every man in town. Except Willie Jack, of course."

We sat there, looking at each other. "We know who it was, but we can't prove it, can we?" Reba Lu asked.

Geraldine made a groaning sound. "Who would believe us if we told a story like that? Don't you remember how people welcomed him at the Fourth of July picnic? Like he was some kind of hero?"

"Not everybody," I said. "Mama didn't want him to sit with us."

We were quiet a minute. "What are we going to do?" Reba Lu asked.

"Nothing," said Geraldine. "If we accuse him, no telling what he might do." She scowled and began pulling long runners of devil's grass from the tomato bed. I knew Geraldine, and I could tell by the way she yanked at the weeds how nervous she was.

"I wish he'd never come back to Messina," Reba Lu said. She tried to sound angry, but I noticed her voice trembled.

I was about to get my things together and go home to

see Buster when I looked up and saw Dr. Thomas hurrying down the street. "Look there," I said.

We watched as he crossed over Palm Avenue and began climbing the steps that led to the Clements' front porch.

I thought about how sharp Buster's teeth were when he chewed a bone, and how loud the man had yelled last night when Buster got him in the backside. I smiled to myself thinking how much it must have hurt.

"Buster took a good bite out of somebody last night," I said.

We three sat there looking at each other. Finally, Geraldine said, "If we accuse Jefferson Clement, a lot of people won't believe us."

Reba Lu nodded. "And if we accuse him, he might try to hurt us."

But I had the last word. "There's no *might* about it," I told them.

CHAPTER THIRTEEN

By that afternoon, the word was out that a prowler was loose in Messina.

"Some vagrant, no doubt," I heard Miss Barnable, the librarian, say. I was in the library waiting to return an overdue book. I had to stand in line behind three of Messina's biggest gossips: Miss Hallie Harper, my least favorite teacher; Mrs. Eunice Abbott, the mailman's wife; and Mrs. Mildred Hewitt, who was still talking about being scared by Miss Emma's snake.

They hovered around the librarian's desk like three crows picking at dead meat in the road.

"A bunch of tramps are camped south of town in the

dry river bed under the sycamores," Miss Harper said. "Those hobos don't have anything better to do than stir up devilment. As bad as Gypsies, that's what they are." She put her little fingernail between her two front teeth and picked out a piece of her lunch.

"A lot of people are homeless these days," Miss Barnable put in. "Just because they're broke doesn't mean they're—"

"Imagine one of them getting in the preacher's backyard and killing a chicken!" Mrs. Hewitt interrupted. She sounded excited, and the way her eyes got big made me think she was wishing she could have been there to see it.

I cleared my throat. I wanted to return my book, but I couldn't get near Miss Barnable's desk until they moved. I wasn't really surprised when they ignored me, so I just stood off to one side and waited some more.

Mrs. Abbott shook her head. "I don't know, Mildred. There's plenty of others right here in Messina who wouldn't think twice about prowling. Take that Willie Jack, for instance. He's never been right since the Great War." She tapped her head and looked like she knew something nobody else did.

"Willie Jack is a war hero!" Miss Barnable exclaimed. "He saved a lot of lives. It's not his fault that he got shell-shocked doing it!" But those other three didn't pay any attention.

"I believe you're right, Eunice," Miss Harper said. "Willie Jack always was trouble, even before he let himself get shell-shocked." Miss Barnable tried to interrupt, but nobody could get in a word once Miss Harper got started.

"I had him in the sixth grade," she went on, "so I

should know. He never paid a lick of attention to anything I told him. Not even when I kept him after school. I always thought it was Willie Jack who put the mouse in my bottom drawer."

Hooray for Willie Jack! I thought. I must have made a noise, for they all stopped talking and turned to look at me.

"Angelina Wallace, you ought to mind your own business," Miss Harper said.

"I am minding it." It was sass, and I knew it, but I figured Miss Harper couldn't give me any more bad grades.

Then I remembered that she was on our list and we were supposed to tell her she was a good teacher. I opened my mouth, but those words got stuck and wouldn't come out. Instead, I stepped up to the desk and held out the book I was returning. "I'm sorry it's a day late," I told Miss Barnable. "I brought two pennies for the fine."

Miss Barnable tried to turn the book facedown before the others could see it, but they already had. Miss Harper leaned way over and read the title out loud. "*Tarzan, Lord of the Jungle*? Is this what you allow children to read? An immoral tale of a savage who cavorts with apes and calls himself *Lord* with a capital *L*?"

Miss Barnable turned pink. "Her mother lets her read anything she wants."

"Not *anything*," I protested. "I'm not allowed to read the magazines behind the counter at the drugstore."

"You shouldn't even *know* about those!" Miss Harper exclaimed. "Those aren't nice magazines!"

Ha! If that was true, I wondered how Miss Harper knew about them. I couldn't wait to tell Reba Lu and Geraldine that I'd discovered another reason for Miss Harper to be on our list of sinners.

"No wonder we're having trouble in Messina," Mrs. Hewitt said. "When our young people are allowed to read filth and sleep outside, boys and girls together in the same backyard, they're liable to make up all kinds of stories." She looked at me sideways, and I knew by *stories* she meant *lies.* "We might not have a prowler at all," she told the others. "We might have a child with an over-stimulated imagination."

I almost bit my tongue off trying to keep still, but the words wouldn't stay inside me. "If you're talking about me," I told her, "I don't make up stories. My folks taught me to tell the truth. And as far as boys and girls in the same backyard—Charles Adams was the only boy and he slept in his own tent, clear over on the other side of the yard."

My voice was shaking, but I couldn't make it stop. "We roasted marshmallows and sang camp songs, and our folks were there till it was bedtime." I couldn't believe I'd spoken up like that, but I wasn't a bit sorry.

They looked at me, little cat smiles on their faces, and I knew what I was going to do. "Excuse me," I said. I walked over to the stacks and chose a new book to check out. I took it back to the desk and handed it to Miss Barnable. She glanced up at me, then opened it quick, stamped the date in it, and gave me the card to sign. I slapped the cover shut so the ladies could get a good look at my choice. *Tarzan the Untamed* was standing, half-naked, on the cover, one hand gripping a hanging vine and the other on the back of a snarling lion.

I was heading for the door, but stopped when I heard Mrs. Hewitt say, "I hope Reverend Wallace doesn't let Willie Jack come on the church outing next Saturday. He needs to be kept away from the young people."

"You don't need to worry," Mrs. Abbott told her. "I heard Mr. Clement volunteer to be a chaperone. He'll keep an eye on things."

"That's all right then," Mrs. Hewitt said. "Jeff Clement is a gentleman. Do you see how he dresses? And that red carnation he wears shows real class. Why, I remember when he began courting Ruth Clement—she was Ruth Mahoney then and stepping out with another young man. Well, let me tell you, Jeff charmed her away from that fellow and married her himself. Yes, indeed. He always knew what to say to make people smile. I believe he could charm the apples off a tree."

Miss Harper was nodding her head. "I remember him when he was younger than that. He was always so nice and friendly, always smiling at people and never too busy to stop and pass the time of day. Even when he was a boy, he always had a smile on his face and a compliment up his sleeve." She reached up and patted her hair like a lady does when she wants someone to tell her how nice she looks. "I reckon it's a good thing for our town that he decided to come home."

Miss Barnable closed her desk drawer with a sharp click. "Don't you remember how Jeff got to drinking and carousing? Mrs. Clement said he was a disgrace and she was glad when he left. I can't imagine her celebrating his coming back."

Miss Harper's face got red and she made a hissing sound between her teeth as she headed for the door. The other two followed her.

Miss Barnable stared at the door a minute, then gave a long sigh and turned back to the book she had been reading. I liked Miss Barnable, and I thought she had more sense than those three gossips, even if she had taken a fancy to Brother Otis when he preached at the revival.

Those other ladies sure puzzled me though. How could they think Mr. Clement was a dependable gentleman? I knew Mama didn't think much of him. Miss Emma was plain scared of him. Even Mrs. Crumper didn't want to do his laundry anymore. Of course, Miss Emma wasn't quite right in her head, and Dodie's mother wasn't what you could call dependable. But Mama's mind was perfectly fine, and she had finagled out of sitting with him at the Fourth of July picnic.

Mr. Clement might have been a friendly young man, and he could dress up in a suit and wear a carnation, but I was positive Willie Jack in his oldest clothes would make a better chaperone.

The next morning, though, the prowler was far from most people's thoughts after Reverend Adams made his announcement from the pulpit.

"The Annual All-Church Picnic will be held next Saturday, July 29, at La Mirada Beach. The deacons have put sign-up sheets in the narthex, and the trustees will hire buses."

I thought about how the Baptist minister was probably making the same announcement over in the other church at that very moment.

The "All-Church Picnic" didn't mean a picnic for all the people in one church. It meant a picnic for all the churches in Messina. There were only two, so the Catholics and Lutherans who lived in Messina and went to church over in West Camptown were always invited to come along, too. The "Holy Rollers" were also invited, but they never came. They didn't believe in bathing suits.

Reba Lu and Geraldine and I did though, and we decided we had to have new ones. That Sunday afternoon, we got together to figure out how to convince our mothers.

"My old one is raggedy," Reba Lu said, "and the elastic is so loose the seat sags."

Geraldine wanted a two-piece one so she could get a better tan. "I don't know how to bring it up without giving Mama a hissy fit," she confided.

I didn't much care what kind of bathing suit I ended up with so long as it was blue and brand new.

Finally, we came up with a plan. Reba Lu and Geraldine would tell their mothers, *We've been invited to go with Angie and Mrs. Wallace to shop for bathing suits.* That much was true because I was the one who had invited them.

Then I would tell Mama, *Mrs. Adams is busy helping plan the picnic, and Mrs. Murlock is working most of the time, so Reba Lu and Geraldine need to come with us when we shop for my new bathing suit.* That part was mostly true.

When I told Mama, she looked at me hard and said, "What new bathing suit?"

I tried to look surprised. "The one I need for the All-Church Picnic. My old one doesn't fit anymore." I hoped this wasn't a lie. It was almost a year since I'd last worn it.

"Just you go and try it on," Mama told me.

I went to my room and pulled it out of a drawer. It was the least favorite of all the bathing suits I had ever owned—bright yellow with a three-inch green ruffle around the neckline in front and back. I always felt like a sunflower with wilted leaves when I wore it. When I held it up to me in the mirror, it looked pretty small, but the stretch was still in it. I said a prayer, *Please let it be too tight,* and stepped into it. When I pulled up the straps, it felt a little snug. I tugged the ends through the metal buckles and it got even tighter. I took a deep breath, felt like I was going to split up the middle, and went to show Mama. She took one look and decided we'd all go shopping.

The next afternoon, we piled in our Plymouth and drove to San Andreas. "I forgot to ask if I could get a two-piecer," Geraldine said from the back seat.

I turned around and saw Reba Lu rolling her eyes. She and I knew Geraldine wouldn't forget a thing like that. She knew her mother would say no, so she didn't bother to ask.

"I can tell you exactly what your mother would say," Mama told her.

That settled Geraldine's problem, but I had one of my own. Dodie. We hadn't asked her to come shopping with us. Guilt niggled at the back of my mind, the way a moth flutters around a light bulb. I was glad when Mama pulled into a parking space, turned off the engine, and said, "Come on."

We climbed the stairs to the second floor of J.C. Penney and tried on suits in little rooms with curtains instead of doors. We all went in the same room together but were careful to turn our backs on each other when we undressed. Geraldine picked out a two-piecer that was so tight it barely covered her bottom. She didn't have much on top, so she picked up some tissue paper from the floor and stuffed it into the bra.

When she showed it to Mama, Mama's eyes got big, and she said, "Geraldine Murlock, you take that off. Whatever would your mother say if you went to the beach looking like that? On the church picnic, too!"

When we were ready to head home, we three piled into the back seat together, Reba Lu in the middle, as usual, and pulled our suits out of the shopping bags so we could admire them.

Geraldine's was flowered. It had two triangles cut out of the midriff, which showed a little skin and was as close as she was going to get to a two-piecer. Reba Lu's suit was red with white stripes on one side. She thought it made her look slimmer.

"That's a pretty blue," she said, looking at mine. "Blue is Charles's favorite color." She squinted her eyes at me and asked, "Didn't I already tell you that?"

I didn't have to answer because Mama gave a gasp and slammed on the brakes. She forgot to put in the clutch, so the car bucked, the engine died, and the car behind us started honking.

"Jehoshaphat!" she exclaimed. She pushed in the clutch with her left foot and pressed the starter button on the floor with her right. The car coughed once and died. She waited a few seconds and tried again. When the engine was running good, she put it in gear and edged out of the traffic toward the sidewalk.

Walking along the side of Meridian, the main road between San Andreas and Messina, was Mr. Jefferson Clement. He had one hand on his hip and was limping along worse than usual. He would take a couple of steps and rest, then start out again. It was almost like he was doing a little two-step and couldn't quite decide which foot to put down next.

Geraldine leaned over and whispered to Reba Lu and me, "He doesn't look much like a war hero to me."

Mama heard her. She turned around and gave us one of her looks. "Geraldine Murlock, I'm surprised at you, making a joke of somebody who served our country and got injured doing it. That man is in pain."

Still, she didn't seem in a hurry to catch up to him. She sighed. "I don't have any choice, do I?"

I saw Geraldine open her mouth to answer and gave her a poke. I knew Mama wasn't asking a question. She was thinking out loud. She revved the engine a little, to keep it going, then slowly pulled up alongside Mr. Clement. This time, she kept the clutch in when she put on the brake. She leaned over and rolled down the passenger window.

"Jefferson . . . Jefferson Clement," she called. "What are you doing walking along this busy street so far from home?"

He glanced over toward our car. At first he looked surprised, but then he gave Mama a big smile.

"Well, if it isn't Sally Wallace. You are an angel. A sign from heaven in my distress! I went to San Andreas to . . . attend to some business. Wouldn't you know it? I missed the bus back."

Mama began drumming her fingers on the steering wheel. "Well, Jeff, I can't just leave you here, can I? The next bus won't be along till after dark. You could get run over by a car, and your family would have to pay for a funeral."

"Well, I—," he began. But he didn't get a chance to finish.

"Get yourself in this car, Jeff. We're holding up traffic."

I groaned and leaned over the front seat to whisper in Mama's ear. "Mama, do you *have* to give him a ride?"

She turned around and gave me the same kind of look she had just given Geraldine.

"If he's getting in, I'm getting out," Geraldine whispered. Reba Lu's head went up and down in agreement. But they didn't get out. They scooched as far back in the seat with me as they could and got ready to listen.

Mr. Clement got in and slammed the door. "It isn't often I get a ride with such a pretty lady," he said. He turned around and looked in the back seat. "And three lovely young girls."

I wondered what my father would say to *that* if he heard him.

"Don't you 'pretty lady' me," Mama told him. "Just roll down your window. Artie Longmire must have spilled the whole bottle of aftershave on you!"

Mr. Clement just laughed. "Yes, indeed. Artie likes his customers to smell sweet."

Mama didn't answer. Just made a choking sound and rolled down her window. We did the same. The breeze blew in from the dairy we were passing. It smelled of manure and the sweet grass the farmer fed his cows. We girls took deep breaths just to cover up the smell of Mr. Clement. We must have made some noisy breathing sounds because Mama twisted her head around, even in traffic, and looked over the seat at us, one at a time. I knew that look. It meant business.

"You have plenty to talk about back there," she told us.

I grabbed hold of Reba Lu's hand, and she got a grip on Geraldine. Even though Mr. Clement was up in the front seat with Mama, I got the creeps having him in the same car. I could see that Reba Lu and Geraldine did, too. We began to whisper as soft as we could among ourselves. I was glad our car was old and made so many coughing sounds.

"It was him, Angie, wasn't it?" Geraldine barely moved her lips. "He tried to get in our tent. Let's tell your mama to let us out, and we'll take the bus home."

"Don't be stupid," Reba Lu hissed, but her voice was shaky. "He won't try anything with Angie's mama right here with us." She leaned over and looked a question at me. "Will he, Angie?"

"Mama wouldn't have picked him up if she didn't think she could handle him," I said.

Privately, I wasn't so sure. I knew Mama was doing this for Mrs. Clement's sake, but if it had been me at the wheel, I'd have driven right by and left him in the dust.

"Anyway, it's too late now," I said, for Mama had her foot almost to the floorboard. I hoped we wouldn't get a ticket.

"Well, as long as we're trapped here . . . ," Reba Lu said, "we might as well not miss anything." So we hunched way down and leaned forward so our heads were touching the front seat.

"Why in the world did you come back to Messina, anyway?" Mama asked him. "You never liked it here."

He looked at her sideways. "No place else to go." Then he laughed. "Everyone but you seems glad enough to see me. Some people have even asked me to run for mayor in the next election."

Mama didn't answer him. She didn't even turn her head in his direction.

Reba Lu put one arm around Geraldine and the other around me and pulled us close so our heads were touching. "I didn't say anything about this before," she whispered, "but I scratched Mr. Clement's name off our list of people to love."

"What took you so long?" Geraldine asked.

I didn't say anything. I was remembering how we had planned to help Mr. Clement get a hobby. Like collecting stamps. It seemed to me that he already had a hobby. I shivered, thinking about what he might have planned to do if he had gotten into our tent.

CHAPTER FOURTEEN

When we got home, Mama pulled up in front of the Clements' house. Mr. Clement made a great to-do about getting out of the car and thanking her. But he didn't call her "pretty lady" again. Just tipped his straw hat and limped up the steps to his front door.

We girls went straight to my bedroom. "What a horrible man!" I exclaimed. "Did you see the way he moves like his backside hurts?"

"Probably from his war wound," Reba Lu said.

Geraldine and I put our hands on our hips and stared at her until she turned pink and said, "Well, that *could* be the reason."

"The trouble with you," Geraldine said, "is you have a goody-goody streak. I just wish Buster had taken a bigger bite."

For a moment, it was Geraldine and me, just like we used to be. Then I noticed how Reba Lu was turning more red than pink and I started feeling sorry for her.

"At least he's off our list," I said. Then, before Geraldine could get started telling us what she thought of that list, I added, "Let's try on our new suits."

We did and admired ourselves in the three-paneled mirror on my little dressing table. The two side panels swung forward or backward so we could see how we looked from the side and the front at the same time.

"I'll bet Dodie doesn't even have a bathing suit," I said. "We should have invited her to come shopping with us today."

Nobody said anything for a minute. "She wasn't very nice to us when we invited her to camp out with us," Geraldine reminded me.

Reba Lu sighed. "We have to try harder. I'll let her use my old bathing suit."

"But you said it's raggedy and has a saggy seat," I reminded her.

"She could have mine, I guess," Geraldine said, "but she's so skinny it would hang loose on her." They both looked at me.

"I could give her mine," I told them. "I'll never wear it again now that I have this new one."

"That sounds real gracious," Reba Lu said.

She was right, and I felt ashamed. We didn't ask Dodie to share our fun that day, but we were willing to give her our leftovers. I wondered how I would feel if I were in Dodie's place, and nobody liked me because I was poor, or didn't want to be around me because my mother was a drunk. I tried to imagine how I would feel if folks just gave me things they didn't want for themselves. I felt real sorry for Dodie. It wasn't her fault she got born into the Crumper family. Then I thought maybe Dodie wasn't looking for sympathy. What *was* she looking for?

I remembered how we had linked little fingers and shared secrets and made promises. Could I have trusted Geraldine and Reba Lu the way I had trusted Dodie?

Geraldine interrupted my thoughts. "Even if we had invited her, she might not even want to go to the picnic." Geraldine always explained things so that she didn't have to feel guilty. She could go right on with life without looking back.

"Let's go out on your front porch," she said now. "We can sit on your steps and work on our tans."

I borrowed Mama's bottle of Johnson's baby oil from the medicine cabinet. She used it for soft elbows, but we intended to rub it all over ourselves. Geraldine wanted to add a few drops of iodine so we would look brown faster, but we were afraid we would stain our new suits.

The three of us sat on the steps and rubbed oil on each other's backs until we felt sticky all over and left grease marks on the cement where our legs touched it. Mama came out the front door carrying a grocery sack rolled up under her arm. "I'll be back in a bit," she said and headed up the street. We tried to stretch out on the steps, but it was too crowded.

"Let's go over to my house and lie on the grass," Reba Lu said.

The parsonage had the biggest front lawn on Palm Avenue. It looked like a cool green blanket and felt like one, too, for about five minutes. Then we began to itch. "I feel like bugs are crawling on me," Reba Lu said.

"They are," I told her. "You've got a couple on your neck right now."

She jumped up and started brushing at herself, scattering bits of fresh-mown grass over Geraldine and me. The thin green blades stuck to the oil on our skin, and we were trying to pick them off each other when the water hit us.

The twins, Violet and Rose, ran out in their bathing suits and started running around in circles as the lawn sprinkler sprayed them and us. "We got you!" they cried.

We sputtered a bit, but the water felt good, and we didn't itch anymore. We leaped all over the front yard and must have made a good deal of noise. The screen door banged open, and Mrs. Adams came out on the porch. She crooked her finger and beckoned to us.

"Not you," she told the twins as they started to grumble. "You go on and play." She handed a pile of bath towels to Reba Lu. "You girls are too old to prance around the front yard in your bathing suits."

"We were working on our tans," Reba Lu said.

"That's a real good idea. You can work on your tans in the backyard."

"You're not sending the twins to the backyard!"

"The twins are five years old. You girls do not look like five-year-olds."

We wrapped the beach towels around us till we got to the backyard, then spread them out on the grass and stretched out on our stomachs. We propped up on our elbows so we could talk.

"Nobody cares if we prance around at the beach in our bathing suits," Geraldine said.

"That's the beach," Reba Lu told her. "Bathing suits are acceptable at the beach."

"But not in the front yard?"

"I guess not. I guess when you get older, you can't do certain things anymore."

"That's a peculiar idea," Geraldine said. "I thought when you grew up you could do anything you wanted."

Reba Lu turned over and sat up. "My conscience is hurting me," she said. "We ought to go invite Dodie to the picnic."

"We?" Geraldine asked.

"We're in this together."

"She told us to leave her alone," Geraldine reminded her.

"She didn't mean it. She was mad about something." Reba Lu stopped and stared over our heads toward the house next door. "What's Mr. Clement doing?"

Geraldine and I sat up. Mr. Clement had a pair of binoculars, and he was pointing them right at us. I put my arms around myself. I felt like my bathing suit didn't cover enough of my skin. "I wonder how long he's been out there," I said.

"Not very long." It was Charles. He came out the back door and sat on the steps. "I just noticed him from the back porch. A few minutes after you spread your towels on the grass, he came limping outside with those binoculars."

"*Brrrr!* He gives me the shivers," Reba Lu said.

"Me, too," Geraldine agreed.

Charles and I looked at each other. Then I began scratching at a mosquito bite.

"Angie, do you know something you haven't told?" he asked.

I didn't answer him right away. I glanced over at Reba Lu, who nodded at me. I guessed it was time to come clean about what I'd figured out.

"It's about that day when Mr. Clement came tearing out of Dodie's house. When he passed me, I smelled something kind of spicy. Like a man's aftershave lotion. Then I smelled it again when someone tried to get in our tent and when Mama gave him a lift in the car. I don't think he wears it all the time. Only when . . . when . . ."

"When he's going visiting?" Charles finished my sentence for me.

Geraldine and Reba Lu and I looked at each other. Charles had put Jefferson Clement's sneaky behavior into words that everybody could understand.

"You need to tell your dad about this," Charles said.

I nodded. I would tell him, but not right now. I needed to think about it first. Mr. Clement made me feel uneasy . . . in a scary kind of way. If he ever found out I was accusing him, I didn't know what he'd do. I didn't want to find out.

"Uh-oh. He's honing in on you girls again."

Hot as it was, we wrapped the beach towels around us and headed for my house, where we had left our clothes. As we walked down the driveway, I looked over my shoulder. Charles raised one hand, and I stopped and gave him a wave.

I knew Geraldine and Reba Lu were watching, but I didn't care. I liked talking to Charles. And I had liked it when he roasted the weenie for my hot dog at the campfire. It felt different to have a boy for a friend for a change. It was the first time that had happened to me, except for boy cousins. And cousins were different kinds of friends. Family friends. Not boy-girl friends.

I turned back around and caught up with Reba Lu and Geraldine. They were grinning. I could see that the two of them couldn't leave it alone.

"Your face is red," Geraldine said. "You must have got too much sun." She poked Reba Lu, and Reba Lu nudged her back. I ignored their little smiles.

"That's good," I said. "I'll have a tan by the time we go to the beach."

Speaking of the beach reminded me of Dodie. "We need to invite Dodie to the picnic," I said. "She might not even know about it."

"She doesn't go to church," Geraldine reminded us. It made me mad the way she said it, as though Dodie wasn't good enough to be invited.

"That's not important," Reba Lu told her. "Loving a sinner doesn't have a lot of rules. You just show your love, and God takes care of the rest."

"Yeah, right," Geraldine said, which meant she thought Reba Lu was carrying this loving thing too far. But I knew she would go along with it anyway, at least for now.

As soon as we had changed into shorts and blouses, we started up the street. "I guess we'd better figure out what to say," Geraldine said.

"We don't have to figure anything!" Reba Lu exclaimed. "We just ask her, that's all." I could tell that Reba Lu was getting irritated with Geraldine. So was I, to tell the truth, but it made me feel kind of good to see the two of them getting testy with each other. I was sick of the way they had been pairing off.

As we walked up the street to see Dodie, I glanced over at the Clement house. It had all the shades drawn against the afternoon heat. Even so, I could imagine Mr. Clement standing behind one of the windows, pushing the shade a little to one side and putting his binoculars up against the crack.

"We'd best keep our distance from that man," I said without even mentioning his name.

"I won't even say good morning from now on," Reba Lu promised.

"I wonder what he did at Dodie's house to make her mother so mad," I said.

"Use your imagination," Geraldine said.

"I'm trying, but I don't know what to imagine," I said. "I don't want Mr. Jefferson Clement inside my head."

But he was there, just the same. I couldn't stop thinking about what had happened. As we walked along the street, I kept seeing Mr. Clement sneaking around, trying to get into our tent. I was pretty sure he did it. Who else would have done such a thing? Then I had a thought: suppose Buster hadn't been with us? I could feel my heart beating faster.

We walked slowly, three across, with our arms linked. Nobody answered when we rang Dodie's doorbell, so we went around back, expecting to see her hanging out laundry.

Instead, she was sitting on the back stoop, cradling a mangy old cat. "Poor kitty," she crooned, and stroked it gently.

"If that cat's sick, you oughtn't to be holding it," Geraldine said. "It might have ringworm or something worse."

"That's not what's wrong," Dodie said. "It got in a fight." The cat turned to look at us, and we saw the torn ear and a bloody place where an eye should have been. Reba Lu put her hand over her mouth and made a gagging sound.

"Nobody was watching out for it," Dodie said. "That's how it got to be a mangy stray. But look here." She ran her fingers gently through the thick fur on the cat's neck, pulling it apart so we could see how white it was under all that dirt. "This is how it will look once I get it all cleaned up. If I doctor its bloody places, I'll bet it will get better. I can't do anything about the missing eye though."

She looked at us. "Someone has to love it," she said.

Nobody knew what to say to that. I couldn't help thinking that Dodie had taken on that sick cat to nurse without any hesitation while the three of us had made a big thing of trying to be nice to her.

"What happened to your legs?" I asked. They were dotted with bloody places only partially covered by pieces of gauze, held on by tape. At first I thought the cat might have scratched her, but she said, "I cut myself."

I looked closer. "You shaved your legs?"

Dodie nodded. "I wanted them to look nice. You don't want to go to the beach with hairy legs."

I looked down at my own legs. Mama would kill me

if I shaved them. "Rub on some lemon juice and sit in the sun" was what she would say.

"I'm invited to the All-Church Picnic," Dodie said. "I got a bathing suit today. It's yellow with ruffles." She looked at me. "Your mama brought it to the house. She said the picnic is free. We don't even have to pay for the bus ride. And the best thing is . . . you don't have to go to church to get invited." She looked at Reba Lu when she said that.

Geraldine turned to me. "So that's what your moth—" I jabbed her with my elbow. Hard.

Dodie didn't pay any attention. She kept petting the cat. "I already tried it on. It fits real good."

"That's fine," Reba Lu said. "We came by to tell you about the picnic. Now that you have a bathing suit, you can go with us. The bus seats are two by two, so we four can split up and sit close together."

"We'll meet at the church," I told her. "If we're early, we can sit at the front. That way, we have a better chance of seeing the ocean first."

Reba Lu put her arm around Geraldine as if they were best friends, and I knew which one of us Dodie would be sitting with. But I wasn't one to give up easy.

"We'll switch around on the way home," I said.

"Sure we will," Reba Lu told me.

I knew she didn't mean it.

CHAPTER FIFTEEN

The next Saturday, we were up early. When I came into the kitchen, Mama was skinning boiled potatoes at the sink. She had already chopped onions and celery and I knew she was putting the last touches on her famous potato salad for the picnic lunch at the beach. She always added a little smashed garlic to the dressing and sprinkled paprika and chopped parsley over the top. There was never a scrap left after folks tasted it and went back for seconds.

I tried to slip past her to the back door because I had seen Daddy heading out toward the toolshed in the side yard. I had thought to tell him last night about that spicy smell that I knew Mr. Clement favored, but somehow the words never found their way out of my mouth. Every time I started to say something, I remembered the way that man looked standing outside our tent and I got a case of the shivers from the back of my neck right down to my tailbone.

I was sure in my own mind who he was, but I kept wondering what would happen to me if I told. What would Mr. Jefferson Clement do if he caught me somewhere alone? I headed for the back door to find Daddy, but Mama stopped me. I was so relieved I felt weak in the knees when I heard her voice.

"Come right over here and give me a hand packing this food for the picnic," she said.

I closed the back door and let out all my breath in a *whoosh* of relief. I felt the same as I did at school once when Miss Harper asked me a question I didn't know the answer to, and just when I was starting to sweat, the bell rang to signal the end of the day.

I thought about telling Mama about Reba Lu and Geraldine and me sunning ourselves in the preacher's backyard, and how Mr. Clement had his binoculars pointed right at us. But I didn't tell her. When I thought about him looking at us in secret like that, my skin prickled with goose bumps.

I was glad when she put her arm around me and gave me a squeeze. She gave a little laugh and said, "I think I'm glad this picnic only comes once a year."

We packed the big wicker picnic basket with potato salad, tomatoes from the backyard vines, deviled eggs made with minced onions and mayonnaise and sprinkled with a dash of paprika and a tiny sprig of parsley on top, and the two chickens Mama had fried last night. Enough for three families, Daddy said.

Eddie came in the back door and reached for a chicken leg and Mama slapped his hand. Then she said, "Oh, all right, but you won't get as much once we get there." I reached for one, too, but then I remembered how I always got carsick when I had a full stomach. I didn't want Charles to see me throw up.

Daddy had bought some dry ice that he packed in dish towels in the bottom of the basket to keep the food cool. I loved the way it made smoky trails in the air, but I knew better than to touch a piece and burn my fingers.

The members of the church choir were supplying lemonade. Miss Lucy Clement told Mama they'd squeezed lemons until their fingers puckered. Old Man Snyder was bringing watermelons from his backyard patch. Mama said she was carrying her fresh-baked lemon cake on her lap, safe in a covered container. People would take turns turning the handle on the ice-cream churn, but Willie Jack always stepped in for the last part, when the cream got frozen thick and the turning got hard.

I wore my new bathing suit underneath a blue cotton skirt and a white Dotted Swiss blouse. Mama had gathered the skirt with elastic running through the waistband so that I could slide out of it in a jiffy. The blouse would take a little longer because it had blue glass turtles for buttons.

When I told Reba Lu what I was going to wear, she grinned and said, "Blue suit, blue skirt, blue buttons. Charles will go out of his mind."

"Why should he?" Geraldine had asked. For someone who knows so much, Geraldine can be a little slow at times. But I did admire the way she got to wear her sandals without socks.

I wanted to wear mine that way, but Mama said I would get blisters. So I put on my white socks with lace around the ankles and fastened the buckles on my sandals. Then I picked up my latest copy of *Calling All Girls* and found the article "Look Your Super Best at the Beach."

A model was standing on the sand with the ocean behind her. She was wearing a skirt like mine, but she didn't have blue glass turtles on *her* blouse. The next picture showed her in her bathing suit, with the skirt draped over one arm. She had pink polish on her toes. I knew I'd never get away with that. I got a bath towel, though, and practiced draping it until I got the hang of it, putting my free hand on one hip and letting the towel almost touch the floor.

"Hurry up, Angie. We're about to leave without you," Mama called. I took a last look in the mirror and grabbed my favorite blue shorts, just in case the skirt got tiresome.

At the church, three yellow school buses had pulled up alongside the curb. Reba Lu said, "My daddy told me this picnic is a way for all the people in Messina to come together and be God's family."

Geraldine looked at her, then at the three buses. "You don't mean we should sit with the Baptists or Catholics, do you?"

"Why not? It's a good way to meet folks from other persuasions."

Geraldine sighed. "That would be fine, I guess, if everybody would do it. But they won't. You just wait and see, Reba Lu. This isn't Heaven. It's Messina."

Dodie came hurrying along the sidewalk, and I grabbed her by the arm. "Come on," I said. "Let's get a good seat."

When Dodie climbed on ahead of me, I could see a

few scabs on her legs, but the bandages were gone. She had tried to brush her hair—I could see places where the bristles had smoothed it down a bit. But she had given up on most of the tangles. I wondered how long it had been since she had washed it.

She was wearing a white blouse and faded navy blue shorts that looked like they could have been somebody's old gym uniform. The blouse looked freshly ironed, but the two bottom buttons were missing, and the gap was held together with large safety pins. She gave a loud sniff and pulled a tissue from her pocket. I hoped she had an allergy to her one-eyed cat and not a summer cold that she would spread around.

I did have to admit that Dodie was making an effort to clean herself up, but she still had a long way to go. As far as I was concerned, my sitting with her all the way to La Mirada Beach was just as much missionary work as Reba Lu would *ever* do.

Jefferson Clement was sitting alone about halfway back. As soon as we got on, he turned his face away and started looking out the window. Geraldine and Reba Lu took the first empty seat, three rows behind the driver, and Dodie and I slid in behind them. I went first so I could have the window seat and regretted it before I even sat down. Charles Adams had the aisle seat right across from us. I whispered to Dodie that we should change places.

"What for?" she demanded. Then she saw Charles and said in a singsong voice he couldn't help but hear, "Angie's got a boyfriend . . . Angie's got a boyfriend . . ."

"Shut up!" I hissed. "You be quiet, or you can take your shaved legs and find yourself somebody else to sit with."

Dodie's mouth dropped open, and she gave me a little half smile. "What do you know? You *can* stand up for yourself." She got up and crawled over me till she was next to the window. She scooted over so far there was almost room for another whole person between us. I couldn't tell if she was mad at me or not.

Reba Lu turned around and looked at us. She had heard the whole thing and was probably thinking I had broken our promise to love Dodie Crumper.

I sighed. Even though Dodie had embarrassed me, I had been rude to her. Normally I wouldn't have cared, but it didn't seem right to spoil the picnic for anybody. Not even Dodie. I reached out and gave her a poke.

"I'm sorry I yelled at you," I said.

She leaned way over and looked at Charles, gave me a wink, and wiped her nose on the back of her arm.

"Use your tissue," I whispered. She dug in her pocket and brought out a tissue. It was already soggy, so I gave her one of mine. She blew her nose on it and started to hand it back to me.

"That's OK," I said, trying not to gag. "You can keep it." We were quiet for a couple of minutes. "Have you got your bathing suit on under your shorts?" I asked.

Dodie nodded.

"Good. When we get to the beach, you can slip your clothes off, and we'll go jump waves."

Dodie raised an eyebrow. "Do you have to go out deep to do that?"

I stared at her, and it came to me that Dodie had never been to the beach before. "Don't worry," I told her. "We'll hang on to each other. And there are lifeguards. You don't have to be afraid."

She gave me a long look. "I'm not afraid. But I'll have to think about it," she said.

I turned to glance behind me and saw that Geraldine had been right. Every year it was the same. The Congregationalists sat together on one bus, the Baptists on another, and all the leftover religions on the third. Once Reba Lu figured that one out, she was going to have plenty to say about our town.

Mrs. Clement hurried down the aisle with Miss Lucy and Miss Martin, their boarder. She eased into a window seat in front of Mr. Clement. She was hugging a casserole wrapped in layers of newspaper, folded down at the edges and tucked under the bottom, the way Mama does when she wants to keep her scalloped potatoes warm. Lucy and Miss Martin looked at each other. Quick as a wink, Miss Martin slid into the seat next to Mrs. Clement. That left Lucy only one place to go. She didn't look too happy about having to sit by her father. I didn't blame her a bit.

I noticed Dr. Thomas and Miss Emma sitting way at the back, in the long seat that stretched clear across the bus. There was plenty of room for a few more back there, but neither Gisele Martin nor Lucy Clement had made a move to join them, even though it was obvious they weren't very happy sitting near Lucy's father. If it was me, I'd choose Miss Emma over Mr. Clement any day. Even if she was tetched, I thought she was harmless. And nice, in a different kind of way.

Dodie twisted to see what I was looking at. "Don't Mr.

Clement look dapper!" she said. "He's wearing the shirt that I ironed for him." She started biting at her thumbnail, chewing until she had a ragged piece loose that she could peel away with her front teeth.

"You better quit that," I told her. "You'll make your thumb bleed."

She ignored me and said, "I was doing fine until Mama chased him off. I liked making some money on my own." She chewed a bit on her index finger, then turned to me. "I keep it in a pickle jar that I hide in the mattress springs of my bed. She'll never find it there. I'm the only one who changes the sheets."

In front of us, Reba Lu and Geraldine were whispering, their heads close together, the way Geraldine and I used to do. I closed my eyes and leaned my head against the seat. We had an hour and a half before we got to the beach, and I was spending it with Dodie Crumper. I began thinking how Dodie and I had waded in the cold water of the park and shared secrets. When I was alone with her, she didn't seem so bad, but when we were with Geraldine and Reba Lu, it seemed like I was seeing her through their eyes. I didn't like the way that made me feel.

Somebody touched my arm. I turned and saw Charles holding an open box of graham crackers across the aisle. "Help yourself," he said.

I was afraid to take one and afraid not to. What if I got carsick and threw up? That would be awful. What if I hurt his feelings? That would be worse. I reached out and took a graham cracker and bit into it. One cracker couldn't hurt.

Charles grinned. "Have another," he said.

I grinned back at him. The first one seemed to be going down all right. And I was getting hungry because I hadn't tasted any of Mama's fried chicken that morning. I decided to take a chance.

I reached for a second cracker. "Thanks," I said. Charles grinned again. Then he reached across me and offered one to Dodie. She took it and broke it into four pieces. She took a bite out of one and put the others in her pocket with the snotty tissue.

The bus *whooshed* and *wheezed* and ground its gears, and Mr. Sadler, who sang tenor in the church choir but was the driver for the day, turned the wheel and pushed on the accelerator. The bus gave a jump or two, then settled down as we swung away from the curb and headed down Main Street toward the river road and the highway beyond.

We still had a long drive, but we were on our way.

CHAPTER SIXTEEN

"**I** see it! I see it!" yelled Violet. She stood up in the aisle and began hopping up and down.

"Sit down right this minute," Reverend Adams commanded.

She sat. I was surprised. I didn't think anyone ever told either of the Adams twins what to do.

Rose gave a smirk that said she was glad she wasn't the one in trouble. "You're not supposed to get out of your seat when the bus is moving," she reminded her sister.

Violet glanced at her. "Shut up, Miss Goody-Goody." Then she began pointing again. "I win!" she shouted. "I win because I saw it first."

We all craned our necks and looked out the front window. Sure enough, there it was, just visible over the rise of a hill. A stretch of blue, darker than the sky and tipped with white flecks.

"That's the Pacific Ocean," Violet told us, "and I win."

"Just smell that salt air," Reverend Adams said, and we all took deep breaths.

"There's nothing like it," Miss Emma piped up from the back of the bus. "Is there, Papa?"

I looked back and saw Dr. Thomas put his arm around her and pat her on the shoulder. "That's right, Emmy. Nothing like salt air to cure what ails us." His words carried over the noise of the bus.

I wondered if salt air could cure what ailed Miss Emma. Maybe other people were thinking the same thing, for it got quiet, and the only sounds for the next few minutes came from the chugging of the engine and the *thud* the bus made whenever it hit a pothole in the road.

Then the ocean came into full view and everybody cheered. Charles looked over at me and grinned. He offered me another graham cracker.

I reached out and took one from the package. "Thanks," I said as my fingers brushed the side of his hand. There *was* something special about a day at the beach.

As soon as Mr. Sadler found a place to park, we piled off the bus and stretched our arms and legs. Then we found a good spot near the pier to open up our big umbrellas and spread beach towels on the warm sand. Reba Lu and Geraldine and Dodie and I stripped off our clothes and stood in our bathing suits in the sun.

Mama motioned us over to where she was settled against a folding wooden frame covered with red-and-blue striped canvas. She stopped rubbing lotion on her arms long enough to pass around a tube of zinc oxide for our noses.

"I don't want to look like a clown," I protested.

"You'll look more like one if your nose burns red," Reba Lu said. She squeezed some zinc oxide on one finger and dabbed it all over her nose. "Here, let me do yours," she said, and she smeared some on mine and Geraldine's.

Dodie stood there, waiting. Reba Lu tried to smile as she covered Dodie's nose with the thick white cream, but her mouth was squinched up like she was sucking a lemon. I wondered what she would do if Dodie gave one of her huge wet sniffs.

We ran across the hot sand, not stopping until it became cool and damp where the waves splashed over it and turned it wet and brown. Glistening seaweed cluttered the shoreline in stringy clumps. I pulled off some of the shiny brown bulbs and popped them between my fingers.

A wave broke and swept up the shoreline, splashing our feet with cool water and white foam. Hundreds of tiny sand crabs dug headfirst into the wet sand, leaving little holes that bubbled and popped, then turned smooth and disappeared.

Geraldine, Reba Lu, and I fell to our knees and scooped out handfuls of sand, laughing as the crabs scurried around our fingers. I caught one and put it in Dodie's palm. She watched it a few seconds, then set it gently on the sand.

"Its shell is pearly pink," she said. She smiled at me, making me feel I had just given her a gift—like she had opened a package and seen something she had always wanted.

"I never noticed that before," Geraldine said. She waited for another wave to wash the sand, then began to dig. She came up with a dozen or more crabs, and each one did have a shiny pink tone to its delicate shell.

"Pearly pink," I said. "That's like the name of a fingernail polish."

The three of us looked at Dodie awkwardly. The person we knew who picked her nose and had sore hands from doing other people's washing didn't seem like this Dodie at the beach who could see a pearl in a crab's shell. It was like she was starting to be somebody we didn't know at all. Or maybe she had always been like this, and we didn't take time to notice. I didn't know what to say.

"What do we do now?" Dodie asked.

"Get wet!" I shouted. I grabbed her hand and started to run across the wet sand to the water's edge. We didn't get far because she dug her heels in, making deep wet holes.

"Wait a minute," she panted. "I'm not going no farther." She squinted at the ocean. "That's a lot of water out there," she said. And I remembered this was Dodie's first trip to the beach.

"At least you can wade," I urged. I tugged at her hand, pulling her, a few steps at a time, closer to the white foam at the edge of the breaking waves.

"Cut it out! Stop!" she cried. But she kept taking little steps until the water washed over her ankles. "Hey, that's nice and cool, Angie."

A big wave came then and splashed us. "Look, Dodie," I yelled. "We're up to our knees in saltwater!"

She gripped both my hands. "That's good," she said. "But I've gone as far as I'm gonna go."

Geraldine and Reba Lu were already holding hands

and jumping waves that rolled and swelled and touched their waists. "Look at them," I said. "They're out farther than we are, and they can still stand up!"

"I don't care," Dodie squealed. "I don't like this one bit."

But little by little she stopped pulling against me and began making tiny jumps up and down in the water, saying things like, "Oooh, this is a big one," when a gentle swell went higher than her knees.

I motioned to Geraldine and Reba Lu, and they sloshed toward us. "What?" Geraldine asked.

"Dodie's never jumped waves before," I said. I looked hard at Reba Lu. "We can show her how."

"Of course we can," Reba Lu said in her missionary voice. "Everybody take hands."

We made a circle around Dodie. She reached out and put her hands on my shoulders just as a larger wave rose up and crashed on us. It reached all the way to our chests. "Aghhh!" Dodie yelled, but she hung on. "Whoa!" she exclaimed. "I thought I was a goner."

We didn't have time to answer. The tide was coming in, and another wave was on top of us, pounding and crashing, pushing and pulling. We three held tight to each other's hands, with Dodie still in the middle holding on to me.

Her face was flushed, but she was grinning. She jumped up and down, letting the water buoy her. "I'm ready for the next one," she said. And she was. We jumped high before it hit us, and I saw Dodie rising above the foam, floating for a second, then sinking to her neck into swirling, salty water, laughing and hollering.

"By the sea, by the sea, by the beautiful sea," Geraldine

began singing, shouting the words out so the splashing waves couldn't drown the melody.

"You and me, you and me, oh how happy we'll be," she went on.

"That's *you and I,* " Reba Lu yelled. "*You and I* are the correct words."

"Who cares!" Geraldine yelled back. "It sounds better my way."

"Yeah," put in Dodie, grinning at me. "*You and me* makes me feel real good."

So that's the way we sang it. *You and me . . . you and me . . . you and me.*

CHAPTER SEVENTEEN

We had plopped down on our beach towels to dry off on the warm sand when Charles appeared. He stood in front of me, blocking the sun, and said, "Come on, Angie. I want to show you something."

He reached out a hand. I put my hand in his and let him pull me to my feet.

Geraldine made a snickering sound behind me, and I heard Reba Lu shush her. I glanced at Dodie, but she was looking out at the sea.

"Where are we going?" I asked, but Charles wouldn't tell me. We walked together to the water's edge. Sometimes his hand brushed mine as we swung our arms along. We turned toward the pier, splashing in the shallow waves and leaving watery footprints in the wet sand.

Miss Emma and Dr. Thomas were climbing on the breakwater. Charles told me that all those huge rocks reaching out into the sea were put there to break the force of the waves near the pier. Miss Emma's arms flapped as she tried to keep her balance and peer into a tide pool. Closer to shore, Lucy Clement and Gisele Martin were collecting blue mussels and putting them into a straw bag.

The wet brown sand beneath our feet was flecked with small stones. As we neared the underside of the pier, they covered the sand thickly, washed up by the tides and piled in layers of different colors and textures and shapes.

Charles bent over and scooped up a handful. "There was a storm in the Pacific a few weeks ago," he told me. "That's why there are so many. Nice, aren't they?"

The beauty of wet stones always surprised me. Saltwater seemed to make the colors brighter, more vivid. Those farther up the shore looked sun-dried and dull.

Charles sifted them through his fingers, letting some fall and bending over to rinse others in the lapping water.

I thought of the moonstone in my cigar box at home and remembered that I had found it after a storm. Could I find another one today? I dropped to my knees and cupped my hands around as many wet stones as I could hold. They felt sea-scrubbed, as smooth as glass.

We were hunting and picking, sorting out the prettiest ones, when Dr. Thomas and Miss Emma joined us. Miss Emma kicked off her shoes, tucked up her skirt, and squatted down beside us. She lifted a handful of stones to her face and sniffed them. Then she touched the tip of her tongue to one. "Salty," she said, and smiled.

She offered me a smooth brown one with white flecks. I took it and thanked her. "Put it in your pocket," she said. So I did. Dr. Thomas nodded his head at me and smiled.

"Hello!" Miss Emma cried out, grasping a piece of polished blue glass between two fingers before the tide could wash it out of reach. She held it up to the sun, turning it slowly to catch the light. "Look, Papa," she said. "See what Emmy found. It's bluer than the sky. It's as blue as Angie's bathing suit."

"You're right, Emmy," he said. "You hold tight to it so you don't lose it." He took her hand and led her like a child along the beach. She kicked her feet, splashing water into the air. Then she stopped and began waving to a seagull.

"Miss Emma is happy today," Charles said. I thought how nice he looked with his hair mussed by the breeze. His nose was white with zinc oxide, just like mine.

I smiled up at him. "I'm glad," I said, but I was thinking, *Poor Miss Emma. Life is good one minute and bad the next.* She had been happy the day we visited her until she looked out the window. What could Jefferson Clement have done to frighten her so? He was a menace, a dark cloud hanging over our town. I made up my mind not to think about him today.

But I wasn't through with him. I had a plan to find out more. The first chance I got, I was going to go visit Miss Emma by myself. I thought she might do better if just one person came to visit her. I'd talk to her about her animals. Then I'd say something about the wonderful view from her bedroom window. I would ask her questions about Messina when she was young. I hadn't planned what else I'd say, but

I hoped I could find out why she had been so scared that day we went to visit her.

Of course, Miss Emma wasn't quite right, so I couldn't depend a whole lot on what she said. But I was going to visit her just the same.

"I'll bet Miss Emma would like to catch that seagull and take it home to be company for Henry," I told Charles.

"Henry?"

"That's her parrot. She also has a monkey called Joseph and a snake named Cleopatra. Lily-Poo is that ugly little pug dog that's always looking out the upstairs window."

He grinned at me. "You're kidding, aren't you?"

"No, I'm telling the truth! We saw all her animals when Reba Lu, Geraldine, Dodie, and I went to visit her. I'll take you there sometime, if you like. Miss Emma enjoys company."

Charles's eyes were wide. "It's a date!" he exclaimed, then turned red in the face and went back to sifting stones.

A date. Charles had said a date! Of course, I had started it by offering to take him to visit Miss Emma. But he could simply have said, "I'd like to do that," or "Sounds like a good idea." Instead he called it a date. And he blushed when he said it.

I felt myself starting to blush, too, and went back to hunting pretty stones, keeping my head down so he couldn't see my face. Just then, I spotted a bluish-white stone, about the size of a quarter, with chalky marks on it. I plunged my hand into the water, but the outgoing wave pulled it away from me, rolling it over and over until it disappeared.

I kept my eye on the spot where I had seen it last and waded out almost to my knees, then bent over and scooped up a double handful of stones. I let the seawater flow through and dropped them a few at a time. When I saw the white stone again. I nudged it away from the others with my thumb, pushing it into the palm of one hand.

I had it between my fingers when a big wave came, rising from the ocean floor in a blue-green surge, creeping toward the shore like a hungry sea creature with foam where its teeth should be. It crashed a few feet away and rushed toward us with a force that made me stagger. I dug my heels into the pebbly sand, but a broken shell stabbed into the sole of my left foot.

"Oh, ouch!" I cried and hopped on my right foot. The undertow pulled at me, and I lost my balance. Charles reached for my arm, but I fell, pulling him down with me. The stone flew out of my hand, sailed in a perfect curve, and sank into the water without even a splash.

Charles got to his feet. "I'll get it for you, Angie."

He fell to his knees where the stone had disappeared. The sea seemed to hold its breath in that silent pause between wave-in and wave-out. Charles reached into the water and came up with a double handful of stones.

He laughed. "I just scooped up as many as I could hold."

We walked up the shore a few steps, and he dumped them on dry sand. We began searching. Round stones, oblong stones, irregular stones . . .

"There it is!" We said the words at the same time.

Charles picked it up and handed it to me. "Here's your white stone, Angie. But are you sure you really want that one? It's got chalky spots on it. Look, here's a blue-green one and another the color of your hair, kind of sunny brown." He looked at me like he was seeing my hair for the first time.

Nobody had ever called my hair sunny brown before. I avoided his eyes and looked down at the colored stones.

"Those are real nice," I told him, "but this is the one I want."

I held it up to the light and saw the glow of the inner stone. "It's a moonstone," I said. "Here, see for yourself."

I handed him the stone. "Hold it up to the sunlight and see what's behind those chalky places."

He held it up, turning it slowly between his fingers, looking at it from every angle. "Amazing," he finally said. "It's like the chalky spots are clouds, and the moon is shining through from behind them. I can see the ball of light inside."

It felt good to know that Charles looked at moonstones the same way I did. He wasn't at all like Reba Lu, even if he *was* her brother. She would probably look at a moonstone and say something like, "It's all splotchy white on the outside, like a pigeon pooped on it." Even though she was into loving sinners, I didn't think she looked very far beneath their surface.

That made me wonder about the people in our town. How many would pick up a moonstone and throw it away because it looked ordinary on the surface? Miss Hattie Harper would. So would Mrs. Mildred Hewitt. But Willie Jack would sit by the Bank of America and hold it up to the sun, turning it slowly so he didn't miss a thing. It came to me that the way people looked at things told an awful lot about them.

I moved my feet in the water, feeling all the different stones shift and slide. I wished I could scoop up bucketfuls and take them home with me. But I remembered how dull they looked when we tossed them up on the shore. They belonged here, where the sea would reveal their hidden beauty.

I felt older all of a sudden. I was starting to understand things I had hardly thought of before. Things I couldn't talk about with Geraldine or Reba Lu. They would laugh and say, "Oh, Angie!"

Dodie wouldn't laugh though. She would probably sit right down among the stones and feel right at home.

I realized Charles was looking at me, a kind of question in his eyes. "You can keep it if you want to," I offered. "After all, you're the one who rescued it."

He held it up to the sun, then reached out and caught my hand. He placed the moonstone in my palm and pressed my fingers around it. "This is yours," he said.

Then he grinned. "Race you to the top of the pier," he challenged.

We took the stone steps two at a time. Charles won. "But not by much," he admitted.

He dug into a buttoned pocket in his swim trunks and brought out a nickel to buy an extra-big pink cotton candy for us to share.

"I love this stuff," I said and pulled a sticky handful of sugary fluff away from the paper cone.

"Me, too. It's pure sugar. Supposed to rot our teeth."

"Who cares?" I asked. We each took another handful. We walked along the pier, high above the water, watching fishermen pulling in their catch: perch, halibut, sole. It was nice to walk along together, eating cotton candy and not talking unless we had something to say.

Then we heard the carefree sound of the organ grinder's music. A crowd was forming around a man with a black moustache and a big smile. His little monkey wrinkled his nose like he was sniffing the corn dogs and popcorn from Molly's Snack Shop behind him. He took off his tiny hat and began collecting pennies from the crowd. Dodie was there, grinning at him and holding out a penny. But when Charles and I broke away and walked toward the merry-go-round at the shore end of the pier, she came with us. Geraldine and Reba Lu were walking ahead, paired up like best friends.

For a second, it felt like I'd lost my place. After all, I was the one who had introduced them. I had known both of them before they knew each other. Now it seemed I wasn't Reba Lu's top choice, or Geraldine's either. They leaned their heads close together, whispering and laughing, then whispering some more.

So let them, I thought. A little while ago, I would have said it wasn't fair that I was stuck with Dodie. But now she was walking along with Charles and me, and I really didn't mind.

Except that she was talking a mile a minute, and I wished she would shut up so Charles and I could talk.

"That was a cute little monkey," she said. "Did you see how smart he was? No wonder Miss Emma has a pet monkey." It seemed like she'd never stop talking.

She finally paused for a breath, and it came to me that Geraldine, Reba Lu, and I had been trying to love Dodie because we wanted to get on God's good side. But we hadn't really gotten to know her. Not the things she liked, or didn't like.

We hadn't tried.

CHAPTER EIGHTEEN

The ticket booth for the carousel was painted bright red with a yellow sunburst across the front and orange lion heads in the four corners. Green starfish danced in the bursting rays of the sun. A large glass dome fit on top of the booth, and a man in a red-and-white striped shirt stood inside it selling tickets.

We started to get in line when I remembered I didn't have any money with me. I poked Geraldine. She looked a little put out that I had interrupted whatever she was telling Reba Lu, but I got her attention when I asked, "What are we going to use for money?"

She felt around for a pocket until she remembered she wasn't wearing anything but skin and latex.

"You got any money on you?" she asked Reba Lu, who

stared at her for asking such a rude question, then shook her head. I shook mine, too. Geraldine turned to Dodie and didn't even ask. When she looked at Charles, he held up a dime.

"Only enough for two rides," he said. "I left the rest of my money with my dad."

"We'll have to go down to the sand," Reba Lu said.

We three had been saving our allowances and had about fifty cents each. Ordinarily that would buy a hamburger, fries, and a soda and still leave enough for ice cream and five rides. But since we were eating at the picnic where the food was free, we could spend all our money on having fun.

We had put our coins in little cotton drawstring bags that Reba Lu made from material in her mother's scrap bag. But when we arrived at the beach, we had taken them out of our pockets and tied them to our shoes.

All but Dodie. None of us had wanted to ask her if she wanted a drawstring bag for her money because we weren't sure she had enough for a day at the beach. So we had put it to a vote and agreed to share what we had. At first it had been two to one, with Geraldine holding out, but Reba Lu told her she had a sinful attitude, and she backed down.

Now we were astonished when Dodie reached down the front of my old bathing suit that she was wearing and pulled some coins out of a tiny bag. It was pinned into the neckline and never even showed because of all the ruffles.

"Where'd you get so many nickels and dimes?" Geraldine exclaimed. "You've got enough there to eat hamburgers for a week!"

"Mr. Clement gave them to me for doing his shirts,"

Dodie said. "My mama never liked him, so I waited until she was asleep, then hung a white handkerchief on the oleander bush by the side of the house to signal that he could come over and pay me. He was real nice to me, but then Mama went and chased him off."

"She sure was mad," I said.

Dodie shrugged and didn't say anything for a minute. "She just doesn't like him," she finally said. "Mama has strong opinions about people."

We were all quiet for a minute until Geraldine blurted out, "Oleander bushes are poisonous. Didn't you know that?"

Dodie shrugged. "I wasn't planning on eating one." She turned and walked toward a bench. "You go on and get your money. I'll wait for you."

We walked back along the pier, Reba Lu and Geraldine in front and Charles and me in back. Charles took hold of my arm and stopped me. "Oleanders aren't the only things that are poisonous. You'd best keep your distance from Mr. Clement," he said.

"Don't worry. I intend to," I told him.

We hurried across the sand to get our money. When we got back to the pier, Dodie was waiting by the merry-go-round, tapping one foot to the music. I put my moonstone in the bag of coins for safekeeping and took out a nickel for a ticket. The music began to slow and the merry-go-round stopped. Before I knew it, Dodie had climbed on the platform, put one foot on the mounting piece and swung the other leg over until she was sitting in the saddle of a white stallion on the inner circle. It had a black mane studded with stars.

I climbed onto a pink horse with large green eyes next to hers, and Charles chose a black one on the outside where he could lean out and reach for a golden ring.

"You can hang on to the pole with one hand and wave to people with the other," I told Dodie. "It's fun, riding to the music. There's nothing in the world like it!"

Charles asked if either of us needed help fastening our seat belts. Dodie made a kind of smirking face and said, "I can figure it out." She gave the belt a pull, then clasped her pole with both hands and waited.

The music started, and the merry-go-round began to turn. The horses quivered, then slowly began to move. Faster and faster. Up and down. Around and around. Dodie held tight to the pole. "Whoa!" she cried. "This is just like riding a real horse!" She watched, open-mouthed, as Charles loosened his seat belt, held tight to the pole, and leaned way out, stretching his right arm toward a metal contraption attached to the wall. It stuck out like a long arm with a shiny loop about as big as a silver dollar at the end.

"He's trying to catch the golden ring," I said, raising my voice over the music. "It's really brass, but it looks golden and shiny. It's a winner. If you catch one, you get a free ride."

"You don't say." Dodie loosened her belt and practiced leaning to one side. Then she wrapped both arms around the pole and watched Charles put all his weight on one of the stirrups, lean way out, and snatch at the ring holder as his horse sped by. He held up a silver ring and groaned.

"Better luck next time," I called.

"I bet I can do better than that," Dodie said.

The horses went around lots more times. Dodie began hanging on with one hand and waving to the people in line just like she knew them. Her cheeks were flushed with excitement. The carousel played "Oh My Darling, Clementine," and we all began to sing along. We knew most of the words. We had learned them in school last year. Dodie sang louder than any of us.

Charles caught several more rings, but they were always silver. I noticed how closely Dodie watched him. Once, she even leaned sideways on her horse, clutching the pole tightly with one hand and stretching as far as she could with her free arm.

As the horses slowed, the attendant came around to collect the rings. "Too bad you didn't catch a gold one," he said to Charles. "Want to ride again?"

We each paid him a nickel, except for Dodie, who handed him a quarter. He was about to push the lever to count out change when Dodie said, "Never mind. I'm going to ride five more times."

Geraldine grinned. "Easy come, easy go," she said. We each handed the attendant our money. If Dodie could ride five more times, so could we.

None of us was ready for what happened next. Dodie undid her seat belt and climbed off her horse. She walked over to a purple charger in the outer circle. It had flaring nostrils and a silver mane. "Purple is my favorite color," she said.

She put her left foot in the stirrup, swung her right leg over the charger's back and settled herself in the saddle. "What are we waiting for?" she yelled. I turned to look at Reba Lu and Geraldine. Both of them had their mouths open. We didn't know Dodie Crumper as well as we had thought.

I was sure of it when she tightened her seat belt as the platform began to move, and her horse started rising. "Yippee!" she shouted. If she had been wearing a cowboy hat, I think she would have waved it the way Roy Rogers did in *Days of Jesse James*.

The first time her horse went past the ring holder, her seat belt kept her from leaning out far enough, and she came away with a handful of air.

"Loosen your belt a little," Charles told her. "When you're ready, hold tight to your pole, put your weight on your right foot and lean as far out as you can. Don't worry, you won't fall. Watch me."

He reached for the ring and caught it. "Silver again," he yelled, waving his ring in the air.

When that ride was over, Reba Lu and Geraldine and I climbed down and chose outside horses, too. I could see our reflections in the long mirrors in the center of the carousel as we stretched out our arms. Reba Lu's cheeks were flushed. My hair was flying in the breeze. Geraldine looked sweaty, but determined. Charles was laughing out loud.

Dodie didn't look like herself. She sat up straight like somebody who knew where she was going. When we passed the post that held the rings, she leaned so far out that I held my breath. She caught a ring, but it was silver. Even so, she looked at me and grinned so hard her mouth seemed to split almost to her ears.

We were on our last ride when she screamed. Looped around one finger, held high above her head, was a gold ring. Of course, I knew it was only brass, but at that moment, it seemed like pure gold.

Dodie held onto that ring like her life depended on it. "I did it! I did it! I did it!" she yelled.

Charles clapped. "Good for you, Dodie!" he shouted. And then we were all clapping and shouting, smacking our hands together so hard it hurt.

Dodie was red in the face when we climbed down from our horses.

"Don't you want to get your free ride?" Geraldine asked her.

Dodie shook her head. "I'm saving it."

"What for?"

Dodie tucked the ring into her money bag. "I want something to look forward to," she said.

CHAPTER NINETEEN

We walked around a while, stopping to lean against the railing and look down at the whitecaps on the sea below. Reba Lu slung an arm around Dodie's shoulders, and Geraldine started talking to her like she was some kind of celebrity. The two of them were making me sick. But Dodie turned and gave me a huge wink, letting me know she was on to their tricks.

Suddenly, Charles put his hand on my arm and said, "Look there."

Mr. Clement was crouched down talking to a small child—a little girl. "I can't find my mother," she told him.

She sounded close to crying, but his voice was soft, almost crooning, as he answered, "Don't worry, honey. I'll help you." He reached down and took her hand. "I'll bet she stepped inside Madame Zola's to get her fortune told. Let's go and look."

The two of them walked toward a booth draped with a brightly painted sign.

MADAME ZOLA'S FORTUNES
TEN CENTS

Tacked on it was a hand-printed note that said,

BACK IN 30 MINUTES.

I got a bad feeling because he was pulling her toward the booth, and she was trying to pull away from him. He glanced around quickly, but he didn't see us.

Charles took a step forward, but Miss Martin, the Clements' boarder, got there before him. She held a paper cup of steaming coffee in one hand. She reached for the little girl's free hand.

Mr. Clement looked up, surprised. The little girl tried to pull away from him. She looked anxiously at the crowd on the pier. Still Mr. Clement held on to her hand.

Miss Martin lifted her arm to take a sip of her coffee, then bumped against Mr. Clement's free arm, spilling it all over his shirt.

"Oh, how clumsy of me!" Miss Martin exclaimed. But I didn't think she looked sorry at all. "Come on," she said to the little girl, "let's go to the lifeguard station. They'll know how to find your mama."

For a second, Mr. Clement just stood there. Then he saw Charles and me watching him. He pulled out his handkerchief, dabbed at his coffee-drenched shirt, then put it wet back in his pocket. As he walked past us, he stopped for a second, staring first at Charles, then at me. Then he said four words, hardly moving his lips.

"You—didn't—see—anything."

We stood there until he had disappeared into the crowd. I kept thinking of the way he had watched us sunning ourselves in Reba Lu's backyard. And the angry look on Gisele Martin's face when she spilled her coffee on him. Could she know something about him that made her step up and take charge of that little girl?

Even though he tried to dress nice—dapper, Dodie had described him—his niceness was all on the outside. I thought if I could look inside Jefferson Clement's head, it would be all dark and creepy, like the open can of sardines Mama accidentally put in the pantry instead of the refrigerator. When we found it several days later, it looked rotten and smelled worse. Once again, I was glad Jefferson Clement was off our list of people to love. I just wished he was out of our town.

I put my hand on Charles's arm. "I think Mr. Clement did something bad to Miss Emma a long time ago," I said. And I told Charles how happy she had been when we visited her—until she looked out the window and saw Jefferson Clement standing on the corner.

He frowned. "That man is nothing but trouble," he muttered. "I wish he had never come back to Messina."

We stood together a moment, neither of us speaking. Then Charles said, "Let's walk," so we did. We passed game booths and food booths and watched Reverend Adams put each of the twins in bumper cars. They sped around the track, steering frantically, trying to bump each other. Charles tossed two pennies at fishbowls with live fish, but didn't win anything. We had just decided to go down to the beach for lunch when we saw a shark that one of the fishermen had hauled in and thrown onto the board planking of the pier.

It was about as long as my father's arm. Still alive, it struggled for breath, thrashing wildly, opening its mouth wide to show its killer teeth. Then it lay quiet.

Charles pulled me back a few steps. "You'd best stay a distance away," he said. "Those are shifty creatures. When they get quiet, they're just biding their time. Don't let them fool you. They can stay alive a long time out of water."

I took several steps back. Suddenly, my mouth felt dry. That shark seemed to be watching me. It reminded me of Jefferson Clement. Not the way it looked, but the way it waited.

CHAPTER TWENTY

After church on the day after the beach trip, I decided to pay a visit to Miss Emma. Geraldine's mama was making Geraldine clean her room, which, her mama said, was about to get up and walk away. And Reba Lu had to help Mrs. Adams polish the living room floor where the twins had scuffed it up. Charles had gone somewhere with his father, which was just as well because I wanted this visit to be just between Miss Emma and me.

I found the rock she had given me at the beach—the smooth brown one with white flecks—and put it in my pocket. Then I sliced up a red apple, took out the core and seeds, and wrapped the pieces in waxed paper. I figured parrots ate apples, and maybe monkeys did, too. I wasn't about to feed that snake, though, or that ugly little Lily-Poo. Miss Emma would have to tend to them.

I brushed my hair and put on my favorite navy blue shorts and my blouse with the turtle buttons and walked up the street to Dr. Thomas's house. Mrs. Dawson answered the door. "Why hello, Angie," she said. "Did you need to see the doctor?"

"No, ma'am. I thought Miss Emma might like a visit." She started to shake her head, and I knew she was thinking of the last time Miss Emma had visitors.

I put in my two cents before she could say Miss Emma was resting, or feeling poorly. "I'm real sorry she got upset last time we were here," I said. "But she did seem to like the company. I thought maybe one visitor at a time might be better."

She hesitated, and I thought she was going to say no.

"I wouldn't stay long," I promised. "Just a few minutes. You know, to pass the time of day and see her animals. And I want to show her that I still have something she gave me at the beach." I pulled out the brown stone and showed it to her. "Miss Emma was the one who found it," I said. "I never really thanked her the way I should have."

Mrs. Dawson looked at me a long minute. "Well, don't stay long, and try to keep the conversation nice and light."

I thanked her and slipped right by her and up the stairs before she could change her mind. The smell was still there, and I thought no matter how much Mrs. Dawson cleaned that room, she would never get rid of it. It had seeped into the walls and rugs, and even if Dr. Thomas and Miss Emma moved away, it would be there as long as the house stood.

I knocked on Miss Emma's door, and when she said,

"Come in," I did. I was surprised to see how glad she seemed to see me. I guessed I was a welcome change from things with four legs, scales, and wings. She was sitting in a chair with Joseph on her lap. As soon as he saw me, he commenced chattering, but I went right up to him and patted him on the head. "Can I give him some apple?" I asked.

Miss Emma beamed at me. When she smiled like that, she looked like she had good sense. "Joseph loves apples," she said. "And so does Henry."

She took a piece and held it up to Henry, who was on a perch near the window. Henry took it in his claw and tasted it. Then he began squawking.

"See how happy you made him," she said. I didn't see how she could tell the difference between happy or unhappy parrot talk, but I just smiled and nodded.

Joseph decided he liked me, and when I sat down on the edge of the bed, he hopped over and got on my lap. He brought his piece of apple with him, looked at me and went, *chicka-chicka*, which seemed to be his total vocabulary.

So far, so good, I thought. Now how was I supposed to bring up the subject of Jefferson Clement without upsetting Miss Emma? I decided not to mention him at all—just talk about the old days in Messina and then maybe about camping out and roasting weenies and other things kids like to do.

"Did you have Miss Harper for a teacher?" I asked.

"Indeed I did," Miss Emma said. "And I didn't like her one bit. She loved it when one of us made a mistake, and she liked to tell the whole class about it. She couldn't pick on my penmanship, though. I could write better than she could!"

I laughed out loud, happy to hear about Miss Harper's failings. "Tell me some more about the people you knew," I urged Miss Emma. She smiled and gave my arm a little pat.

"Well, we were all together in the old two-story schoolhouse in those days. First grade through eighth. After that, we had to take the bus to San Andreas for high school."

She didn't say anything for a minute, and I thought her mind might be wandering. But when she spoke, I could tell she had just been thinking about what to tell me next.

"Sometimes we had school picnics at the American Legion Park. And we had spelling contests and sports competitions. Oh yes, Messina was a good place to live when I was young. Until . . ."

"Until what? Did something happen to change things?" A shiver went down my spine. I was scared she might start carrying on and Dr. Thomas would come. Then I would be sent home. And I wasn't ready to go home yet.

Joseph nibbled at his apple. Henry looked out the window. Finally, Miss Emma began to speak.

"Once," she said. "A long time ago. When I wasn't any older than you . . ." She looked up at the ceiling for a minute, then she grinned and looked almost like a little girl.

"Some friends came over after school to play. At first we hopscotched, and jumped rope, and played those kinds of games. Then somebody got the idea we should be shipwrecked on an island. We got a white towel and tied it to a pole. That was to help somebody find us if they were flying over in an airplane."

I had never heard Miss Emma say so much at one time.

She came over to the bed and sat by me. "Then the others went home, and Mama called me to come inside because it was bedtime. But I begged her. Then I begged Papa. 'Just a little longer,' I said. 'Just till the moon comes out and the crickets start singing. It's always safe in Messina, Papa. You told me that yourself.'"

She wasn't smiling now. She got a worried look on her face, and I didn't know what to say. I didn't want her to start wailing again so that Dr. Thomas would come and send me home. So I took the brown stone out of my pocket. "See here," I said. "This is the pretty stone you found at the beach."

She reached for it. Rubbed it between her palms. "It's nice and smooth," she said. "That's why I chose it. Nice and smooth. The way life ought to be."

I took the stone and held it up to the light. "We had a good time at the beach, didn't we?" I asked, to change the subject.

She seemed to be far away in her thoughts—back in a time when her mama and papa were calling her to come in for bed. Then she began to whisper.

"He came."

She hesitated. But she didn't start wailing like I was afraid she would.

"He told me not to tell. Not ever."

She reached out and took my hand and patted it. "You and your friends—be careful."

She got up and walked to the window and looked out.

I wondered if she saw him out there, and I went to stand beside her. No one was there. Only an old stray cat rummaging in an overturned garbage pail.

I cleared my throat. "I'd best be going now," I said.

She nodded. "I enjoyed our little visit," she said. But when I got as far as the door, she came over and put her hand on my arm. "You go straight home, Angie," she told me.

She didn't have to say it twice. I made it home in record time. Not running, because that would have attracted attention, but walking fast and not looking to the right or left.

I had learned two important things. Messina wasn't safe anymore. And Miss Emma wasn't as crazy as everyone said she was.

CHAPTER
TWENTY-ONE

I was sitting at the kitchen table finishing a bowl of Rice Krispies and reading the funny papers when Eddie pushed open the swinging door from the dining room.

"Somebody you know is out there," he said, jerking a thumb toward the front door.

I took a piece of buttered toast with me and went to look out the window. Dodie was sitting on the top step of the porch. She started going down the stairs on her bottom. I had done the same thing myself lots of times, but I pulled open the front door and said, "What are you *doing?*"

"Waiting for you." She kept on scooting and plopping without even looking at me. "This is a good muscle builder," she said, checking the tops of her arms to see if her biceps were growing.

"What do you want muscles for?"

"You never know when you'll need to be strong." She got up and brushed off the seat of her shorts. "Let's go," she said.

"Where?"

"Up Sycamore Creek," Dodie said. "I know a good place."

I told Mama where we were going, and we started off.

"Hurry up," Dodie told me, "or those other two will be butting in."

"You mean Reba Lu and Geraldine?"

She nodded. "I don't want them tagging along."

I felt a little guilty for not including them, but I told myself they wouldn't want to go up the creek with Dodie anyway. I couldn't help feeling a little pleased that Dodie had chosen me to see her "good place." It struck me that this was the first time Dodie had invited any of us to go anywhere with her instead of the other way around.

I followed her down the front steps and we started up Palm Avenue. Was anybody watching us? I wondered what they would say if they were. I could imagine Miss Barnable saying, "There goes Angelina Wallace and that Crumper girl."

If people saw me hanging around with Reba Lu or Geraldine, they wouldn't pay the least attention. They would never call Reba Lu "that Adams girl" or Geraldine "that Murlock girl." But with Dodie it was different. She wasn't exactly what most folks would call *respectable*. I wondered if they saw me with Dodie a lot, would they start calling me "that Wallace girl"?

Then I asked myself why I cared. It shouldn't matter what people thought so long as I knew I wasn't doing anything wrong.

When we came to her house, she slowed down and grabbed my arm. "Come in for a minute," she said. As soon as I stepped inside, Dodie pointed at the fishbowl. Hanging from a string that was tied to a stick laid over the top of the bowl was her golden ring. Her free ride. To my surprise, the water was clean.

As we watched, a little goldfish nudged the ring and sent it swaying, then swam right through the middle and out the other side.

"That's the way!" Dodie shouted. "I knew you could do it."

It was a few seconds before I realized she was talking to the fish, not me.

"That's great," I said. But I was always uncomfortable in Dodie's house, not knowing what condition her mother might be in. I grabbed Dodie by the arm.

"Come on. It's getting hotter outside by the minute."

She reached over to the fishbowl and picked up the stick with the ring dangling from it. Quickly she untied the string and slipped the shiny loop into the pocket of her shorts.

"For good luck," she said, grinning.

We walked on up the street, and when we came to Dr. Thomas's house, we both looked up at the window where Miss Emma usually sat. Nobody looked back at us, but we could hear Henry squawking, "Help! Help! Somebody save me."

"We *could* stop and say hello," I said. Miss Emma had seemed so happy at the beach, and she had talked like a normal person when I visited her. I wondered if the sea air had cured her of her ills, like Dr. Thomas said it would.

"I'd rather eat worms," Dodie replied. She grabbed my arm and started to hurry me past the house.

But the front door opened and Mrs. Dawson came out. She turned the spigot, picked up the hose, and began watering the red geraniums that grew in clay pots by the front door.

"Morning," I called. "How's Miss Emma today?"

Mrs. Dawson turned off the water. "Miss Emma isn't well," she said. Then she fumbled in her apron pocket, brought out a wadded-up handkerchief and blew her nose on it. Afterwards she wiped her eyes. I wished she'd done it in a different order.

"I wonder what's the matter with Miss Emma," I said, after Mrs. Dawson had gone back into the house.

Dodie gave a little twitch of her head that told me to look across the street. "There's the trouble right there. Didn't you see him?"

Someone moved quickly behind one of the tall cypress trees that grew in front of Miss Barnable's house.

"Mr. Clement stands over there where she can see him from her window. As soon as she starts carrying on, he gets out of sight so people think nobody's there. I expect he'll be happy if they put Miss Emma away in the sanitarium."

"The sanitarium? You mean where crazy people go?"

She looked at me a few seconds, then began shaking her head. "You live on a cloud, don't you, Angie?"

"What do you mean?" I asked. I was getting tired of hearing this. Geraldine was always telling me I didn't know much about the world. "Why would he be happy?"

"Because if they put her away in the crazy house, she can't point a finger at him and tell people what he did to her."

"How do you know so much?" I was thinking of what Miss Emma had told me. Dodie didn't have any way of knowing about that. But she acted like she knew *something*.

She paused and scrunched up her face, then looked away from me, down at the geraniums. She picked one and began pulling off the petals.

"Dodie?" I said. But she didn't look up. She kept dropping those petals in the dirt, one by one. Something had changed. She used to go on and on about how nice Mr. Clement was to her. Now she sounded like she didn't like him anymore.

I really wanted to know more, but I wasn't taking a chance on looking dumb. Instead I put some authority in my voice and changed the subject. "Dr. Thomas would never put her away. Never!"

Dodie didn't answer me, and I felt uncomfortable, wrapped in her silence. Wrapped in the memory of a dark figure looking into a tent. I glanced over at Miss Barnable's house, at the tall cypress trees. Nothing moved. I supposed that Jefferson Clement had slipped away through the alley next to the house. He was gone. But he had invaded our day just the same.

Dodie nudged me. "We need to move along or we'll be too late."

I knew better than to ask *Too late for what?* I was learning that Dodie was the kind of person who wouldn't tell anything until she was good and ready.

I looked down at my feet and started side-stepping cracks. "Don't step on a crack," I told Dodie. "You'll break your mother's back."

She grinned and put one foot on a crack wide enough

to have a dandelion plant coming out of it. "Ha!" she said. "Let's see how she likes that!"

I was shocked that she would talk that way about her mother. I guess I looked it because she said, "Just kidding."

We both zigzagged up the street. It was hard not to step on cracks on our sidewalk. Tree roots had grown into the concrete and split it wide enough for red ants to dig their nests and leave pyramids of dirt behind them.

I glanced up at the clock on the front of the Bank of America. Nine a.m. and already hot. "I wish I'd brought a thermos of ice water," I said.

"Too much trouble," Dodie answered, twisting one foot sideways so it would fit onto a smooth piece of sidewalk. "Plenty of cold water up the creek."

"Just how far is up?" I asked.

"As far as you want to make it." She gave me a sideways look. "I got a place I like. It's secret, but I decided to let you see it."

I didn't know what to say, so I kept quiet. We reached the American Legion Park and walked through the eucalyptus trees, past the place where Dodie had built her little fort. I looked under the trees for it. All that was left was a dried mud wall and a scattering of acorns.

"Your fort is almost gone," I said.

"It wasn't built to last."

I thought back to that day when Dodie had told Geraldine she built it without a door so nobody else could get in. But something was different about Dodie today. She was taking me to her special place. She had opened a door, and I felt like she was letting me in.

We walked out of the park, into the shade of the orange groves, and all the way to the high cliff above the creek. It was irrigation day, and water rushed down the stone ditches, through openings in the sluice gates, and into the furrows among the trees.

"Remember that time we went to the picture show?" Dodie asked. She picked up a stick and squatted down, dragging it through one of the furrows, back and forth, muddying the water.

I squatted down beside her. "I remember," I said, waiting for her to go on.

"When we saw the Fox Movietone News, it showed a picture of that man who wants to do away with all those people. What's the word for that, Angie? The word for doing away with someone."

I pictured the trainloads of Jews that Hitler shipped off to work camps. I had heard Daddy say they would be lucky to come out alive. And I remembered the voice on the newsreel. "Eliminate," I told Dodie. "Hitler wants to eliminate all the Jewish people in Germany."

"That's it," she said. "That's exactly the word I was trying to remember. Hitler's pretty bad, isn't he?"

"He's worse than bad. He's terrible. Eddie says he's the reason there's a war in Europe. He says America might have to fight, too. But when he was in the grocery store, he overheard Mr. Flannery telling Reverend Adams that it's not our battle."

"What did Reverend Adams say to that?"

"He said evil is everybody's battle and that man Hitler needs to be stopped."

Dodie was quiet for a moment, then she said, "I think Reba Lu's daddy is right. I think we should fight Hitler. And other countries should, too. I don't get it, Angie. How can people turn their heads and let that man get away with doing terrible things to people?"

I didn't have an answer. To tell the truth, I hadn't thought much about it. I always felt safe at home in Messina. Europe was far away. Then I remembered how Hitler had invaded other countries. If he did come to America, he would bring a lot of trouble with him.

I thought about how Jefferson Clement had come to town, bringing trouble to Messina. Why did good folks put up with that? Was that the way people were putting up with Hitler, just ignoring him and hoping he'd go away?

I felt like I was getting a headache. If America couldn't figure out what to do about the war in Europe, how were we supposed to know what do to about the bad thing that was happening in our little town?

Dodie kept dragging her stick through the muddy water. "Do you suppose I'm bad like that Hitler person because I want to eliminate somebody?"

"What are you talking about? Who in the world would you want to eliminate?"

She mumbled something I couldn't hear. I nudged her with my elbow. "Come on, Dodie."

She raised her head and looked right at me. Her lower lip trembled, but when she said the words, her voice was clear. "I wish I could eliminate Mr. Jefferson Clement."

"You mean *kill* him?"

"I didn't say that. I just want him to go away and not come back."

She shivered and hugged herself, even though it was such a hot day.

"I thought you liked Mr. Clement because he pays you for ironing his shirts."

"I changed my mind." She was quiet for a few seconds. "He's a real bad man. I got mad at my mama for chasing him off, but she was right, after all. He does things he shouldn't ought to. I think that's why Miss Emma's afraid of him."

"What kind of things?" I asked, even though I thought I knew.

"He watches until he sees me hanging out the clothes. Then he figures Mama's asleep. He comes over and pretends to help me, but all he wants to do is put his hands on me."

She stopped and looked at me. When I didn't say anything, she yanked up her shirtsleeve and showed me an ugly purple bruise on her arm. "See what he did yesterday when I told him I was going to tell?"

"Oh, Dodie! That must have hurt. Do you suppose that's what he did to Miss Emma?"

She stared at me. "Angie, you don't get it. A bruise on my arm is a little thing compared to what he wants to do. He wants to touch . . . he wants to touch me where he hadn't ought to." Her voice cracked and she jabbed her stick furiously into the furrow, splashing mud on us both.

When she finally looked at me, I saw how red her face was, and her eyes were all watery. She rubbed the back of her arm across them and gave a loud sniff.

"Dodie, you have to tell your mother! If you don't, I'll tell my dad. He'll do something about it!"

But that didn't seem to be what Dodie wanted to hear. She got up and turned around without answering, then started walking along the edge of the grove.

"Dodie?" I called. I wanted to tell her I was sorry about her arm and what Mr. Clement had tried to do to her, but she walked fast and didn't give me a chance. I followed her until we reached the clearing that led to the cliff above the creek bed.

We stood there a minute, together. I started to say something more about telling my dad and what he would do, but when I looked at her and saw her raising her face to the sun, her eyes closed and her head thrown back, I stopped. She seemed to be trying to put Jefferson Clement out of her mind, and I didn't want to bring him back into our conversation.

"I like it when things are warm and bright," she said. "Remember how I told you that sometimes I'm afraid of the dark?"

"Sometimes I am, too," I admitted, thinking about that night when I camped out with Reba Lu and Geraldine.

I peered over the edge. "It's a long way down there," I said, glad to have something else to talk about.

"There's a path," Dodie said. "Follow me, and you'll be all right."

It wasn't much of a path: more like a downhill skid through dirt and rocks. Dodie went first, bending low and inching her way, so she could hold on to the large rocks in the cliff wall. She reached the bottom and pumped both arms above her head. "Your turn!" she shouted.

I hated high places. They made me feel helpless. I imagined something was crooking a finger, beckoning, pulling me forward. I stepped over the edge, feeling for a foothold. A rock jutted out from the cliff, and I put my weight on it. It held me for a few seconds, then gave way and crashed down the incline. I slipped several feet, before I could grab hold of a dead limb poking out of the side of the cliff. My leg was stinging where I had scraped some of the skin off.

"Come on, Angie!" Dodie sounded like the captain of our fifth grade baseball team. "Just skid on down!"

I dug my heels into loose dirt and let go of the limb. Stones scattered as I took a few steps. I slipped and slithered down the steep slope, groping for footholds I never found. When I finally landed, I was sitting down.

"Yay, Angie!" Dodie yelled. Then she held out her hand to help me up. I thought for a second about the day she had put that same hand in my popcorn. *Please, God, let it be clean,* I prayed as I reached out and felt her skin against mine. I pulled myself up slowly, surprised that all my parts were still there.

"Nothing to it!" I lied.

We grinned at each other like we had just climbed down a mountain. I thought of that day at the beach when I'd shown Dodie how to jump the waves and ride a painted horse and dig for sand crabs. Now it was Dodie's turn to share something new with me.

"Come on," she said. "I have lots to show you." She led the way, and I followed her.

CHAPTER TWENTY-TWO

Hiking up the creek was just like she'd said. We followed the water upstream, sometimes walking in the sand, sometimes jumping from rock to rock. Dodie was good at this.

"When you hold your arms out for balance you look like a dancer," I told her.

She grinned at me, but then I slipped and skinned an elbow on a sharp-edged granite boulder. "Ohhh, that hurts!" I said. I twisted my arm to get a better look. "I think I'm bleeding."

Dodie laughed. "It's just a scrape. Stick it in the creek for a minute. That'll help the pain."

I did. At first I was shocked by the feel of icy water on my skin. But soon my elbow felt better, kind of numb, but not hurting.

"Come on," Dodie yelled. "Try to jump on the flat places." I did, and got a little better as I practiced.

Finally, we stopped at a turn of the creek where sun-bleached boulders glittered as bits of mica caught the light. Sycamores spread bent branches, forming shady patches over the water, and late cottonwoods were dropping seeds covered with the soft white tufts that gave the trees their names. "We're here!" Dodie said. Her smile stretched across her whole face.

We tried to catch the snowy fluff before it touched the ground, then took turns picking it out of each other's hair. "We ought to save this stuff for Christmas," Dodie said. "It would look like snow on a Christmas tree, and it wouldn't cost us a penny."

I tried to imagine a Christmas tree in Dodie's house. Where would they put it? What would they use for decorations? Then I wondered if Dodie had ever had a Christmas tree. I reached out and caught some more cottonwood fluff. Maybe this was the closest Dodie ever got to celebrating Christmas. I made up my mind to bring this up to Geraldine and Reba Lu.

After a while, we were sweaty from all that jumping around. We squatted by the side of the creek, trailed our fingers in the cold water, and watched tiny minnows swimming in a shallow pool, where an offshoot of the creek had trickled into a low, sandy spot in the shade of a giant twisted sycamore.

"I'm thirsty!" I complained.

Dodie waved her arm. "There's plenty of water right in front of you."

"I'm not drinking anything that has live fish swimming in it."

"Would dead fish make it any better?" She laughed at her own joke, then got up and walked over to where the creek was running fast, splashing over smaller rocks in the streambed. "This is the best water in the world," she said, and she put her face right down into the stream and drank.

"You don't know where it comes from," I said, hearing Mama's voice in mine.

"Sure I do. It comes from snow in the mountains. Come on, Angie. It's nice and cold." She cupped her hands and threw some at me to prove it.

I squealed and splashed some right back at her. We pulled off our sandals and waded into the creek. The cold water made me hop up and down, but it didn't take long to get used to it. Dodie showed me how to drink where the water rushed over rocks. "It cleans itself," she said. "Go on and try some."

I did, against my better judgment. I'd never thought about water having flavor before, but this really tasted good. Cold and fresh, almost as good as lemonade. I took another drink and let the water wash my sweaty face. I splashed it on my arms and legs and felt cool all over.

We hiked on up the creek, and sometimes in it. Dodie pointed out plants like sage and manzanita and wild lilac. "You can boil wild lilac leaves to stop your skin from itching if you walk through poison oak. And sage tea is good for a fever," she said.

"How do you know all that?"

"Dr. Thomas told me. He said the tea tastes pretty bad though. He knows lots of things about plants."

I nodded. I wondered why Dr. Thomas had told *her* and not *me*. I didn't even think he knew her that well.

Dodie broke off a stem of sage and rubbed the gray leaves between her palms. She raised her cupped hands to her face and took a deep breath. Then she held out her hands to me. I bent over and sniffed. "Whew!" I said. "That's strong stuff."

Dodie grinned. "Dr. Thomas says it's *pungent*. That's why Mrs. Dawson only uses a little in her beef stew. She let me taste it one day, and it was real good."

The truth began gnawing at me that Dodie Crumper knew more about some things than I did. It didn't bother me especially. It just took me by surprise.

She tossed the crushed sage to the wind and spread her arms wide. With her white-blonde hair blowing, she looked, for a second, like an angel ready to fly. But when she started to talk again, she was plain Dodie Crumper.

"This here chaparral is like a miniature forest. Did you ever notice?"

I hadn't.

"See, the lizards are like prehistoric creatures prowling around under giant manzanita trees. The creek is like a great river to them, and the rocks must seem like giant boulders."

She pointed up the canyon. "The coyotes live up there," she said. "They only come down at night, so you don't need to worry."

"You can come here with me early in the morning and hear the bird songs. All different kinds come to nest here.

There are squirrels, too, and sometimes I see a raccoon washing its face upstream or a red-tailed hawk just flying along looking for its breakfast. Once I saw a mama deer with her fawn. They stood up there at the head of the canyon and watched me. We just looked at each other for a bit, and then they went away. I think they were telling me they owned this place. We're the visitors, but I don't feel like one. I feel right at home here."

She stood there, the sun shining on her pale hair, and she didn't look like the Dodie I had known before. The one who picked her nose and didn't have anything polite to say. Here, in this place, she was another person altogether.

She took a deep breath. "Can you smell that? Go on, Angie. Fill up your lungs."

I did, and I had to admit I'd never smelled anything like it. The heat of the day hadn't settled in yet, and the air was cool and sweet, full of the scents of growing things. I closed my eyes and listened to the breeze rustling the big leaves of the sycamore trees.

When I opened them, Dodie was getting down on her knees. She stretched out so her face was only inches from the ground. "Look here." She pointed to tiny yellow flowers growing so low that I probably would have stepped on them and never known it. "See these little belly flowers?" she said.

"Belly flowers?"

"You know. Flowers so tiny and close to the ground that you have to get down on your belly to see them." She laughed. "They grow knee high to a lizard, and that's not very high."

She shaded her eyes and squinted. "If you half close your eyes, you can imagine this is a separate little world."

I squinted, too, but it still looked like regular bushes and lizards and rocks to me.

Dodie got to her knees and reached out toward a rock. When she stood up, she had both hands wrapped around a squirming lizard. She turned it over carefully. "It's a blue belly," she said, holding it out to me.

I took a step back.

"You can touch it," she said.

I didn't want to touch it. I didn't like things that hid under rocks. "That's OK. I'll just look," I told her.

I got a little closer. It really did have a blue belly. "I never saw one like that before," I said.

She looked surprised. "I'll bet you did. They're common around here. Maybe you never bothered to look at their undersides."

I sure hadn't. The closest I'd been to a lizard was when Buster caught one, and it lost its tail on our front porch. I hadn't held that one in my hands, and I sure hadn't turned it over to look at its belly. But I was sure Charles would have.

Dodie squatted and put the lizard on the ground, but she didn't stand up again.

"Don't move," she whispered. The tone of her voice told me not to talk either.

Just ahead of us, sunning itself on a large, flat boulder— the kind I'd been thinking it would be nice to stretch out on—was a snake.

It was thicker around than my daddy's arm. Its scaly skin was reddish-brown and looked as rough as the granite it lay upon. Darker scales formed diamond shapes on its back and about seven or eight rattles were attached in a neat bundle at the end of its tail. As we watched, it moved slowly and began to wrap itself in circles until it was coiled, with its head raised, ready to strike.

I watched as it flicked its blackish forked tongue, in and out, testing the air. Its head swayed from side to side. I felt like it was staring from Dodie to me . . . again and again . . . from Dodie to me. It was close enough that I could see that its eyes were glassy looking, and the black pupils were shaped like a cat's.

I let my breath out slowly and was afraid to breathe in again. Finally, I had to, but I did it slowly, carefully. I concentrated on standing perfectly still. I didn't even let my eyes move to see what Dodie was doing. I wished a squirrel would stick its head out from behind a rock or a rabbit would hop by, and the snake would look at them instead. I counted my shallow breaths. One . . . two . . . three . . . four . . .

It seemed like forever that we didn't move or make a sound, but I guess it was only a couple of minutes. Finally, the rattler began to unwind. It eased itself off the rock and slid toward the thick chaparral. Only then did we dare move.

I picked up a large stone and lifted my arm.

"Leave it alone," Dodie said. "It's not hurting anybody."

"But it might," I argued. "Don't you know that rattlesnakes are bad?"

"Who says so?"

"Everybody knows that. They're poisonous. They can kill you."

"So can lots of other things."

We watched the snake slink away and disappear.

"At least a rattler warns you," Dodie said.

We hiked on back to the place where the cottonwoods were dropping their white fluff and sycamores bent over the water. Thanks to the snake, I had lost my taste for resting on a boulder, so I went over and sat on a branch that jutted out over the pool where the fish swam. I leaned my head against the trunk. It was nice here. Nobody but Dodie and me.

Not long ago, that would have been an unsettling thought: *nobody but Dodie and me.* Now, I felt the sun on my legs and listened to the water bubble over the rocks, and I had to admit that Dodie could be pretty good company.

She went over to the little fish pool and got down on her knees to watch the tiny minnows swimming in the shallow water. "I have to come back here tomorrow," she said. "You coming?

"I guess. But why do you *have* to?"

"I need to move these fish."

"What for? They seem happy to me."

She gave me an exasperated look. "They're trapped. They can't get back into the creek, and even if they did, this water will likely dry up before the rains come again. We need to carry them upstream and put them back in deeper water, where they belong."

"OK," I said. "But how?"

I pictured myself jumping from boulder to boulder, clutching a slippery, wriggling fish in my hands, dropping it back into the creek, then going back to the little fish pool and doing it all over again.

"Don't worry," Dodie said. "We'll scoop them up in a sieve. You can get one from your mother. Then we'll dump them into a pail of creek water and carry them in that. We'd better do it first thing in the morning while it's still cool."

She cupped her hands now, filled them with creek water, and carried the water over to the shallow pool. When she went back for more, I started helping her.

"This is going to take all day," I said.

Dodie frowned. "But they're going to die if we don't help them. They'll lie there in their little pond until there's no more water. They'll gasp and their eyes will bulge out. Doesn't that matter to you?"

I looked at Dodie, at her blue eyes, as pale as creek water. "Yeah," I said. "I guess it matters."

We worked in silence until the little pool held enough water for the fish to swim more freely. Then we made plans for the next morning.

"You bring the sieve, and I'll bring the pail," Dodie said.

"And I'll make some peanut butter and jelly sandwiches," I offered.

"The fish won't eat them."

"They're not for the fish, silly. They're for . . ."

She gave me a poke. "Gotcha!" she said. We looked at each other and grinned. As we started back toward the cliff, I kept thinking, *Dodie Crumper has a sense of humor! Who would have thought?*

It wasn't noon yet when we climbed the cliff. When I reached the top, I stopped and looked back over the side. It was a long way to the bottom. I remembered Dodie saying, "Just skid on down!" I was real proud of myself for having done it.

We cut through the orange groves, walking between the rows of trees, glad for the shade. They had started blossoming early in the spring, but a few trees still wore the waxy white blooms like decorations. They smelled sweet in the warm summer air.

As we walked on, we made our plans. I wanted Reba Lu and Geraldine and maybe even Charles to help us move the fish, but Dodie wouldn't have any part of that. "Charles might be all right," she said, "but those others would get to fooling around and ruin things."

"Ruin things, how?"

"Oh, I don't know. Just ruin things." She seemed to be thinking it over. "I might let them come another time."

Might? I stared at her. She was talking like she owned the whole creek. In a way, I could see how she felt like she did. She had made it her own. It was her getting-away place. I didn't say anything, and she went on.

"But not tomorrow. Tomorrow I want it to be just you and me."

I looked at her, and for an instant I saw the old Dodie. She was clenching her fists, and she had her jaw set in that determined way that made her whole face go rigid. She looked ready for a fight.

"I mean it, Angie," she said. "I won't have those others messing with my fish."

It came to me that this was the Dodie—the old Dodie—who needed to protect herself from getting hurt, and I wondered if she was afraid the others might laugh at her for trying to carry some fish upstream so they could swim in deeper water.

I could imagine Geraldine saying, "Let's just cook them instead." Or Reba Lu wanting them baptized. Dodie had said Charles might be all right, but I remembered that he was going to help Reverend Adams paint the parsonage kitchen starting first thing in the morning.

"OK, then," I agreed. "Tomorrow it will be just you and me."

"Remember, you need to be at my house by eight o'clock in the morning. After that it will be too hot for the fish. And don't forget the sieve," Dodie told me.

"I'll do the best I can, but it will be hard to get by Mama without eating breakfast first."

"So get up a little earlier. If you're late, I'll go on by myself and meet you up the creek." Dodie was using her stubborn voice again.

"Why don't you wait at your house until I get there?"

Dodie made a little sound that could have been a sigh. She hesitated a second before she said, "I don't think that's such a good idea. My house is the kind of place you don't want to wait around in."

I couldn't argue with that.

CHAPTER TWENTY-THREE

The coyotes howled that night. They often do in the summer months, but this time they came down farther out of the hills and sounded like they were in the backyards of Messina. *Ya-ooo. Yipyipyip ya-ooo.* It seemed like they would never stop. Every now and then, their howls changed to excited high-pitched yelps, and I could hear the frantic squeals of a rabbit that had not managed to outrun them.

Of course, they got most of the dogs in town barking. Not Buster, though. I put my hand on him, and he settled down next to my bed with his paws over his ears. Daddy had explained that coyotes are predators, and they get their food by hunting smaller, weaker creatures. "It's the way of things in the animal world," he said.

Maybe so, but I didn't have to like it.

I was worried that this would be a night when I'd never get to sleep, and that I'd miss my early morning with Dodie. But after the coyotes finally stopped hunting their prey, the crickets began to sing. It was like a lullaby, telling me everything was safe now. I finally did drop off and didn't wake up until quarter of eight in the morning. I put on the same clothes I had taken off the night before and hurried to the kitchen.

I sat down and swallowed corn flakes as fast as I could. Then I had to brush my teeth and make the sandwiches because I'd forgotten to tell Mama we needed some. I was almost to the door when I remembered I was supposed to bring a sieve. I could only find a small one, but it was big enough to hold a few fish. By the time I slammed the front screen door behind me, the clock on the mantle said ten after eight.

I hoped Dodie might have changed her mind and waited for me even though I was late. I ran all the way up the street to her house. When I knocked at the door, nobody answered, so I lifted the latch and walked right in. I never thought I would do such a thing, but by now, I had decided the rules were different at the Crumpers'.

"Dodie?" I called. Nobody answered.

Mrs. Crumper was on the sofa, as usual, lying there barefoot, with her eyes half closed and an empty glass dangling from one hand.

"Mrs. Crumper," I said. I put a hand on her shoulder and gave it a little shake. "Mrs. Crumper, when did Dodie leave?"

She screwed up her face and thought about it. "She slammed out of here a couple minutes ago. Said she couldn't wait no longer. Said to tell you . . . something . . ." Mrs. Crumper closed her eyes.

"I told her . . . not to . . . slam . . . that door," she murmured. "The girl's got no respect. No respect . . . at all."

The empty glass dropped from her hand and broke into splintery shards that glittered on the bare floor. I would have left them there, but I could imagine what Reba Lu would say. *You could have kept Mrs. Crumper from cutting her feet if you had cleaned up the broken glass.* So I fetched the broom and dustpan from a kitchen corner and swept up the pieces.

On my way out, I banged the screen door on purpose. I was that put out with Dodie's mother. Dodie had left a message for me, and her mother couldn't even remember what it was. I started up the street. I figured Dodie didn't have too much of a head start. She would probably be at the park by now. If I hurried, I might be able to catch up while she was still in the groves, and we could climb down the cliff path together.

But when I got to the park, it was empty. Dried eucalyptus leaves covered the place where her little fort had fallen apart. "Dodie?" I yelled. But there was no answer.

I started to run, following the irrigation ditch through the orange groves. Filtered shade sifted in the morning light like dark butterflies among the trees. A big horsefly followed me, buzzing around my face. I swatted at it, but it kept coming back. A patch of stinging nettles brushed my bare ankles. I quickly got a double handful of water from the irrigation ditch and made some mud to plaster on the hives that were already forming and starting to itch and burn.

Then I heard voices. I recognized Dodie's right away. The other voice was deep, talking low. The sound of it made me feel like I had hives all over my body, not just my ankles.

I came to the last row of trees and stepped out onto the bare dirt that stretched from the groves to the cliff. The sunlight blinded me for a second, and I put up my hands to shade my eyes.

Mr. Clement stood with his back to the cliff's edge. Dodie was facing him. They didn't see me. I stood as still as I could, trying to look invisible while I listened to what they were saying. My knees started shaking. It made me sick to hear the way he talked to her . . . the things he said. She put both hands over her ears, like she wanted to stop the sound of his voice. When he reached out his hand toward her, she backed away so fast she almost fell down.

"You leave me alone!" she yelled. Her voice was high and squeaky, like she was about to cry. "If you don't, I'll tell everybody what you've been trying to do to me."

She moved sideways away from him, toward the place where the rocky cliff path started down the bluff—where we had skidded down the day before. Yes! Dodie could get away by climbing down that path. She would be all right once she reached the canyon. That was her territory. She knew every rock and bush and all the places to hide.

But I could see he didn't mean to let her get away. He took a step toward the cliff, reaching out for her.

"Dodie!" I shouted. "Look out, Dodie!"

He snapped his head in my direction. When he saw I was alone, he said, "Get away from here, you meddlesome brat!"

He turned, as if to come toward me, but one foot slipped in the loose dirt at the edge of the cliff. He would have fallen for sure if Dodie hadn't reached out and grabbed his shirt. She pulled hard with both hands until he got his balance.

I wished she hadn't bothered.

He steadied himself, then shook his fist in her face. "You stupid girl!" he yelled. "You almost made me fall!" Then he said a lot more. About how he didn't know why he bothered with somebody like her. And how worthless she was. And he called her some names I hadn't ever heard before.

He took a step closer. My knees began to shake, and I had a crawly feeling at the back of my neck. I thought of the coyotes I had heard last night and the way they had cornered a rabbit and made it scream in terror. Coyotes weren't the only predators. Jefferson Clement was a predator, too.

He raised one hand and might have hit her, but she scooted away from him toward the cliff. "You come back here!" he shouted.

"Come on, Dodie!" I yelled. "This way!"

She took a few steps toward me, but he stuck out a foot and tripped her. She put out her arms to stop the fall and landed on her wrist. She cried out in pain, then staggered to her feet, holding her arm up close to her. She was right at the cliff's edge.

She had a confused look on her face. No wonder, after the way she had fallen. She didn't seem to know which way to go. She started backing up—backing away from him. "Stop, Dodie!" I shouted. But she started teetering—back and forth, her feet stirring up loose dirt. Her arms flailed in the air. She looked for a moment like she was trying to fly.

"Help her!" I yelled.

But he didn't move. And then she was gone. Her scream followed her, startling a hawk that rose, sending its shrill cry across the canyon. There was an empty place where she had stood. And Jefferson Clement was alone at the top of the cliff.

I began to moan. "Nooo. . . Dodie . . . Nooo." But it seemed like somebody else was saying the words.

The sun went behind a cloud, and a warm breeze blew across the clearing, carrying the scent of orange blossoms. A few dried-up sycamore leaves blew round and round in a little circle at Mr. Clement's feet. He didn't move.

I heard a sound from beyond the cliff, from down below. It was a whimper, a sound a hurt animal would make. Then there was nothing at all.

Mr. Clement turned to look at me and I could hardly breathe.

Then I heard Willie Jack's voice. "I heard a lot of yelling," he said. "What's going on here?"

I whirled toward him. "Dodie . . . Dodie . . ." I started crying and could barely get the words out. "D-Dodie fell. She's down there at the bottom of the cliff. We have to help her!"

Willie Jack looked beyond me toward the cliff's edge. His eyes narrowed, and he said a word I'd heard before but wasn't allowed to say. Then he put both hands on my shoulders and made me look at him. "Run. Fast as you can. Get Dr. Thomas. Hurry up now!"

He turned me around so I was facing away from the cliff and toward the groves that led back to town. He gave me a little push to get me started on my way, but I turned and looked back over my shoulder.

Jefferson Clement was climbing down over the edge, dirt and stones scrabbling around him as he struggled to get his footing on the steep, rocky path. He turned once and looked at me, before he disappeared over the side. He pointed at me, then put one finger over his lips. His message was clear. I shivered. Nobody had ever scared me with a look before.

I knew Willie Jack hadn't seen Mr. Clement's threat. I started to tell him, but he gave me another little shove. "Go!" he said.

My face was wet with tears. I could hardly see. But I ran faster than I had ever run before. Into the groves. Along the irrigation ditch. Through the park. I jumped over the eucalyptus roots where Dodie had built her little fort.

When I reached Dr. Thomas's house, my chest hurt, and I had a pain in my side. My breath came in quick little gasps that didn't seem to let in any air at all. I put my finger on the doorbell and held it there, resting my head against the doorframe. I didn't want to close my eyes because every time I did, I saw Jefferson Clement putting his finger against his lips.

"What in the world?" It was Mrs. Dawson, her forehead all wrinkled up in little lines of concern.

"Come in, child. Are you sick? Do you need the doctor?"

I still couldn't speak, so I nodded. Then I began to cry. The doctor came running. He put his arms around me and held me tight until my wails turned to hiccups.

"Now then," Dr. Thomas said. "You'd better tell me about it."

"It's Dodie," I said. "She . . . she fell . . . off the cliff."

He moved quickly, handing me over to Mrs. Dawson. "Take care of her," he said, then grabbed his black bag and headed for the door. Mrs. Dawson made me sit down in Dr. Thomas's comfortable chair and tucked a blanket around me because I was shivering so. Then she went out of the room, and I heard her talking on the telephone. In a minute she was back with a glass of cool water, and Miss Emma was with her.

Mrs. Dawson kept saying *shhh, shhh,* and patting me on the back. I tried to drink some water, but my teeth chattered against the glass. Chills swept up my back and down my arms. I couldn't seem to hold my legs still. I wrapped my arms around myself and held on tight. Miss Emma came right up and took hold of one of my hands with both of hers. She stayed that way until the doorbell rang.

The door opened before Mrs. Dawson could get to it. Mama was there. She held out her arms, and I ran to her.

"Dodie," I said. "She f-fell . . ." I couldn't say any more. I was afraid to say what really happened. I just hugged Mama like I couldn't let go. Then there were four of us hugging. Five, if you counted Henry, who was on Miss Emma's shoulder.

"Poor little thing," Miss Emma said. "Something frightened her." Her eyes looked as big as saucers, and her lips trembled. She looked as frightened as I felt.

"Help, help!" Henry squawked.

Mama nodded her thanks at Mrs. Dawson. "We'll be going now," she said, and she pulled me to the door.

When it was closed behind us, I could still hear Miss Emma and Henry.

Poor little thing. Help, help. Poor little thing.

When we got home, I crawled between the sheets with all my clothes on and pulled the covers over my head. I wanted to tell Mama everything, but I couldn't seem to talk. Every time I started, I saw Jefferson Clement's face in my mind, and my voice wouldn't work. The words were stuck in my throat, and I couldn't spit them out.

Mama kept patting me. "Close your eyes and rest," she said. But when I closed my eyes, I saw the way he had looked at me, and I was afraid all over again.

After a while, Mama came in with a glass of warm milk. I hate warm milk, especially in the summer. But I pushed the covers back so I could sit up and drink it. Daddy had come home from work as soon as he heard. He came in and sat on a chair by my bed. He looked at me a minute, then reached for my hand and squeezed it.

"Dr. Thomas is here," he said. "Do you feel like talking to him?"

I didn't, but I nodded.

Dr. Thomas sat on the edge of my bed like he always did. Only this time he didn't have his stethoscope. He didn't even have his black bag. He seemed like a different person without them.

"D-Dodie," I said. "How's—"

"Angie," he said, "I have to tell you something sad. When Dodie fell, she must have hit her head on a big rock." He took a deep breath. "She's unconscious. I'm afraid she's in a coma. That means . . . that means we . . . can't wake her up."

"But I can wake her up. I know I can!" I pushed back the covers and sat up.

Dr. Thomas shook his head. "Not now, Angie. Not now. We need to give Dodie a little time to heal. In a few days, you can see her. I'll take you to the San Andreas Hospital myself. I promise."

I gulped to get my breath. The words finally came tumbling out. I looked at Dr. Thomas, then at Daddy. "I saw what happened. I saw how she . . ." I tried to swallow, but I didn't have any spit. I tried again, but I couldn't find the right words. They got all tangled in my head and wouldn't come out right. Then I began to hiccup.

"No need to say any more," Dr. Thomas said. "Mr. Clement already told Constable Mullens what happened. Willie Jack is on his way to the jail." His face had a tight, pinched look that told me he couldn't believe what he had just said.

"No . . . no . . . no!" I moaned. My heart gave a lurch, then began to pound. I could taste the salt from the tears that were running down my face.

"Hush, child," Dr. Thomas said. He held a glass to my lips. I was thirsty and drank it, even though it fizzled and had an odd taste. "Now you lie back in your bed," he said. "That drink will help you sleep."

"But I have to tell you what happened."

He nodded. "Go ahead then."

I told him about how I went to find Dodie. "First, I went to the park. Then through the groves . . ."

Dr. Thomas kept nodding. It was almost like the slow ticking of the mantle clock. *Tick, tock.* Nod, nod. I closed my eyes, but I kept talking.

"Dodie was on the edge of the cliff. She was . . . she was . . ." I started to say *she was arguing with Mr. Clement,* but all I could do was hiccup. I remembered him putting his finger over his lips and the look in his eyes as he did it.

"She lost her balance," I said. Then I started to cry. I felt Daddy's hand tighten around mine. I couldn't get any more words to come out of my mouth.

I opened my eyes and saw Daddy and Dr. Thomas looking at each other. Then Daddy bent over close and kissed me on the forehead. He had that serious look around his eyes, the way he always did when we talked about something important. He gave me a little nod, squeezed my hand, and stood up to go.

Dr. Thomas said, "We'll talk some more, my dear. As soon as you have rested."

The last sound I heard was the doctor's voice. "The poor child is in shock," he said. "She witnessed something horrible . . ." His voice drifted away, and I heard a click as my bedroom door closed.

I needed to get out of bed, tell them what really happened. But I didn't. I remembered the look on Miss Emma's face when she looked out of her window. The way her eyes had grown so big, and her lips had trembled. That must be what I looked like now. Afraid. Just like Miss Emma.

CHAPTER
TWENTY-FOUR

For the rest of the day and all into that night, I kept waking up and going right back to sleep. Sometimes, when I had my eyes open, I could see my room and my bed. Once Mama came in and helped me get out of my clothes and into pajamas. Then she left the door ajar so that the hall light could come in. Other times, I would think it was somebody else's room, and somebody else's soft pillow, and somebody else's head lying on it.

During my waking times, I kept thinking about Dodie. Walking up the street with Dodie. Jumping waves at the beach with Dodie. Looking at pearly pink sand crabs with Dodie. Wading up the creek with . . . Then I would drift off to sleep for a little while.

I felt groggy in the morning, and I lay in my bed without moving until Buster put his wet nose in my hand

and whimpered. Then I remembered every single thing that had happened the day before, and I began to whimper, too. High, wailing sounds came out of my throat and turned to sobs. I tried to stop but couldn't.

Mama came rushing in with Dr. Thomas right behind her. Eddie stood in the doorway. When he saw me, his face twisted up like he might start crying, too.

I swallowed hard and took a deep, shuddering breath. "I-I'm . . . all r-right, Eddie," I stammered.

But I wasn't all right. The world had turned upside down, and I had lost my balance. Dodie had lost her balance, too. She had stepped backward off the edge of the world . . . falling . . . falling . . .

I sat up suddenly. "I need to talk to Dodie!"

"Oh, Angie, honey," Mama said. "Dodie is still unconscious. She can't talk to you." She sat on the edge of my bed and held my hands tightly in hers.

"I know that!" I was shouting now. "But I can talk to *her*, and maybe she can hear me. Maybe she'll know she's not all by herself. Mama, I have to try."

I put my feet over the edge of the bed and started to get up, but Dr. Thomas put his hand on my shoulder. "Listen, Angie. We're only letting Dodie's mother and father visit her right now. But I promise you that I'll tell you the minute you can go and see her." He gently squeezed my shoulder. I wished he would sit down and pull me up on his lap, but I was too old for that.

I looked at him and nodded. "I can sit with her even if she doesn't know I'm there. She needs somebody to sit with her. If she wakes up alone, she'll feel trapped in that hospital."

Trapped!

Like those minnows in their shallow pond with no way to get back to safe water. I'd forgotten all about the fish, and now it might be too late.

I wiped my nose. "I need to go back up the creek," I said.

"My dear, you're spending the day in bed," Dr. Thomas told me. He opened his black bag. "I'm going to give you another sleeping powder."

"I won't drink it. I don't need to be in bed, and I don't need to sleep. I need to be up the creek. Dodie's fish are going to die if somebody doesn't save them."

Mama and Dr. Thomas exchanged a glance. I had been sassy and expected a talking-to, but I didn't get it. "Eddie will go with me, won't you, Eddie? He won't let anything happen to me."

Dr. Thomas looked over at Eddie, who gave him a little nod. "I'll make a bargain with you, Angie. You stay here and rest this morning. If you feel like getting dressed and taking a little walk this afternoon, I won't stop you."

He stood up to go. "It might be just as well if we encourage her to get on with life," he told Mama. "Moping around never cures anybody." Then he patted me on the head, the same way he used to do when I was a little girl.

"Take care, child," he said. His eyes looked watery. He got out his handkerchief and blew his nose.

Mama left to walk Dr. Thomas to the door. Eddie turned to go, too, but I called out to him. "Eddie, don't go. I have to talk to you." I motioned for him to come close to the bed. "I need you to go and tell Geraldine and Reba Lu to come over here. Get Charles, too. We're all going up the creek as soon as I can get dressed and convince Mama. Hurry up, Eddie. We don't have a lot of time!"

"But the doctor wants you to . . ."

I tried to keep my voice low so that Mama wouldn't hear us. "I don't care what he said. I know what I have to do. Are you going to help me or not?"

Eddie nodded. "I'm going," he said, "but I hope you know what you're doing."

As soon as he left, I got out of bed and pulled on some clean shorts and my new blouse that I had been saving for a special occasion. My knees felt wobbly, probably from whatever Dr. Thomas made me drink last night, but I felt stronger the more I moved around. I brushed my teeth and splashed my face with cold water. Then I combed my hair and fastened it back on one side with a barrette.

The screen door banged, and the front room filled with voices. Good. Eddie had found Reba Lu and Geraldine. And he had found Charles, too.

As soon as I went into the front room, they stopped talking. Reba Lu's eyes were swollen, and Geraldine kept biting her lower lip to stop it from quivering. "Willie Jack's been arrested," Geraldine said.

"I know." I had to bite my tongue to keep from telling them the whole story.

Reba Lu and Geraldine looked back and forth at each other in a way that said they had inside information. "He's in the jail," Reba Lu said.

"I heard that," I told her.

"You were there. You must have seen the whole thing."

Geraldine sounded like she wished she had been there, too. "Angie, what really hap—"

I was glad when Eddie interrupted her. "Mr. Clement is claiming he saw Willie Jack arguing with Dodie at the top of the cliff. He says Willie Jack lost his temper and pushed her. He's telling that story all over town."

I looked at them—my friends and my brother—people I was pretty sure I could trust with a secret. But if I told what really happened, would one of them accidentally slip up and let somebody know what I had seen? And if Mr. Clement found out I was accusing him, what would he do? I couldn't get that picture of him out of my mind: The way he had stared at me when Willie Jack's back was turned. The way he had warned me with that look.

So I just looked at them and said, "Eddie and I are going up the creek this morning. We have something important to do, and I want you to come and help us."

"You mean you're going back to where Dodie fell?" Reba Lu sounded scared.

"Why do you want to go *there?*" Geraldine asked.

"Because Dodie and I didn't get to finish what we started," I told them. "She was trying to save some little fish that got caught in shallow water. All we have to do is move them to a deeper place. It won't take long with all of us working together. I just have to get another sieve. I must have dropped the one I had yesterday. Eddie, can you find a pail that we can fill with creek water?"

Before he could move, Geraldine had her hands on her hips and was exclaiming, "*Fish?* We're walking all that way to save some *fish?*"

Reba scowled at her. "They *are* God's creatures, Geraldine."

Charles raised an eyebrow at me. Eddie shrugged. "I'm just along for the ride."

We started up Palm Avenue together. Nobody said much. I guessed we were all thinking our own thoughts. When we came to Dodie's house, a beat-up pickup truck was pulling up in front. We slowed down and watched a man get out. His hair was whitish-blond, like Dodie's, and scraggly looking. His clothes looked like they came from somebody's scrap bag. On the side of the truck were the words, *CRUMPER'S SANITATION SERVICE.* I had a pretty good idea who he might be, and so did Geraldine.

"I saw him once before," she whispered. "That's Dodie's father."

We walked on in silence, up to the end of the block, through the park, into the groves, and out onto the clearing by the cliff.

I started down the cliff first. "Be careful," I told them. I concentrated on blocking Dodie's screams from my mind, trying instead to think about the way we had climbed down the cliff together. How I had skidded, but she was sure-footed. How she had encouraged me. I tried not to, but I remembered her voice when she fell. I remembered her screams. I listened hard for the sound of running water. I was glad when a bumblebee got too close and buzzed in my ear.

We hiked upstream to the spot where Dodie and I had seen the rattlesnake. There was no sign of it now, but the minnows were there, flapping around in a pool that had only a little water in it.

"There they are," I said. "Poor things. Look, there's barely enough water for them to move around in. I hope we got here in time."

Charles went and filled the pail with fresh creek water. Eddie handed me the sieve.

"We can each lift a few out of the pool," I said. "That way we'll all be saving them together."

I wondered what Dodie would think about "those others" saving her fish. She had been so determined not to let anyone but me in on her secret place. But it wasn't safe now for me to come up here alone. Not when Jefferson Clement was walking the streets free. Anyway, I had a good feeling when I thought of all of us doing something for Dodie.

I dipped the sieve into the pool and caught three tiny fish. Quickly, I transferred them to the pail and handed the sieve to Geraldine.

She caught only two, then one of them got away. "Gotcha!" she said when she finally captured both of them. When she put them in the pail, I saw that her face was red, and her lips trembled. I stopped looking at her for fear she would get me crying, too.

After all the fish were caught, we hiked up the creek until we began to see scrub oaks growing along the sides. The water deepened here. "This is a good place," Eddie said.

"Ready?" Charles asked.

I nodded, and he handed me the pail. It was heavier than I expected. He helped me lower it into the water, then tilt it so that the fish spilled over the rim and splashed into the creek. They swam slowly at first, then faster, darting freely back and forth. Some went in circles. Others started upstream. A few hid in the shade of big rocks.

"We did it," I said softly. I was talking to Dodie, but nobody else knew it.

We walked single file back to the bottom of the cliff. Geraldine looked around curiously, but I didn't. I tried not to think about where Dodie might have fallen and hit her head.

"Look here," Charles said. He bent over and picked up something half hidden under a manzanita bush. He held it in the palm of his hand, where it glittered in the sun.

"It's Dodie's golden ring," I said.

Charles handed it to me. We all stood together a few minutes looking at it. I closed my fingers around it and put it in my pocket. Then we climbed the cliff and headed for home.

CHAPTER
TWENTY-FIVE

The *Messina News* was published every Friday, and there was a big article about Dodie on the front page. Right next to the article was an invitation by Reverend Adams for the whole town to come together to send up prayers for her recovery. They would meet at the Congregational church at twelve o'clock sharp, right after the regular service. The way the church filled up on Sunday, you would have thought it was Easter.

Mr. Wilcombe, the janitor, put extra seats down the side aisles, then turned on three big rotating fans, two in the back of the sanctuary and one up front where the altar flowers were already drooping from the heat. Some of the church ladies handed out carnations, one to each person. It smelled like somebody had opened a box of cloves.

"After the prayer service, we're all going to walk up

to the altar and put our carnations there," Reba Lu said. "Then my daddy will take them to the hospital for Dodie. I hope Dodie likes that smell," she added. "I sure don't." She gave a big sniff and wiped her nose with her hankie.

Reba Lu and Geraldine and I sat in the third row with Eddie and Charles.

Mrs. Crumper hadn't come for the church service, but she came in now, by the side door from Reverend Adams's office.

"Mr. Crumper's not with her," Reba Lu whispered, "because he's staying at the hospital with Dodie."

"How do you know that?" Geraldine demanded.

"I'm the preacher's daughter," Reba Lu said.

Geraldine couldn't top that, so she commenced flipping through the hymnbook. "I'll bet we sing 'Jesus Loves Me,'" she said.

Reba Lu shushed her because her daddy was helping Mrs. Crumper to a seat, all alone, in the front row. Mrs. Adams had offered to sit with her, but Reba Lu had overheard her mama tell the reverend that Mrs. Crumper had said she didn't want any favors from anyone in this godforsaken town.

The service started. We all stood up and sang *Jesus loves me, this I know, for the Bible tells me so . . .* Geraldine poked Reba Lu and gave her an *I told you so* smile.

Then Reverend Adams talked a bit about Dodie and how Jesus loved her. He told about Dodie's wanting to save the minnows in the creek. He said she cared for God's creatures, and I remembered how she'd stopped me from throwing a rock at a rattlesnake. He said everyone should take hands while he said a prayer. I didn't know what to do because Charles was sitting next to me, but he just held out his hand like it was something he did every day, so I took it. It was warm, but not sweaty. Reba Lu glanced over at us and rolled her eyes.

After that, I got my hand back, and we sang "God Will Take Care of You," which sounded like a promise. I hoped it was. Then the church organist played some soft music while people started filing down the center aisle to the front of the church to deposit their carnations on the altar.

"They're showing that they care about Dodie," Geraldine whispered.

I stared at her. I thought of how I had once said I hated everything Dodie Crumper did and had only changed my mind when I got to know her a little better. But most of these people didn't know her at all. It felt fake for everyone here to be pretending how sorry they were about what had happened.

"Who in this town cares what happens to Dodie?" I whispered.

"Dr. Thomas, for one," Geraldine said. "And Reverend Adams, and we three, and . . ."

"OK, OK. But most people don't. We didn't. Remember how hard it was for us to find something about her to love?"

"Some of these people look sad," Reba Lu argued.

Old Man Snyder stood at the altar shaking his head slowly. Miss Hallie Harper, who had given Dodie an even worse grade than she'd given me, sobbed out loud and had to be helped back to her seat by Mrs. Dawson.

"Come on, Angie," Reba Lu whispered, standing up.

I shook my head. "I'm not going up there."

"Of course you are. You have to put your carnation on the altar."

She gave me a shove and said, "Stop being difficult." I was about to tell her she sounded just like her mother when she grabbed my hand and pulled me into the aisle behind her.

We laid our carnations there with all the others and turned to walk back to our seats. Just as we sat down, we heard Mrs. Crumper start to wail. It was an awful sound, like somebody having a tooth pulled without anything to deaden the pain. It made my skin crawl to hear her.

"Oh, my baby!" she cried. "My Dodie! She is all I have to live for. Oh, my precious Dodie!"

She kept on like that. I wished I knew what to do. Finally, Dr. Thomas went to the front of the church and helped her to her feet. He took her by the arm and led her down the aisle toward the back of the church.

The whole place was quiet, everybody waiting out of respect until Mrs. Crumper got outside before they would start to talk. But she never made it to the door. She stopped at the pew near the back where Jefferson Clement sat with his family.

My heart started to pound. She leaned over until she was right in his face and said loud enough for everybody to hear, "I know what kind of man you are."

A low murmuring of voices filled the church. Mr. Clement never looked at her, just stared straight ahead like he hadn't heard what she said. But her words echoed like a church bell gone sour.

I know what kind of man you are. They floated over

the congregation and echoed from the rafters as Mrs. Crumper folded up like a used handkerchief and collapsed onto the floor.

Lots of people stood up to see what had happened. They began to talk all at once. Some gathered round, peering over each other's shoulders to get a better view. Dr. Thomas had to tell them to move back and to give Mrs. Crumper some room. They moved back a little, but not much.

Finally he told them, "Get on outside. You're not helping by standing around watching!"

My dad helped Dr. Thomas stretch Mrs. Crumper out on a back row pew. Mrs. Dawson fanned her with that morning's church bulletin until she began to moan, and we knew she was alive.

Geraldine and Reba Lu and I had twisted around in our seats to watch what was happening in back. I especially wanted to get a look at Jefferson Clement. He was still sitting there in one of the back pews, stony faced, looking neither right nor left.

I seemed to hear Mrs. Crumper's voice again in my head. I was glad she had said those words right out loud so everyone could hear them. But the look on Mr. Clement's face scared me. It reminded me of that day at the cliff when he had put his finger to his lips as a warning.

I felt a little better when I felt Reba Lu's hand in mine. "Let's go on outside," she said, "so we won't have to look at him."

It was cool out there under the spreading elm trees. I took a deep breath and let it out slowly. Reba Lu and Geraldine put their heads together, whispering, but I didn't care. I walked around to the churchyard where the grass around the gravestones was dry and brown from the heat. It felt crisp under my feet. I passed a marble monument with an angel spreading her wings. I sat down on a little bench in the shade.

I wished I could go back to last week and live it over again. If I hadn't been late that morning, would things have turned out differently? Would Mr. Clement have stayed away when he saw that there were two of us? I wanted so bad to have another chance to keep Dodie away from the cliff, away from Mr. Clement. If I just had another chance, I'd get it right this time.

Geraldine and Reba Lu came over and sat on the bench, one on either side of me. "Looky there," Geraldine said.

Jefferson Clement stood to one side with his hat held in his hand. "He's holding it over his heart," Geraldine said in a low whisper.

"He doesn't have one," I whispered back.

As we watched, he put one foot forward and nudged a pink cemetery daisy with the toe of his shoe. Geraldine's hand reached out and touched mine as he put his foot flat on the flower and squished it. I shut my eyes tight and gave Geraldine's hand a squeeze.

Mrs. Crumper was making snuffling noises when she came out of the church and made her way through the crowd. Mrs. Adams put her arm around her and patted her on the shoulder. Just then, a pickup truck pulled up in front of the church, and Dodie's father got out. He had combed his hair and put on a clean shirt. But his pants were too short, and the sole of one shoe flapped when he walked.

Shabby or not, he was a better person than Jefferson Clement, dressed in his Sunday best.

He came up to Mrs. Crumper and stood looking at her. We could tell that Mrs. Adams was asking him a question, but we couldn't hear what he said. He just shook his head slowly, back and forth, back and forth. Then he raised his voice. "She won't wake up," he finally said, loud enough so we could hear him. "I was at the hospital. I talked to her . . . talked a long time. But she won't wake up."

We stood and watched as Mr. and Mrs. Crumper walked away. He fumbled in his pocket and pulled out a soiled cap, putting it on his head and pulling the brim down over his eyes.

Pretty soon, everybody began to wander off. Then we three were the only ones left in the church cemetery. A mockingbird flew from a low branch and began to sing. Up and down the notes went. Up and down like the merry-go-round horses. We waited and listened until the bird flew away. We didn't look at each other. None of us spoke a word.

CHAPTER
TWENTY-SIX

The next morning, Geraldine, Reba Lu, and I picked a big bouquet of sweet peas from Mama's backyard vines. Mama wrapped them in wet newspapers, and we stood out in front of my house and waited for Dr. Thomas to drive up in his Model T Ford. He loved that car. "Over fifteen years old and getting better every day," he said. He had given me a ride one time, and I sat in the back seat because Miss Emma liked to be up front. This time, I climbed into the front seat real quick, and that left the back for Geraldine and Reba Lu.

Dr. Thomas handed me a jelly jar filled with orange blossoms in a little water. I took a sniff. I loved that smell.

"Where did you find those?" Geraldine asked. "Orange blossoms don't bloom in the summer."

Dr. Thomas started the car and stuck his head out the window to check for traffic, even though there was hardly ever any. "Sometimes they do," he said. "When a plant is under stress, it sometimes blooms out of season."

I liked that idea—of a flower sometimes blooming out of season. "That describes Dodie," Reba Lu said.

But Geraldine didn't agree. "Dodie isn't a flower," she said. "She might have been out of season, but I never saw her come close to blooming."

"She was about to," Reba Lu insisted. "Our friendship changed her."

I wondered if that could be true. It seemed to me that *we* were the ones who had changed, especially me. That day up the creek had made me look at things differently. Who would have thought I'd have hiked back up there to save a few little fish? The thing that surprised me most was that I had been the leader.

I had never been a leader before in my whole life.

I was still thinking about that when we arrived at the hospital. Dr. Thomas pulled into a parking space that had his name painted on it in big red letters. I turned around and looked at Reba Lu and Geraldine in the back seat. Reba Lu's eyebrows were raised, and Geraldine had her mouth open. But I wasn't surprised at all. I had always known Dr. Thomas was somebody special.

Dr. Thomas had to go talk to somebody at the front desk, so we three waited by the elevator for him. Reba Lu couldn't wait to start talking about what was going on in Messina. "My daddy says Constable Mullens has asked for a judge to come from the courthouse in San Andreas to hold a hearing next Monday. That will be just six days after Dodie . . . after Dodie . . ."

"After Dodie fell." Geraldine finished the sentence for her. Reba Lu nodded and looked relieved that she didn't have to say the words that meant Dodie was lying unconscious in a hospital bed.

Geraldine went on. "I heard Dr. Thomas say that the judge will have to question people and decide if it was an accident or if somebody caused her to fall."

She stopped and looked at me. "I guess that means you, Angie. And Willie Jack and Mr. Clement. You three were the only ones who were there. Anyway, if they decide it wasn't an accident, there has to be a trial at the courthouse in San Andreas, and *someone* will be in a whole lot of trouble." She took a deep breath. "And that someone is Willie Jack. That's all I know. Just what I heard Dr. Thomas say."

Reba Lu looked put out that Geraldine was acting like she knew so much. "Jefferson Clement is going around town blaming Willie Jack," she said. "But he's not the only one who was there. Angie saw the whole thing." She looked at me. "You'll testify in front of everyone, Angie. You'll probably get your picture in the paper."

That made me mad. "I don't *want* my picture in the paper," I said. "Not for something like this."

"I don't see that you'll have much choice," Geraldine told me. "You're a star witness." She was quiet a minute, until Reba Lu gave her an elbow jab. Then, "Come on, Angie. Tell us what you know. How come it's Willie Jack who's on trial?"

I stared at her. "I can't talk about it," I said, even though I knew I could if I wanted to.

I was glad when Dr. Thomas joined us and pushed the elevator button for the second floor. "Here's what I want you girls to do," he said. "You stand around Dodie's bed and talk naturally—about things that she cares about. Tell her how you saved those fish and how everybody came to church and prayed that she would wake up and be all right."

He made all three of us look him in the eye, one by one. "There's going to be no crying and carrying on," he said. "Any one of you who even hiccups will have to stand in the hall. Do you get my meaning?"

We nodded.

"All right then. We're coming up on Dodie's room now. Number 202. Here it is."

He pushed open the door and held it while we went in. The smell of carnations greeted us, and I knew that Reverend Adams had brought them from the church. But when I saw Dodie in her hospital bed, I almost went right out again. Her head was wrapped in bandages, and a nurse was wiping her face with a wet cloth. A needle was in her arm, and a tube was connected to a bottle that hung from a tall metal stand. I hated needles.

Dr. Thomas must have read my mind. "They're giving her nourishment," he said. "And something that will keep her from hurting."

Dodie's eyes were closed, and her face looked as white as the sun-bleached boulders up the creek. She didn't move. It looked like she was hardly breathing.

"She looks pretty good . . . considering," Reba Lu said.

"She does not! She looks like she's about dead," Geraldine snapped.

"There will be no talk like that!" Dr. Thomas said. "How would you like it if your friends stood around your bed and said you looked dead?"

Geraldine didn't have an answer for that. She looked at the floor. Reba Lu edged in between the two of us until she was standing right next to the bed. She put one arm around Geraldine and the other one around me. "She looks real nice," she said. "Peaceful, like." Then she began to hiccup.

"Now that's enough," Dr. Thomas said. "She may be in a coma, but we never can tell how much she can hear. You girls get busy and talk to her—just like she's awake and can understand what you're saying."

We looked at each other. Nobody said a word. Finally, Dr. Thomas said, "I have to see some other patients, so I'll leave you here with her for a little while. Remember what I said."

As soon as the door had closed, we gathered closer around Dodie's bed. "We're all here," I told her. "Reba Lu and Geraldine and me. We brought you some sweet peas from Mama's garden."

I poked Geraldine. She was holding them, and she looked around for a place to put them. "There's an empty vase," she said. "I'll just go outside and put some water in it."

"You don't need to go outside," I told her. "There's a sink over there in the corner."

"Oh, yeah. Now I see that."

I knew she had seen it all the time and was just looking for an excuse to leave the room. She filled the vase with water, stuck the sweet peas in it, and came back to stand by the bed.

"The church had a prayer service for you," I said. "Everybody wants you to get better, Dodie. That's why there are so many carnations. People sent them to you."

I poked Reba Lu. She jumped like I'd lit a firecracker under her. Then she calmed down and said, "Please wake up, Dodie. Things aren't the same without you. We . . . miss you, Dodie."

"Yeah," Geraldine said. Then she made a choking noise and starting biting her lower lip.

We three stood by the bed without saying another word. I wanted to close my eyes, but I couldn't seem to blink. Dodie looked so different. Her hair had been washed and brushed. And she was wearing a white gown without a spot on it.

"Somebody got Dodie cleaned up real nice," Geraldine whispered. Then she bent closer. "Look there," she said. We all bent over to look at Dodie's fingernails. The ragged edges had been trimmed, and I had never seen them so clean.

I looked at Dodie with her eyes closed. I waited for her to open them, though I knew she probably wouldn't. I thought of her in the eucalyptus forest with leaves in her hair. I remembered the way she had jumped from rock to rock in the creek looking almost like a dancer. I pictured her at the beach singing "you and me . . . you and me."

I turned away. The body in that bed might look real nice, but it wasn't anybody I knew. The Dodie I knew had dirt under her fingernails so thick that seeds could have sprouted. Her hair was as untamed as a horse's tail on a windy day. And she had never had a peaceful look about her as long as I'd known her.

I reached into my skirt pocket and took out the golden ring, then I tucked it under her clasped hands so it looked like she was holding it. Her free ride.

"You better not leave that here," Reba Lu said. "It might get lost."

She was probably right. I picked it up and put it back in my pocket. I would keep it for her.

Pretty soon, Dr. Thomas came in and said we had stayed long enough. We walked down the hall to the elevator and took it to the first floor. Nobody said a word. Not even when we got in Dr. Thomas's car and he drove us home.

I went to bed that night and lay in the dark without closing my eyes. I tried to imagine myself being questioned by the visiting judge. I wondered if I would have to swear on a Bible to tell the truth. Then I remembered the look on Jefferson Clement's face when he stood at the edge of the cliff and put his finger over his lips, warning me not to tell.

I began to shiver and pulled my blanket clear up around my ears. When I finally slept, I dreamed about the little fish we had moved into the creek. But when I looked at them closely, I saw that the creek water had all dried up and we hadn't saved them after all.

CHAPTER
TWENTY-SEVEN

Even though Judge Withers, the visiting judge, only wanted to question the people who had been at the cliff the day Dodie fell, it seemed like half of Messina crowded into the Woman's Club building that Wednesday morning. Judge Withers sat at a long table in the front of the big room. At one end of the table, a lady sat with a notebook in front of her and a pencil in her hand. A pile of sharpened pencils lay nearby. An empty chair stood at the other end of the table, turned so it was facing all the people. The rest of us sat on metal folding chairs. A man wearing a uniform and a badge stood in the doorway. Willie Jack sat in a chair off to one side, where everybody could get a good look at him.

The August heat seemed to fill the room. The big rotating fan in the corner made a soft humming sound, but it only stirred the air. It didn't cool it.

Judge Withers picked up the gavel that he had borrowed from the Woman's Club president and pounded it on the table. Everybody stopped talking, except for Mrs. Eunice Abbott, who was busy pointing at Willie Jack and telling anyone who wanted to listen that he had never been right in his head.

The judge cleared his throat. "Does everyone understand that I am ready to start these proceedings?" He looked right at Mrs. Abbott when he said that. She clapped her mouth shut and turned red in the face. "Well then," Judge Withers said. "If everyone is through talking, I will continue."

He explained that he had gone to see Dodie in the hospital and talked to the doctors about the seriousness of her injury. Then he said it was up to him to question witnesses about the *manner* of her injury. That meant he needed to find out what made her fall. He would decide if it was an accident or if someone was to blame. He made sure everyone knew that this was not a trial. It was an inquiry—a time for asking questions and getting the answers that would tell him if a trial was necessary.

Judge Withers looked like his name. His face was wrinkled, and his hands had gnarled fingers, bent like old driftwood. But his blue eyes were bright and quick, and he looked like he could spot a liar when he saw one.

Dr. Thomas was the first one to come up front to sit in the witness chair and answer questions. He told the judge what the whole town already knew and a little bit more, about how I had told him that Dodie had fallen over the cliff, and how he'd found her at the bottom, lying in the sand.

"The little girl was scratched up pretty bad and had a

lot of blood on her. We got her right to the hospital, but she's still in a coma. There's no telling when she might wake up . . . or if she ever will."

"Did you see anyone else?"

"Jefferson Clement and Willie Jack Kelly were there with her. Willie Jack was squatted down by Dodie, patting her shoulder. He kept saying, 'Poor little lamb, poor little lamb.' Jeff Clement was crouched down, too. I noticed his shirt was all torn apart in the front. He saw me looking at it and said he'd caught it on some thornbushes when he skidded down the cliff path. Then he jumped up and started shouting."

"Can you remember his words?"

Dr. Thomas took a deep breath and let it out slowly. "Jeff pointed at Willie Jack and shouted, 'Willie pushed her. I saw the whole thing!'"

The doctor looked around the courtroom. When he spoke, his voice was steady. "I don't believe a word of it."

Judge Withers tapped on the table with his gavel. "What you saw is important, Dr. Thomas. What you believe is not."

"Dr. Thomas isn't supposed to give his opinion," Geraldine whispered. We knew all about court cases from listening to *Mr. District Attorney* on the radio.

"I don't care," I whispered back. "I'm glad he did."

Dr. Thomas went back to his seat, and Judge Withers shuffled some papers. Then he called out, "William John Kelly."

For a second I wondered who that was, then Willie Jack came forward to give his testimony. He wore a clean shirt and a leather belt to hold up his pants. I was glad he didn't have handcuffs on. It seemed strange to see him without his brown paper bag.

He took his time, easing himself into his chair until it seemed to fit him better. He looked around the room, taking note of who was there. His eyes rested on Mr. Clement until the judge gave a little cough and told him to go ahead and tell his story. You could have heard a pin drop. Even Mrs. Abbott didn't make a sound.

"Last Tuesday morning, I was standing on my corner by the Bank of America talking to the Lord. Amos Snyder was with me, weren't you, Amos?"

Heads turned to look at Old Man Snyder, who nodded and made some throaty sounds that only Willie Jack seemed to understand.

"That's right, Amos," he said. "Old Duke was there, too. We saw the Crumper girl heading up Palm Avenue. A couple of minutes later, here comes Jeff Clement going the same direction, toward the park.

"Then Angie Wallace raced up the street like she was going to a fire. I thought about it a bit, then told Amos to stay put—he moves a bit slower than I do—and I headed out to see what was up.

"I had reached the grove when I heard somebody yelling, so I started to run toward the sound. Jeff Clement and the Wallace girl were at the clearing. Jeff was starting down the old cliff path. When Angie told me Dodie had fallen, I sent her running for the doc. Then I climbed down the cliff to see for myself."

He hesitated, and it was like a shadow passed over his face, making his eyes darker, his brows closer together.

"Little Dodie Crumper was there," he said. "She was twisted like somebody had used her and tossed her away."

Mrs. Crumper began to whimper. There wasn't another sound in the courtroom, except for the little *click* the wall clock made when it advanced one minute. Finally he went on.

"Jeff Clement was hunkered down next to her little body. He had his hand on her arm. He started crying. I swear, he blubbered like a baby.

"We both looked up when some stones skittered to the ground. Doc Thomas was climbing down the path. Soon as Jeff saw him, he got right over his crying spell. A few minutes later, he was jumping up and pointing his finger at me. 'There's your villain!' he yelled. He told Doc Thomas he saw me push that little girl. He said he saw the whole thing."

Willie Jack stopped and stared over at Mr. Clement. "Miserable liar," he said.

Mr. Clement stared straight ahead. He stayed that way even after the judge called a short recess so people could get up and stretch their legs. The only time he changed his expression was when the door opened, and Miss Emma came in with Mrs. Dawson beside her. He looked at Miss Emma, and then he didn't. His mouth tightened until it seemed like he'd swallowed his lips.

Miss Emma was white as a bleached sheet, but she held her head up high. Dr. Thomas walked her and Mrs. Dawson over to a couple of empty chairs next to Mrs. Adams. I saw Reba Lu's mama reach out and pat Miss Emma on the hand.

Miss Emma wore a blue dress with tiny white flowers all over it. Her hair was pulled away from her face and held at the sides with tortoiseshell combs. It looked like Mrs. Dawson might have taken her up to the beauty parlor and told Verna to do something to smooth the frizz out.

"She'd look real nice if it wasn't for the foxes," Geraldine whispered.

Even in this hot weather, she had her fur pieces draped around her neck. I saw her reach up and pat one of the little heads, but she didn't talk to it.

"You don't suppose she's going to testify, do you?" Geraldine asked.

"Of course not," I said. "She wasn't there when Dodie fell."

I glanced at Mr. Clement. He looked like a spider was crawling down his back. Whether Miss Emma said anything or not, her being here in the room was making a difference. It was bothering Mr. Jefferson Clement a whole lot.

CHAPTER TWENTY-EIGHT

Mr. Clement came to the front of the room and swore to tell the truth, the whole truth, and nothing but the truth. He sat down in the witness chair and straightened his tie. It was dark blue with yellow dots and made him look like a swarm of bees had landed on him. Mrs. Clement had starched his white shirt so stiff it hardly moved when he did. I could just imagine Mrs. Hewitt admiring the way he dressed.

He faced Judge Withers and nodded his head like he was happy to see him. The judge didn't nod back.

"Do you recall where you were the afternoon of the first of August?" Judge Withers asked.

"I do. I went for a walk. I walk regularly."

"Do you always follow the same route?"

"No, indeed. I like to wander through the byways of our little town looking for surprises."

"What kind of surprises?"

"Pretty things," he said. He spoke directly to Judge Withers. "Wildflowers, for example."

Judge Withers cleared his throat. "Our wildflowers are past their season by July."

"I was merely giving you a 'for instance.'" Mr. Clement frowned and sat up straighter. "Let me see. On that particular day I noticed a red-tailed hawk in the sycamores. I admire hawks, don't you?"

Geraldine leaned over and whispered, "He's really laying it on thick, isn't he?"

I nodded. Mr. Clement had a way of charming people. I wondered if he had acted polite like this when he started helping Dodie hang out her laundry. "He's a good actor," I whispered back.

But I thought he was putting on the charm this time because he was desperate. He might be an evil man, but he wasn't stupid. He was determined to convince everyone that he was a good citizen.

When Judge Withers didn't answer him, Mr. Clement tapped his chin with one finger. "I came across some watercress growing in a wet spot near the park. That was a happy discovery. My wife has a fondness for watercress sandwiches. Don't you, Ruth, my dear?"

He looked hard at Mrs. Clement. She glanced helplessly at Lucy, then looked down and stared into her lap.

"I would have picked some," he went on, "but I heard loud voices. The sounds seemed to come from beyond the park, way up by the cliff. Of course, I headed that way to see if anyone was in trouble." He put a solemn look on his face. "I couldn't just turn my back and walk away."

Liar! Liar! I knew he must have seen Dodie and followed her all the way to the cliff.

He looked around the room at the spectators. His eyes seemed to glow with concern. You never saw such a model of public-spirited kindness. It made me sick.

From the poke Geraldine gave me, I knew she felt the same.

"Halfway through the grove," he continued, "I came upon this child." He stretched out his arm and pointed at me. "Angie, is it?"

I glared back at him. He knew who I was. He knew that I was there and that I saw everything that happened.

"The poor girl seemed frightened," he told the jury. "I called out and asked what had upset her, but she just kept running through the grove, right past me toward town."

Liar! Liar!

He looked at the judge. "I continued on toward the cliff." He shook his head sadly, letting us know he couldn't bear to remember what he had seen.

"Willie Jack Kelly was there with the Crumper girl. They were arguing. He took a step toward her and grabbed her arm. She tried to back away from him, but he held on. She said something that I couldn't hear. It must have angered him because he gave her a shove that sent her over the edge. She screamed. Then it was quiet, except for the sound of Willie Jack scrabbling down the side of the cliff. He never saw me, never knew I was there.

"I walked to the edge and looked over." He covered his eyes with one hand, like he was trying to block out a terrible sight.

People leaned forward in their seats to hear what he would say next.

"Poor girl," he murmured. "Little Dodie Crumper, who lived across from our place on Palm Avenue. She lay there, all bloodied up. I tell you I could hardly look at her."

There was a heavy silence in the courtroom. Then the judge asked, "Did you see Mr. Kelly?"

Mr. Clement's voice grew stronger. "Yes, I did. He was standing over her. 'Dodie . . . Dodie,' he kept saying. Then he reached down and put his hand on her throat. I figured he was going to finish the job he had started."

"What happened then, Mr. Clement?"

"Why, I climbed right down that cliff path yelling at him to get his hands off her. It was hard going, I can tell you, but I made it to the bottom. I had to get down there to see if there was any chance of helping that poor girl. But she was unconscious. Barely breathing. And we don't know if she'll ever wake up. That man is to blame. Him. Sitting right over there." He pointed a long finger. "Willie Jack Kelly!"

The metal chairs in the courtroom creaked as spectators turned to look at Willie Jack. A low murmuring filled the room as people began talking in low voices.

"There's your villain, folks. Sitting right here among us. Willie Jack Kelly threw little Dodie Crumper off the cliff, and he never shed a tear."

I knew it was a lie, and so did Mr. Jefferson Clement.

The two of us looked at each other and the truth passed between us.

That didn't stop the murmuring that grew into a sound like thunder gathering before a storm. Some people sprang to their feet, shouting and pointing at Willie Jack, who sat in his chair staring at Jefferson Clement. Others held tightly to each other, shaking their heads.

Judge Withers picked up his gavel and pounded it. "Please, everyone. This inquiry is still in session."

"That's all for now," the judge told Mr. Clement, who went to sit beside his wife. She didn't look at him, but Lucy Clement did, and her mouth twisted like she had just rinsed it with vinegar.

"We'll take a short recess," Judge Withers said. He stood up and walked out the side door. A lot of people stood up and stretched. Then they put their heads together and whispered. I tried to hear what was said, but their voices were too low. Mr. Clement sat in his chair, looking straight ahead. I sat in mine. It seemed like the murmurings went on and on, filling my head with sounds without meaning.

Someone touched me on my shoulder. I looked around to where Daddy was sitting behind me. Mama was beside him, and so was Eddie. But Daddy was the one who spoke to me.

"You can do this, Angie," he said. "All you have to do is tell the jury exactly what you saw." He gave my shoulder a squeeze. "Just tell the truth."

I nodded, but I was thinking about that word. Truth. The truth was that Jefferson Clement didn't actually push Dodie. But the truth was also that it was his fault she fell.

I wanted to put my hands over my ears to stop the memory of how he had yelled at her and called her terrible names. I closed my eyes, then wished I hadn't. Because whenever I closed them, I remembered the look on his face when he put his finger to his lips, his unspoken warning coming through loud and clear.

I opened my eyes quick. I looked around the room and saw Miss Emma. I concentrated on her furs. Three little fox heads waiting to be petted. *Go ahead and pet them, Miss Emma. It's all right.* That's what I wanted to say.

But I felt my throat kind of close up and my eyes begin to burn. I didn't want to cry. Not here. Not now. I wouldn't!

I was just reaching behind me to take hold of Daddy's hand when Judge Withers came back in, took his seat, and rapped on the table.

"Angelina Wallace," he said.

I jerked a little in my chair and swallowed hard. Even though I knew I was going to have to testify, it gave me a start to hear my name called.

Reba Lu squeezed one of my hands, and Geraldine the other. Theirs were as sweaty as mine were. I stood up and wiped my palms on my skirt. I tried not to wobble as I walked to the front of the room.

Judge Withers had me swear to tell the truth, and I sat down in the witness chair. It was still warm from Mr. Clement, and I scooted forward and sat on the edge to get as far away from his heat as possible.

Willie Jack gave me a little nod that told me he felt fine about my being up there telling the whole truth and nothing but. Everything was going to be all right. That's what the nod said. But Willie Jack didn't know all that was going on in my head.

Not about him. I was going to tell the truth about Willie Jack. It was Mr. Clement I was worried about. Mr. Clement deserved to be punished, but I was afraid if I told the truth—the exact truth—they might let him go free.

I reminded myself to just answer the questions and to tell it the way it happened. That's what my dad had said. Charles had said the same thing. But answering the questions might not tell the whole truth, and that was what I had promised to do. My head began to ache. I wanted a drink of water. I wanted the big light fixture in the ceiling to fall on Jefferson Clement's head so we could all go home.

"Now, Angelina," Judge Withers was saying, "there's no need to be nervous."

"Yes, sir," I told him. "I'm not." But I felt a twitch starting in my right eye. Then I saw that I had taken a tissue out of my pocket and torn it into narrow shreds. I wadded the torn bits up and hid them in one fist.

"I'm going to ask you some questions," Judge Withers told me, "but you can feel free to add any details that might help us understand what happened."

I nodded.

"Mr. Kelly has said that you were in a hurry last Tuesday morning. Why was that?"

"I was meeting Dodie," I said. "I mean, I was supposed to meet her, but I slept late, and she'd already left her house when I got there."

"Why didn't she wait for you?"

"She said her house wasn't the kind of place you'd want to wait around in."

The words came out before I thought about how they would sound. A few people tittered, but Judge Withers gave them a look that quieted them down.

"We were meeting to save the fish."

The judge looked confused. I guessed he wasn't at the service when Reverend Adams told that story, so I told it again. All about finding the minnows and needing to move them to deeper water.

Judge Withers drummed his fingertips on the table. His nails made a steady clicking sound. He never stopped looking at me. "According to Mr. Clement, he and Mr. Kelly were the only ones there when Dodie Crumper fell."

"That's not right," I said. "Willie Jack wasn't there at all. Not then. He came afterwards."

"After Dodie fell?"

"That's right. He sent me to get help, just like he said."

Judge Withers leaned forward. "Do you have any idea why Mr. Clement would be at the cliff with Dodie Crumper?"

"He . . . he was . . ." I glanced at Mr. Clement. He was staring at me. Staring hard. He put one finger to his lips, kind of casual like, then reached up to scratch his nose. But I knew what he meant.

I hesitated, and Judge Withers said, "What was her relationship to him? How were they acquainted?"

I felt a surge of relief. I could answer that one. "She did his laundry," I said.

"Did Dodie like Mr. Clement?"

"At first she did. He gave her money, and sometimes he helped her hang the clothes on the line. But after a while she didn't want him around her anymore."

People put their heads together and whispered. The judge gave the table a couple of taps with his gavel. The talking stopped, but everybody was looking at me. Especially Jefferson Clement. And I saw the warning in his eyes. A little cat's smile played at the edges of his mouth. The same smile he had worn when he sat up here and told his lies. I wondered if he had smiled like that when he'd found Dodie alone at the top of the cliff.

I tried to swallow, but I didn't have any spit. I kept thinking about how maybe if I had been there with her— if I hadn't slept late—if I hadn't taken time to sweep up the broken glass from the Crumper floor—then maybe he wouldn't have . . .

My eyes started to burn, but I wasn't going to cry. I wouldn't. Even so, I felt a tear form in the corner of one eye. It trickled down my cheek, and another one tried to follow it. I started to wipe them away with my tissue, but it was torn all to pieces and already wet from my sweaty hands. I looked away from Mr. Clement and saw Reba Lu and Geraldine watching me. Charles was sitting next to Reba Lu, and I remembered him saying earlier that day, "Tell it just the way it happened."

Could I?

CHAPTER
TWENTY-NINE

J udge Withers looked at me and smiled. "Do you need a short recess before we continue?" he asked.

I shook my head. I wished I had a glass of water, but I didn't ask for it. I kept my hands on my knees, holding tight to keep them from shaking.

There was a hush in the courtroom, as if all the clocks had stopped and time wasn't ticking by.

Then Judge Withers said, "Tell us what happened at the cliff, Angie. Tell it exactly the way you remember it."

I looked out across the room and saw Miss Emma watching me. She sat up straight and gave me a little nod. She seemed to be saying, *That's right, Angie. You go ahead and tell everybody the truth. Tell them what really happened.*

I pictured the scene in my mind. The fear and anger in Dodie's eyes. The way she had tried to get away from

Jefferson Clement. I remembered the warning look Mr. Clement had given me just before he climbed over the cliff's edge.

I glanced at him now. He wore the same expression he had then. A look as cold as ice. Dry ice. I remembered how dry ice could burn. I looked away from him and began.

"Dodie and Mr. Clement were standing near the edge of the cliff. They were talking loud, and I could hear everything they said. Dodie told Mr. Clement to leave her alone. She said, 'If you don't, I'll tell everybody what you've been trying to do to me.'"

"And what was that?" Judge Withers wanted to know.

I looked down at my lap. Then I looked up at Miss Emma. Her eyes were moist around the edges, but she gave me the tiniest little nod. When I started to answer, my voice was so low that Judge Withers had to tell me to speak up.

"Mr. Clement wanted to . . . to . . . put his hands where he oughtn't."

A murmuring rose in the room. It got louder and louder. I felt my face heat up. I stopped and looked over at the judge. Then I looked at the sea of faces in the room. Everyone was watching me.

I wanted to close my eyes, but I didn't. I kept my head up while he rapped on the table with his gavel. He had to rap quite a while to get people calmed down.

"If there are any more disturbances like that, I will clear this room," he said. Then he looked at me. "Are you feeling all right, Angie?" he asked.

I looked at him. I thought he had kind eyes. I nodded my head. "I want to tell what really happened."

He nodded. "Go on then."

"Dodie tried to get away from him. But Mr. Clement wouldn't let her go. He reached out and tried to grab her. I yelled at her to watch out, and that's when he saw that I was standing there watching. He told me to get away from there, and he called me a meddlesome brat. He started coming toward me, but his foot slipped. He was standing right at the edge of the cliff, and he lost his balance."

"*Mr. Clement* lost his balance?"

"That's right. He almost fell, but Dodie grabbed his shirt. She might be kind of skinny, but she's strong. He would have fallen right over the edge if she hadn't pulled him back up. That's the way his shirt got ripped, not from getting caught on thornbushes."

I heard a kind of murmuring from the audience. *Good,* I thought. They were paying attention.

"When Mr. Clement straightened up and stepped away from the cliff, he never said a word to her about saving his life. He just hollered at her and shook his fist in her face. He called her stupid and said it was her fault he almost fell."

The room hushed. It seemed that everyone had inhaled and couldn't let their breath out. Then I heard a low murmuring as folks nudged each other and put their heads close together. Mr. Clement looked straight ahead, without any expression on his face, as if I had been talking about a stranger.

Judge Withers gave me a nod, so I went on with my story. "Dodie started to walk toward me, and when Mr. Clement saw that, he put his foot right out and tripped her. I know he did it on purpose.

"Dodie put out her arm to break her fall, but her wrist hit the ground hard. I wanted to help her up, but I was scared of what he might do to me."

I looked down at my lap and was surprised to see blood on my finger where I'd been tearing at a hangnail.

"What happened next, Angie?"

Judge Withers's voice was soft and gentle, the way I talked to Buster when I petted him.

"It's important for you to tell us exactly what happened next," he told me. "Take your time. Tell us what you saw."

Jefferson Clement leaned forward in his seat, staring straight at me. He had lied and tried to make people think Willie Jack shoved Dodie off the cliff. Lying in court was a crime, wasn't it? Would they put him in jail for that? Jail was where I wanted him to go.

Tell the truth, Angie. Tell it just the way it happened.

All I had to say was that Jefferson Clement put out his hand and gave Dodie a shove. That's all it would take to get him out of our lives forever. I looked straight into his face and saw the fear in his eyes. I looked away from Mr. Clement and faced the judge.

"Dodie got up. She was holding her arm up against her chest. She started walking backward to get away from Mr. Clement and she backed right up to the edge of the cliff.

"When she started to fall I yelled at Mr. Clement to help her. But he never moved. Even when she screamed, he just watched her. Then she was gone."

I couldn't talk for a minute. I clenched my hands until my nails bit into my palms. When I finally said something, it didn't sound like me at all, but like a voice somewhere outside myself.

"I'm telling the truth," I said. "Mr. Clement never reached out to help Dodie. He put his hands down at his sides and watched her fall." I swallowed hard and forced out the rest, the bitter-tasting words that would set Jefferson Clement free.

"But he didn't . . . he didn't push her . . . off the cliff."

The spectators seemed to let out one breath in a big *whoosh*. Mr. Clement gave me a thin little smile that made him look as satisfied as a cat that's cornered a mouse.

Judge Withers closed the notebook he had been writing in and stood up. I stood up, too. "I'm not finished," I said.

Judge Withers sat back down, but I didn't. I glanced around the courtroom and fastened my eyes on Miss Emma. She was patting her furs and watching me.

"Mr. Clement did bad things," I said. "Dodie showed me the bruises on her arm that he made when she wouldn't let him touch her anymore. He's the one who tried to sneak into our tent when we were camping out in the minister's backyard. He's got my dog's teeth marks in his backside if you need proof. He used his binoculars to look at us in our bathing suits, too."

People began talking right out loud. Some of the ladies pressed their fingers against their mouths like I'd seen people do when they could hardly believe what they'd heard. Judge Withers had to pound the table with his gavel to get the room quiet enough for me to continue.

"I told the truth when I said he didn't push Dodie over the cliff, but I'm also telling the truth when I say that it was his fault that she fell.

"Mr. Clement knew I heard Dodie say she would tell the whole town what he tried to do to her. He saw me standing there. He knew I had heard everything."

Jefferson Clement jumped up so fast his chair tipped over. "Nobody will believe you, you lying little brat." He was breathing hard, and his face was as red and swollen as an overripe tomato. "I never did any of those things. It was an accident. Nothing but an accident."

He spoke as though Dodie's injuries were no more important than a broken dish or a stubbed toe.

Judge Withers raised his voice. "You are out of order, Mr. Clement. Another outburst like that, and you will be removed from this room in the custody of the sheriff."

Mr. Clement sat down. Nobody spoke. Nobody moved.

I looked at Judge Withers. "I've been wondering," I said, "why it is that people can know that a person has been doing bad things, but they just look the other way and try not to think about it."

He looked at me for what seemed like a long time. Then he turned to the people in the courtroom. Some of them lowered their eyes, and others began to fidget as if their clothes were too tight. Judge Withers shook his head. "I wish I had an answer for you," he said.

The courtroom was silent except for the sound of his nails *tap-tapping* once again on the wooden table.

Finally he said, "Thank you, Angelina. You may be excused."

I walked back to my seat. I was hardly aware of Geraldine or Reba Lu until they each took one of my hands and held them tight. There wasn't a sound in the courtroom until Mr. Clement got up and turned to leave the room. But Judge Withers stopped him.

"Just a minute there," he said. "You're saying now that Dodie Crumper's injury was an accident. But you testified that Willie Jack Kelly pushed her off the cliff. Are you saying that you want to change your statement?"

Mr. Clement didn't answer. He glared at his wife with a look that told her the whole thing was her fault.

The judge waited for him to say something. But he didn't. Judge Withers cleared his throat. It was so quiet in the room, I thought I could hear people breathing.

"A jury will have to make a decision about the cause of Dodie Crumper's injuries. In the meantime, Mr. Clement, you have just convicted yourself of perjury. Lying to an officer of the court is a serious offense. You and I have a few things to talk about." Judge Withers nodded toward the uniformed man who was standing by the door.

The rest of us stood to go, but the man at the door stopped Mr. Clement as he tried to leave the room.

I looked at Reba Lu and Geraldine. They were grinning. Charles held a fist in the air and mouthed the word YES.

Outside, the heat struck me like an oven suddenly opened wide. It felt good. It helped take away the coldness deep in my bones.

Mama and Daddy both put their arms around me, and Eddie gave me one of his crooked smiles. Reba Lu and Geraldine were talking excitedly about what was going to happen to Jefferson Clement now.

I wondered what Judge Withers was saying to him right that minute. Would he eventually be able to go home and live across the street from us again? Would I have to look into his face and see his little cat's smile? I had a feeling that I hadn't done anything to stop him . . . I had just slowed him down.

Charles was suddenly beside me. He put one hand on my arm. "You did fine," he said.

"It was the best I could." We looked at each other a few seconds. Neither of us spoke.

CHAPTER THIRTY

A few days after the hearing, Mr. Clement was officially charged with perjury—lying under oath. Daddy told me this was a serious crime, and he would spend some time in jail for it.

Reverend Adams went to see him at the jailhouse. "It wasn't because he wanted to," Reba Lu told me. "But my daddy practices what he preaches." I took that to mean he tried to hate the sin, but not the sinner. I knew how hard that could be, and I felt sorry for Reverend Adams.

The word around town was that Judge Withers hadn't been easy on Mr. Clement. He made him pay a big fine, and he told him that if Dodie died, he would have to stand trial for involuntary manslaughter. Daddy explained that meant someone's actions caused a death, though they didn't plan for it to happen. He also told me that I might have to testify again, this time at a real trial. If Dodie lived, there would still be a trial, but Mr. Clement would only be charged with assault and battery. That meant that he could be put in jail, but for a shorter time.

I nodded. I hadn't figured we were through with Jefferson Clement right yet.

In the meantime, Daddy said Mr. Clement would have to stay in the county jail unless Mrs. Clement could dig up enough money to bail him out. He smiled at me when he said that, and I smiled back. I was pretty sure Mrs. Clement wouldn't try very hard.

Reba Lu and Geraldine and I were sitting on the porch swing when Reba Lu told us what else Judge Withers had said to Mr. Clement. "He said, 'You'll be smart if you find another place to settle down when you finally get out of jail. Messina has had more than enough of you!' Those were his exact words. My daddy was there, and he heard him."

"Well, good!" Geraldine shouted. I didn't shout with her.

"What's the matter, Angie?" Reba Lu asked. "It's all over now, and you did a real good job when you testified in court."

I didn't say anything.

"Mr. Clement is finished," Reba Lu went on. "*You* finished him. He won't be bothering any little girls again."

I wondered if she really believed that. "Won't he?" I asked. "He'll be punished for what he did in Messina, but eventually he'll move to another town and start all over again."

"But that's terrible," Geraldine protested.

"Yes," I said. "It's terrible."

I was thinking of that day at the matinee when Dodie had wondered about that man—Hitler—who wanted to eliminate a whole race of people. He didn't seem to have any conscience at all. Well, neither did Jefferson Clement as far as I was concerned.

I couldn't help thinking of what might happen in the next town he lived in. Daddy said he hoped his reputation would follow him. I hoped so, too. But mostly I hoped he would go to jail after his trial and not get out for a good long time.

A few days later, Miss Martin moved away, and I didn't blame her. Mrs. Clement and Lucy were the only ones living there now. Lucy did all the errands and directed the choir at Wednesday night practice. Sometimes I heard her singing while she hung out the wash to dry. Whenever she saw me, she waved, but Mrs. Clement always turned her back and looked the other way.

Mama sent me out front one morning to water the lawn because it was turning brown in the summer heat. Charles saw me and walked across the street. I told him about Mrs. Clement not wanting to look at me.

"It's because she's embarrassed," Charles said. "She thinks people connect her to the things Mr. Clement did."

"Well, do they?"

He waited a bit before he answered. "Some might. But most folks have better sense."

I thought about that. Did I have better sense? Mrs. Clement had always been nice to me, but Mama said nobody really knew her that well. I had the feeling that she was afraid of her husband . . . and ashamed of him, too. I decided that I didn't blame her. I just felt sorry for her.

Charles gave me a questioning look. "What's really bothering you?"

"Jefferson Clement ought to be in jail for the rest of his life," I said. "If I'd told Judge Withers that he pushed Dodie, he would have been in a lot more trouble. Maybe he wouldn't have been able to get out of jail and hurt anyone ever again."

"You told the truth is what you did. You didn't have any choice."

"I had a choice."

"Listen," Charles went on, "you're the one who saved Willie Jack from going to jail for something he didn't do. You're not to blame for any of the rest. You didn't cause Dodie to fall off that cliff. You just happened to be there when it happened."

He put one arm around my shoulder and gave it a squeeze. We stood together a few seconds, then Charles gave a little cough and pulled away. "I've got some things to do," he said.

I didn't answer. I seemed to have something in my eye.

Later that afternoon, Dr. Thomas got out his Model T Ford again, and Reba Lu, Geraldine, and I piled in. I let Geraldine sit in the front seat this time, and I got in the back with Reba Lu.

"I hope Dodie will be better today." Reba Lu said it loud enough for Dr. Thomas to hear her. He nodded. "That's what we all hope," he said. But he didn't sound like he believed it would happen.

He had to see another patient, so we took the elevator by ourselves up to the second floor and found room 202. Dodie's father was just leaving when we opened the door. He tipped his hat to us just like we were grown-up ladies, then went down the hall, the loose sole of his shoe flapping on the polished floor.

"He needs to—," Reba Lu began, but I gave her a look that shushed her.

"He cares about Dodie," I said.

"If you ask me . . . ," Geraldine said.

"Nobody did," I answered.

We went into the room, not speaking to each other. Dodie looked about the same. She still had that needle in her arm, and the tube was still connected to a bottle hanging from a tall metal stand. We stood by her bed. She didn't move. She didn't make a sound.

"She looks like she's not breathing," Geraldine whispered.

I stepped on her foot. "Don't you say that. Don't you dare."

Reba Lu swallowed, and I figured she'd gulped down whatever comment she had been about to make.

Dodie's hand was lying on top of the sheet, palm up. I reached out and touched her wrist. I expected her skin to be cool, but it was warm. I could feel her pulse. *Ker-thump. Ker-thump.* I took hold of her hand. "Dodie," I said, "it's me. It's Angie."

It was silent in the room except for the buzzing of a fly on the windowsill. Geraldine stood on one foot and then the other. "She can't hear you," she said.

"You don't know that!" Reba Lu snapped. I could tell they were ready for an argument.

"Shut up, you two," I whispered. It must have been a loud whisper, for they both stopped their bickering and stared at me.

"Dodie." I said her name softly, then a little louder. "Can you hear me, Dodie? If you can hear me, move your hand. Move one finger, Dodie. Just let me know you can hear me."

We stood there in that white room. White walls, white sheet, white venetian blinds. And nothing happened.

I waited for a movement, some signal that she knew I was there. "Dodie," I said, "Geraldine and Reba Lu are here, too. We picked some more sweet peas for you. They smell real good. Mama said to tell you there are plenty more where those came from."

The door opened, and Dr. Thomas came in. He looked at the three of us standing around the bed. "I think that's a long enough visit for today," he said.

Geraldine turned away from the bed and started for the door. Reba Lu was right behind her. I was about to follow them when, under my fingers, I felt a movement. No more than a breath against my skin. I could barely be sure I felt it at all.

"Dr. Thomas," I said.

He looked at me, then came over to the bed. "She moved her hand," I said. "Not much. But I felt her move it."

Dr. Thomas took out his handkerchief and blew his nose. Geraldine and Reba Lu stood close together, their heads almost touching. I looked at them once, then went back to holding Dodie's hand in mine.

"Are you sure?" Dr. Thomas asked.

I nodded. "I'm sure."

He took her other hand in his. "There may be hope," he said. "We'll just have to wait and see."

CHAPTER THIRTY-ONE

A few days later, I woke up early in the morning and couldn't go back to sleep. It was five o'clock, and the full moon was still low in the sky. I put on my shorts and a shirt and left a note on the kitchen table.

GONE FOR A WALK

Buster woke up and begged to go with me, so I fastened his leash and slipped out the front door while a warm August breeze moved through the streets in a river of soft air.

As I walked up Palm Avenue, Buster nose-nudged me, and I reached down to scratch his shaggy head. "Good Buster," I told him.

The light was on in Reverend Adams's upstairs study,

and I knew he would be at his desk, working on Sunday's sermon. A door slammed, and Mrs. Clement scooted across her front porch and down the steps to get the morning paper. She kept her eyes down the whole time, so she missed the sunrise that reached for the sky with fingers of rosy light. As I passed Dr. Thomas's house, I smelled coffee, and I could imagine Mrs. Dawson putting the pot on to boil, then dropping egg shells in to settle the grounds.

Buster pulled at his leash, and I unfastened it to let him run, but he didn't. He stayed near me, going ahead a little way, then coming back to nuzzle my hand. When I rubbed his head, he shivered all over with happiness.

I practiced stepping around the sidewalk cracks for a bit, but soon tired of that. Then I made a game of naming all the people who lived in the houses, going up one side of the street and down the other.

"We know them all," I told Buster. "We know their names and what they do for a living and if they're friendly or snooty." I thought for a minute, trying to work something out in my head.

"What we don't know," I finally said, "is how they feel inside. Are they scared of the dark, like Dodie? Are they crabby, like Miss Harper? Do they have secrets they don't want anybody to know?"

Then I got to thinking about the difficult times everybody was talking about, and the war in Europe, and I wondered if we were going to get involved in that. It seemed an awful thing to send boys not much older than my brother off to war. But it was also an awful thing to let that man Hitler keep killing innocent people. Everybody in our town was talking about how bad he was, but so far nobody I knew had tried to do anything about it.

We reached Main Street and waited for a delivery truck to pass before we crossed the street. I looked over my shoulder and saw Mr. Flannery direct the truck into the narrow alley that led to the parking area behind the grocery store. I never realized that he had to get up so early to go to work.

Buster and I walked on to the American Legion Park. Gusts of warm wind made the eucalyptus branches sway and drop their pods onto the dusty earth. Dodie's fort was almost gone. The wind had blown away the roof, and somebody had stepped on the rest. All that was left was a mound of dirt like a sand castle that has almost washed away. I sat down and collected a fistful of long, spear-shaped leaves. I rubbed them between my fingers until they smelled like Mentholatum, then tossed them away.

Buster chased a ground squirrel, but it escaped up a tree. He made some whining sounds and came back to me.

I got to my feet and began the hike through the groves to the cliff. When I got to the edge, I started down the slope, digging in my heels and skidding, raising a cloud of dirt. I walked up the creek until I came to deeper water and saw the pool where we had moved Dodie's fish.

There was Willie Jack, sitting on a boulder talking to the Lord. He had to stop because Buster jumped all over him, licking his face and pawing at his shirt. But when Willie Jack said "Sit," Buster sat.

We watched the minnows swim in the clear water for a while. Then Willie Jack said, "You did a brave thing,

Angie, when you sat in that witness chair and told the truth about what really happened to Dodie. That was the right thing to do."

He picked up a stick and tossed it for Buster to fetch. When he brought it back, Willie Jack petted him and scratched him behind his ears. Then he looked at me.

"What are you going to do with your life, Angie?"

"I've never thought much about that," I told him. "I guess I'll keep going to school until I don't have to anymore." I thought for a minute. "If there's a war, I'd want to go and fight, but I guess that wouldn't be possible."

"Is that so?"

"Of course. You have to be born a boy to fight in a war."

Willie Jack shook his head. "If war comes, women will be in the army, and the navy, too." He was silent a few minutes. "But there are lots of other ways to fight the wrongs in this world, Angie. You're a strong girl. You'll always find a way to stand up for what's right."

I didn't know what to say to that. I thought about how I'd felt that day when we went up the creek to save the fish and I'd felt like a leader, but I didn't know how to put my feelings into words right then. Willie Jack and I sat there a while, not talking. Then Buster and I headed for home.

CHAPTER THIRTY-TWO

On the way, I was passing the Crumper house when I saw a light in the window. I thought Dodie's mother might be sitting in the front room—all alone except for that poor trapped goldfish. I tried to make myself walk on, but something tugged at me, and I found myself at the front door.

Mrs. Crumper opened it so quick I almost fell off the steps. "Come in," she said.

It was the last thing I wanted to do, but she had me by the arm and was pulling me inside. "I just finished a load of wash," she told me. "It's hanging out to dry."

The sun was just up, and a cool breeze was blowing. It wouldn't be drying any time soon, I thought, but I guessed she was getting some comfort from doing the things Dodie used to do.

She sat on a sofa cushion with its insides coming out and motioned me down beside her. I didn't want to, but I sat down.

"Dr. Thomas says Dodie might not be able to come home for a long time," she said. "We don't know how much damage that fall did to her." She squeezed my hand. "She opened her eyes today. I was standing right there. But she didn't look like she knew who I was."

I nodded. Dr. Thomas had already told me about that. He said that Dodie had a hard road ahead of her. He didn't know how long she would have to be in the hospital. Then she would have to do lots of exercises to learn to walk and talk again. She wouldn't be able to start school with the rest of us. But Dr. Thomas said she would catch up because she was full of grit. I wasn't sure exactly what that meant, but it did sound like something Dodie would be full of.

"I have to remember to feed Dodie's goldfish," Mrs. Crumper told me.

I nodded. "Not too much. A pinch every day is enough."

Then she put her head in her hands. She began to moan. "I wasn't a good mother to Dodie." She said the words over again, waiting for me to disagree with her. But I couldn't do that, even if she begged me to.

Dodie's one-eyed cat came from the direction of the kitchen and began to rub against her legs. Somebody—I wondered if it could have been Mrs. Crumper—had given it a bath. Except for the missing eye, it didn't look too bad.

I wondered what it must be like for her to live in that house with nothing but a goldfish and that cat to keep her company, and a tub full of someone else's dirty clothes to scrub.

I thought of Miss Emma living in her upstairs bedroom, looking out the window and waving to anybody who passed by. And I remembered what Geraldine had said about putting Miss Emma away. That would be a terrible thing. I remembered how she had nodded to me at the trial, and I thought that on her good days, Miss Emma could act just like other people. She probably would be better if more people would drop in to visit. That was something Reba Lu and Geraldine and I would have to do. Then another thought struck me.

"Do you like animals?" I asked.

Mrs. Crumper raised her head and looked at me. At first she looked surprised. Then she smiled her crooked smile. "I think they often have better sense than people," she said.

"Miss Emma has lots of animals."

"I heard about that."

I crossed my fingers and waited. She didn't say anything more, so I told her, "She likes people to drop in and visit. Mrs. Dawson has all she can handle with cooking the meals and taking messages for the doctor. I think she would be happy if Miss Emma had more visitors."

"Is that right?"

"I'll bet she'd show you her parrot if you visited her."

I got up to let myself out of the house. Just as I opened the front door to leave, Mrs. Crumper called out, "Can that parrot talk?"

I smiled at her. "Henry is a regular chatterbox," I said.

That night, it was so hot inside the houses that half of

Messina came outside to sit on their porches or walk along the sidewalks, trying to find a little cooler air to breathe.

Geraldine came up the front walk and plopped down on the cool concrete steps. "Ahhhh," she said. "That feels good."

Mama brought out some fresh-made lemonade. Then Reba Lu and her whole family joined us.

We sat around on the front porch pulling pieces off Mama's angel food cake that was still warm from the oven.

"It's the end of August," Reba Lu said. "School starts in three weeks."

Geraldine groaned. "Why did you have to bring that up?"

"I'll be glad for school to start," Reba Lu told us. "This year we get to study world geography."

Geraldine made a face. "Maybe you'll decide where to go on a mission."

The two of them kept it up, but I was more interested in Charles. He was learning to play the ukulele, which was a lot better than practicing his spitting. He strummed some chords and looked right at me when he began to sing.

Then the full moon shifted among drifting clouds. We both looked up and saw how bright it was. Even when it was partially covered, the light shone through.

He shifted keys and began to hum. We all picked up the tune and began to sing together.

> By the sea, by the sea,
> By the beautiful sea!
> You and me, you and me,
> Oh, how happy we'll be . . .

I swallowed hard. The August night floated on honeysuckle breath, carrying memories with it. My eyes welled with tears, and one escaped, trickling down my cheek. It went all the way to my chin, where I touched it with one finger.

The music stopped, and we sat in silence for a little while. Buster curled up next to me and settled down with a sigh. Then the crickets began to sing.

AFTERWORD

When the Crickets Stopped Singing takes place in the United States during the latter part of the Great Depression. Although many people were poor in 1939, it was a time of peace. This was not true in Europe. Adolf Hitler was invading Poland, forming an alliance with Italy, and beginning devastating air raids on Britain.

In the beginning of the story, Angie is thinking about the long, carefree summer days ahead of her when a voice on the radio says, *"escalation of the war in Europe . . . only a question of how long America can stay out of the conflict."* And her response is *"But not now. Not here."* She was echoing the general feeling in our nation. To people in small-town America, the war seemed a world away.

Yet, when Angie goes to the matinee and sees a newsreel showing people being loaded into trucks and carried away, she begins to wonder if Adolf Hitler (or someone like him) *could* come to her town and try to do the same thing. Would Americans fight him then?

Why did our country hang back? Why did we hesitate to jump right in and stop the wrongs that were occurring? Was it because we had our own problems? Why did we not join the conflict until the Japanese attack on Pearl Harbor on December 7, 1941? These are questions historians try to explain and the rest of us try to understand.

By the same token, why did so many of Messina's citizens turn a blind eye to the activities of Jefferson Clement? How could his actions toward Dodie go so far without anyone noticing? Why did the townspeople of Messina look the other way? Why did they hesitate to believe that there was evil in their midst?

Today, people speak more openly about predators like Jefferson Clement, and children are taught to tell responsible adults if anyone bothers them or threatens them. Times were different in 1939. A feeling of innocence prevailed in the lives of ordinary people in small towns like Messina. *Molestation* was a seldom-used word. Citizens dealt with people like Jefferson Clement more quietly. He might be asked to move to another town, for example. This might not have been the right way to deal with the problem, but it was very often the way things were done. In towns like Messina, people liked to think that, although terrible things were happening in Europe, their town was, as Angie's mother says ". . . *a good place to live—full of good people.*"

Just as Adolf Hitler has become a symbol for an evil that threatened to destroy the world, so does Jefferson Clement symbolize an evil that could stalk the streets of any small town anywhere—an evil that might be harder to recognize in a starched shirt and wearing a red carnation.

Angie's problem is clear. She can tell the truth and let Jefferson Clement go free. Or she can tell a lie and send him to jail, which is where she believes he belongs. Do you think she made the right decision?

Acknowledgments for
WHEN THE CRICKETS STOPPED SINGING

First, heartfelt thanks to my wonderful agent, Kelly Sonnack, who read my first draft and recognized its potential. She nurtured me through innumerable rewrites until the story began to speak for itself. Her support kept me going through the tough times.

Next, I am eternally grateful to Mary Colgan, my editor at Boyds Mills Press, who shared my vision of Messina and led me through the final revisions that illuminated setting, character, and plot. Guided by her expertise, *When the Crickets Stopped Singing* became the book I wanted to write.

My critique group listened patiently through chapter after chapter, making suggestions for changes and applauding me when I finally got something right. I might have faltered along the way without you: Rilla Jaggia, Beulah Colvin, Julie Brett, Judy Tschann, Nancy O'Connor, Patricia O'Brien, and Marge Flathers. You are the best!

Finally, I offer thanks to my daughter, my sons, and their families. They believe in me and tell me so. Margaret and Lyn Rippetue, David and Michael Gunther; Tom and Pam Donahue, Wesley and Daniel Donahue; Michael and Barbara Donahue, Stephen and Brandon Donahue; John and Jana Donahue, Allison and Chris Donahue.

MARILYN CRAM DONAHUE is the author of *Straight Along a Crooked Road* and its sequel *The Valley in Between,* as well as sixteen other books for children. Marilyn says, "My earliest memories are of words, a gathering of voices that came from a family of storytellers and singers. Their rhythms surrounded me and nourished me. My mother often read aloud to me when I was young, and when she finished a story, she encouraged me to think about what might have happened to the characters after the last page. My imagination soared, and so . . . I became a writer!" She lives in Highland, California. Visit marilyncramdonahue.com.